普通高等教育高职英语系列教材

INNOVATION
COLLEGE ENGLISH

创新大学英语
教师用书·高职高专版·
An Integrated Course

总 顾 问◎何自然

总 主 编◎高等职业英语教材编写研究会

何 刚

本册主编◎卢 敏

华东师范大学出版社

总序

何自然

语言理论研究和语言教学关系紧密显而易见,如何使我们的研究和思考更好地服务于我们的教学?

思考需要碰撞才能产生火花。很幸运碰到华东师范大学出版社高等职业英语教学研究的团队,提供我的想法给他们思索。

我的希望是,在一套教材里既融入语言学的语用学、语块理论、英汉语对比、认知语言学、二语习得里与教学相关的智慧,又吸收交际法、任务型教学、自主学习等理论的精华,让英语教学更有效果。

这无疑非常不容易,但这套教材做到了。

需要特别指出,本系列的编者不仅将这些理论和实践体现于教材编写之中,还贯彻了高职高专英语教学改革的新思路,在"工学结合、职业能力发展"和"任务型教学"理念的指引下,以"外语是学会的"作为终极目标,使这套教材有了闪光的东西。

我也很高兴看到,这种探索突出职业特色,以贴近生活与职场实际的各类主题来安排教学内容,循序渐进地将基础英语、职场英语介绍给学生,选材来源于真实的图表数据、应用文书、产品规格说明、广告宣传和商务案例等,让学生在学期间就能接触到社会语言实际,同时增长他们的职场、行业见识。教材注重实践教学,将语言实践、职业(商务)实践和综合能力实践有机结合起来,为如何在高职高专院校中有效开展上述三种实践(实训)流程的外语教学起示范带头作用。它不仅能提高学生的英语水平,还能提高他们的职业素质和人文素养。

此外,具有积极意义的是,本套教材重视当代信息技术的应用,不但在课文里介绍日常交际以及工作实践中普遍应用的电子信息交流方式,而且除提供综合教程及学生自主学习用书之外,还配有教师用书和多媒体教学光盘以及网络学习系统,实现课堂教学和学生自主学习一体化,便于组织灵活的网络教学和开展互动的网络学习。

最后,研究团队归纳提出了指导思想:让学习者"学得更有效"、"在做中学,在练中学",并认为高等职业英语教学应该置于课程、教育、社会大背景下综合思考,将教学要求、教材、教学、学习、评价进行一体化思考。这对其他层次的英语教学亦有启发,应该得到更多的关注。

让我们期待她的成功。

2010 年 6 月 于
广州白云山

前言

《创新大学英语综合教程(1—2)》(高职高专版)是公共英语类课程规划教材之一。这是一套由英语教学专家、高职英语教学一线骨干教师、企业培训专家共同编写的高职公共英语综合教材,旨在通过由浅入深、循序渐进的综合(读、写、听、说、译)训练使学生在工作中能轻松自如地运用英语进行交流。

在经济全球化浪潮的冲击下,大部分工作对人才的外语水平要求越来越高。英语语言运用能力在公共英语教学中的重要性是显而易见的,这些都对教学和教材编写提出了更高的要求。然而由于高职高专公共英语教学研究起步时间不是太长等原因,出现教材不能满足教学需要、教材跟不上时代发展和随意拼凑出版教材进行教学等现象。针对这些状况,着眼于推动高职公外,我们编写本系列教材,希望能对高职公共英语教学改革做出我们微薄的贡献。

本系列教材是以高职高专公共英语教学的最新改革精神为依托,以"任务型"教学理念为指导,贯彻"工学结合、职业能力发展"的思路而编写的创新教材。从学生的学习兴趣、生活经验和认知水平出发,倡导体验、实践、参与、合作与交流的学习方式和任务型的教学途径,发展学生在职业场景中运用英语进行交际的能力,同时兼顾学生人文素质培养。教材编写突出在任务型教学理念指导下来尝试采取多维度的改进措施:以学生为中心,面向全体学生,注意个性特征;增强自信心,激发学习兴趣;情景、结构、启发、交际的学习模式;积极主动参与在任务或情景中进行生动活泼、相互合作的小组活动;指导学生学会学习方法;扎实语言训练,足量的听读输入;在实用性、趣味性、夯实英语学习基础、开阔学生视野等方面做到平衡。简言之,教程根据日常生活和职场活动中的实际需要,创设真实情景和接近真实的交际任务,提高学生的语言能力、职场沟通能力。

本系列综合教程共分 2 册,根据高职教学的实际需要突出语言运用训练、职场交际与沟通能力。每册分为 8 个单元,每单元由 6 部分组成:第一部分是单元热身。第二部分为语言能力任务(Unit task),贯彻任务型教学理念,包括但不限于小组讨论(口语)、词汇、语法、听读、翻译与写作练习。第三部分为语言精读(Reading,或文体精读),选取难度合适、长度适当,同时具有艺术性(指语言美)、思想性并兼顾时代性的短文、典范作品或名篇。选文主要选取国外同类教材、报刊及与职场、商务活动相关的短文,尽量围绕单元主题把真实任务与阅读结合起来。第四、五部分为听说能力拓展(Listening & Speaking)。第六部分是写作,含句子拓展和实用写作两部分。另外每单元还有三大补充模块:表达文件夹(Portfolio),呈现单元相关实用背景知识及培养跨文化意识;语言练习(Language practice),词汇、翻译和结构的练习;寓教于乐(Learning for fun),简短的笑话和趣味知识,给学生学习带来乐趣。此三大模块均有规律地安排在各单元中。

本系列教程具有如下特点:

(1)丰富而实用的选材与任务设计。本书以主题方式安排,力求内容丰富,题材各异,主题贴近生活与职场实际,视角触及面广。实用性的突出体现是每单元第一部分的语言能力任务。因此,任务的真实性和选材的真实性是我们对实用性最好的注解。本教程充分利用了国外教材与互联网的丰富资源,其中相当部分数据、图表、商务文件、信函、产品说明书、广告、公告、通知及案例等均来自一些企业、公司或因特网,并配有相当数量的练习或交际任务,旨在努力创造条件为学生提供真实的语言输入和输出机会,使学生真切地掌握相应的英语语言基础知识,熟悉商务实践的技能、策略以及相关的现实职场的真实场景,从而可以使学生真切地掌握相应的英语及商务实践的技能。

(2)精心而系统的语言练习。教程在听、说、读、写、译各方面均精心设计形式各异的练习。比如口语活动就包括:双人讨论、角色扮演、小组讨论、模拟活动、辩论、口头汇报、调查问卷、口译等。丰富多样的练习活动为学生提供了更多提高听、说、读、写、译等各项技能的机会,可以极大地增强学生学习语言的兴趣。本教程特别突出对学生语言交际能力的培养,强调教学过程中的互动性,为学生提供了诸多在现实生活中灵活运用英语语言的场合、情景及任务等,以期达到学以致用的教学目的。

(3)结构清晰、易于教学。教程形式活泼多样,与众不同,图文并茂,互动性强。每册教材的侧重点不同,但注意系统性和独立性的有机结合。本系列教程可成套使用,亦可根据使用者的实际情况选择使用。

综合教程按照每单元 8 个教学课时设计,使用时可根据具体情况灵活掌握。系列教程均含学生用书、教师用书和配套磁带(或光盘)。

各部分的编写思路和使用中应注意的问题,分别说明如下:

1. 编写上力求以人为本,以任务为中心,以交际为目的,把语言知识的传授和英语技能的培养有机地结合起来。以循序渐进的方式,通过内容丰富、专业面广、程度适宜、饶有趣味的材料,帮助学生了解职业英语独特的语言现象(包括词汇、用语、语言结构等)和文体风格,促使学生切实掌握英语语言的基本技能。此外,教程从学生的实际水平出发,参考最新的《高等职业英语教学要求》,扩大输入量,进一步巩固、深化语言基础,提高语言应用能力。

2. 教程在课文选材上力求新颖有趣,力戒过深过细,旨在帮助学生掌握基础知识,培养新的思维方式,拓宽视野,了解职场新动向,获取新的认识。

3. 选文以语言典范、优美的范文为主,选文尽量出自国外教材或国际英文主流媒体报刊,注意内容新颖、文字典型、文体多样、语言地道、趣味性强,具有强烈的时代气息和前瞻性。

4. 表达文件夹(Portfolio)模块包含一些实用性强的背景知识、数据、图表、案例以及应用性(practical learning)较强的资料拓展阅读。

5. Text B 之后的 Language practice 部分的语言练习是对 Unit task 和 Text B 的语言点的巩固。其中包括词汇拓展、词组、重点词、翻译和结构以及 1—2 个灵活的练习。词汇练习针对课文中的重点词汇及词组设计,要求学生反复操练,重点掌握。翻译练习偏重于选实用的句子,注重活学活用,逐步增强学生的翻译技能。写作策略则着重各类商务信函的写作。教材还兼顾了学生今后的就业需求,将基础教学同全国大学英语应用能力 A、B 级考试、大学英语四级考试及其它英语等级考试的写作要求有机结合。

6. 认知水平、系统性与可读性兼顾问题。在选材时,我们特别注重科学性与可读性的关系,既不失其科学的严谨性,又要考虑到学生学习心理方面的要求,力求将职场知识用浅显易懂的方式表现出来,使教材的内容具有可读性,教师愿意教,学生愿意学。

7. 文化教育与语言教学兼顾,在选材时注重培养学生的"跨文化意识",注意语言材料和文化内容的融合,注意中西文化的对比,使学生在学习语言的同时,了解文化差异,多角度、多纬度地获取西方文化的精髓。

8. 教材中的人文关怀意识主要通过有思想性的文章体现,对学生的审美提高也有一定的帮助。

　　为了方便教师使用,本教程配备了较为详尽的教师用书。每单元的教师用书由两部分组成:第一部分是单元教学目的、步骤与建议;第二部分是单元参考教案,由热身活动(Warm-up),任务创设(Unit task),语言讲解(Language points),课文译文,练习答案,听说活动,写作指导等部分组成。其中语言讲解部分为教师提供了进入课文教学时引导性的问题和讲解词汇时所需的例句;练习答案在必要之处我们对所给答案作了简单的解释。我们的意图是把教师用书变成一本十分实用、使用方便的教学参考书。

　　本教程第一册主编为卢敏老师(湖州职业技术学院)。参加本教程第一册编写工作的有胡卫卫、沈丹铧、王俊凯、王秀娥、王艳、张辉、陶玥君、黎蓉等老师。

　　本教程在编写过程中得到何自然教授(广东外语外贸大学)、邹为诚教授(华东师范大学)、夏纪梅教授(中山大学)、王大伟教授(上海海事大学)、蔡基刚教授(复旦大学)、井升华教授(南京理工大学)等多位英语界专家的支持,在此一并对他们表示衷心的感谢。

编者

2010 年 2 月

致教师

您应该怎样用好这本书？

请您充当导游的角色。如果学习是一次旅行，作为教师，我们的职责是介绍、提示和引导。请尽量不要以本书中提供的内容，结合自己找的资料，在讲台上读自己的讲稿。我们的工作重点应该是介绍结构性的知识，引起学生的求知意向，乐于与学生交流与分享观点，善于发现学生的问题并尽力提供帮助。

请您充当主持人的角色。尽管本书做得也许还不够好，还不是主持人的好脚本，但我们确已努力过。"Tell me, I forget. Show me, I remember. Involve me, I learn."因此我们在本书中对任务型教学模式进行了尝试，以丰富、多元的活动形式为载体，鼓励学生去看、去听、去说、去写，在真实的交际过程中达成教学目标。您可以根据我们提供的东西，改编成您想要实施的学习活动，让任务与活动成为课堂的基调，这样您就是主持人、组织者。

请您充当研究者的角色。"学然后知不足，教然后知困"，教学是教育者和学习者共同提高的过程。我们特别在每单元任务之后设置了"教师教学行动研究"版块，让您记录下任务活动中的观察和反思，留下宝贵的第一手资料，与我们一起为有效教学进行更多的思索。

您应该怎样规划这门课程？

您需要编写一份课程纲要，它是课程计划、认知地图，也是交流工具。

请您围绕课程目标精心设计教学过程，并思考在此过程中，学生如何：

(1)学会运用每课的关键表达方法和核心词汇；(2)能把所学知识应用于新的情境，解决实际问题；(3)通过丰富的学习活动，养成积极的学习习惯，提高主动获取知识的能力；(4)在与同伴完成任务的过程中，体验合作、分享、互惠的教育意义。

我们还打算为您做些什么？

我们深知教师工作的不易，为此我们探索、建立了教学分享网络。我们开设了网络自主学习中心，建设资源库，鼓励学生上网进行自主学习，并教师提供每一课的 PPT 课件和补充资料，让您有更多的选择，在组织教学时更加得心应手。

高等职业英语任务型教学研究项目　总策划
李恒平
2010 年 5 月

Bookmap

Content	Theme	Unit Task	Text A	Text B	Grammar	Writing
Unit 1	Reception	Entertaining clients in business reception	Tips for Business Reception	Luxury Treatment Can Give You Wings after a Long Flight	Tense (1)	Email (1)
Unit 2	Fashion	Working in a fashion retail	How to Discover Current Fashion Trends	China Outsourcing Boomerangs on Brands	Nouns & pronouns	Invitation card
Unit 3	Advertising	Designing advertisements	3 advertisements	Advertising Good or Bad?	Modals	Poster
Unit 4	Finance	Investigating a robbery	Recession Easing, but Many Americans Still Afraid to Spend	The Role of Money in Society's Development	Verbal agreement	Bank account application
Unit 5	Expo	Participating in a trade fair	Canton Fair	Another Coming-of-Age Party for Brand China	Tense (2)	Business card
Unit 6	Travel	Organizing a group trip to Hong Kong Disneyland	How to Organize a Group Trip	Business Travel: Cruising on the Yangtze River	Adverbial Clauses	Itinerary
Unit 7	Public Relations	Arranging a press conference	How to Hold a Press Conference	Twitter Do's and Don'ts for Brands	Inversions	Email (2)
Unit 8	Entertainment	Creating a good story	What Makes a Good Story?	Hip-Hop World	Review test	Movie review

目录

Unit 1 Reception

Objective

- **Career skills**

  Picking up a client at the airport; planning a business reception; knowing some intercultural business reception skills; writing an invitation via email.

- **Reading**
  1. Reading for main idea(s)
  2. Skimming/Scanning
  3. Reading for key word spotting
  4. Reading for finding out the cause
  5. Reading for guessing word meaning from context

- **Writing**
  1. General writing: sentence patterns
  2. Practical writing: emails

- **Listening**
  1. Listening for key words
  2. Listening for general information and details
  3. Listening for note-taking

- **Speaking**
  1. Making recommendation on what specialty to buy
  2. Seeing off a client at the airport

- **Language focus**

Key words and phrases				
reception	activity	track	flight	pick up
entertain	available	greet	plan	invite
hospitality	spa	land	serve	baggage
dinner	specialty	recommend	see off	celebrate

Teaching Arrangement

Warm-up & Unit task (Text A)
1) Time schedule: 2 periods
2) Suggested lesson structure
   Warm-up: 10 – 15 minutes
   Text A: 10 – 15 minutes
   Unit task step 1 (pre-task):
   10 – 15 minutes
   Unit task steps 2 – 5 (while-task):
   45 – 60 minutes
   Unit task step 6 (post-task)

Reading (Text B)
1) Time schedule: 1 period
2) Suggested lesson structure
   Language points: 20 – 25 minutes
   Language practice: 20 – 25 minutes

Listening
1) Time schedule: 1 period
2) Suggested lesson structure
   Listening exercise 1: 10 minutes
   Listening exercise 2: 10 minutes
   Listening exercise 3: 10 minutes
   Listening exercise 4: 15 minutes

Speaking & Writing
1) Time schedule: 1 period
2) Suggested lesson structure
   Speaking: 20 – 25 minutes
   Writing: 20 minutes

Teaching Procedures

Warm-up

If you are going to entertain your clients during the business reception, what recreational activities would you like to choose? Please match the activities with their pictures respectively. What would you add?

Target:

Ss understand the meaning of each picture and brainstorm the suitable recreational activities during a business reception.

Guidance:

- Ss read Warm-up 1.
- Ask Ss to match the names of different activities with their pictures.
- Invite 1 – 2 Ss to present their answers.
- Ask Ss to read the sample.
- Ask 2 – 3 Ss to express their ideas according to the sample.
- Ask 2 – 3 Ss to add some suitable activities during business reception.

Key

1. hiking ___H___	2. Beijing opera ___A___
3. karaoke ___G___	4. flying kites ___B___
5. tea drinking ___D___	6. rock climbing ___I___
7. foot massage ___F___	8. tennis ___E___
9. golf ___C___	

- I would like to choose Beijing opera, because it shows Chinese culture.
- I would not like to choose rock climbing, because it is too dangerous.
- I would like to add badminton, table-tennis, traveling in or around the city, dinner . . .

Background Information:

······· What is business reception? ·······

A business reception means the first step to impress your client. A good reception can help the following negotiation and the following deals. Reception includes meeting clients at the airport, reserving hotel rooms for clients, planning recreational activities to entertain clients and hosting a dinner for clients, etc.

Try the following quiz so that you know whether you are good at intercultural business reception skills. Choose the right country for each question.

Target:

Ss can know whether they are good at intercultural business reception skills. Ss can learn some skills which may help their career.

Guidance：

- Ss read Warm-up 2.
- Ask Ss to do a pair work. Try the quiz and check the score for their partner.
- Invite a student to present his/her partner's result.
- The teacher may help to explain some difficult language points.

Unit task

Read Text A and practice a series of real tasks of reception supposing that you are a clerk in a company and you are going to impress your client during the business reception.

 Task Map(任务导航)

在商务场合,商务接待是留给客户好印象的非常重要的首要环节。商务接待有一系列的任务,如机场接客户、邀请客户赴宴、邀请客户参加某些招待活动等。商务接待的各项环节里有大量的英语口语、听力、写作等的实际应用。

特此要求学生围绕商务接待可能涉及的任务进行具体实践,通过模拟情景进行模拟实践,巩固学生用英语查询、询问、介绍、建议、提问与回答等能力。

本单元任务分为 6 个步骤,第一个步骤让学生通过合作阅读了解查询航班的步骤、机场接人的步骤以及如何招待客户的注意事项;第二个步骤是学生模拟身份,收到客户来邮,记录客户航班信息,给客户回邮表达去机场接机的意愿;第三个步骤是学生模拟身份,以公司职员间的谈话来口头演示说明如何上相关网站查询航班信息;第四个步骤是主任务,模拟身份,模拟情景,学生角色表演机场接客户;第五个步骤也是主任务,模拟身份,模拟情景,学生角色表演为了准备招待计划而询问客户意见;第六个步骤是后任务环节,供学生课后讨论和演练,主要是针对商务接待的各项任务的典型注意事项进行复习性质的思考,另外还创造了一个情景剧表演的初步剧本。

本单元任务的安排主要根据活动过程顺序来设定,每一任务为后续的步骤做基础。

Process Break-down

Pre-task：

Step 1　A：Jigsaw reading let Ss share the tips for business reception.

　　　　B：Ss need to rank the steps of picking a client up at the airport.

While-task：

Step 2　A：Ss read the email from a client and sort out the flight information.

　　　　B：Ss reply the email in order to inform the client that he or she is going to pick him up at the airport.

Step 3　Ss orally introduce how to track flight information according to Article 1.

Step 4　Ss role-play of meeting at the airport and on the way to the hotel.

Greetings and small talks should be included.

Step 5   Ss work out a reception plan for the client. Give reasons for the arrangements. Role-play of inviting the client to take part in a certain entertaining activity.

Post-task：

Step 6   Ask Ss to discuss questions and make a short play after class concerning the topic of reception.

Step 1

Read the articles and get background information for the following real tasks.

任务过程控制关注点 Minefield

- 提醒学生不要被生词限制住，阅读时需要利用上下文猜测关键词，非关键词可以忽略。阅读时也应引入常识。
- 提醒学生快速阅读时应采用查读法。
- 提醒学生这个步骤的任务是为接下来需要完成的实际任务提供理论依据。

A

Work in groups of three. You are each going to read an article. Tell your group members the main idea of what you have read and try to help Eric to list some key words.

Target：

Know some tips for business reception.

Guidance：

- Divide the whole class into groups of 3 students.
- Each student in each group is going to read an article.
- Tell their group members the main idea of what he or she has read and try to help Eric to list some key words.
- By finishing this step, Ss will have mastered the main steps or tips of tracking flight information, picking up clients at the airport and entertaining clients.
- During this step, Ss can also master retelling the main idea of an article. Also, they learn how to work in a team efficiently.
- Invite one group of Ss to present the answers.
- Teacher can do a little explanation afterwards.

Expressions Pool

1. The main idea of Article ... is that ....
2. The key words can be listed like this ....
3. I think the reasonable order is ... according to the article I have just read.
4. Words and expressions： track, pick up, entertain, flight, baggage claim, recreational acitivity ...

 Key

- Article 1：flight information, track, airport name, flight number, route, enter, click, alert ...
- Article 2：pick up, when, airline, flight number, baggage claim, check, location, vehicle, greet ...
- Article 3：entertain, feed, recreational event, show around the city, creative ways ...

B

Rank the following steps when Eric is going to pick his client up at the airport.

Target：

Know the tips for picking up a client at the airport quickly.

Guidance：

- Ss scan Article 2.
- Rank the steps into a reasonable order according to the article.
- Invite 1－2 Ss to present the answer.
- Teacher can do a little explanation afterwards.

 Key

The reasonable order should be：C F B D A E

Step 2

Read the email and reply it.

A

Read an email and sort out information.

Target：

Understand a typical email from a potential client.

Guidance：

- Ss are supposed to be Eric. Eric gets an email from his potential client. The client is planning to visit Eric's company and try to make a deal.
- Ss read the email.
- Ss sort out the flight information.
- Invite 1－2 Ss to present their answers.

 Key

Client's name	Smith Park
Flight number	AA7951
Airline	American Airline
Departure date	June 22
Arrival time	10：30 a. m. June 24

B

Reply the email in order to inform the guest that you are going to pick him up at the airport.

Target：

Know how to reply an email to the client and inform that you would like to pick him up at the airport.

Guidance：

- Ss are supposed to be Eric. They are supposed to give their reply ASAP, telling Mr. Park that they will be available to pick him up at the airport.
- Ss can follow some instructions from Article 2.
- Give Ss 5 minutes to write.
- Invite 1－2 Ss to read their emails.

任务过程控制关注点
Minefield

- 提醒学生阅读查找信息时应用查读法。
- 提醒学生 email 的格式。
- 提醒学生写给客户的回邮必须及时、礼貌。
- 提醒学生在写邮件的时候一定要把愿意去机场接机的意愿表达到位。
- 提醒学生要注意语言，但同时不要害怕语言错误。

Expressions Pool

1. Email includes the sender, the recipient, the subject, the content, and the ending.
2. It's a great honor to get your email and we are looking forward to your visit.
3. I am available to meet you at the airport.
4. It's my pleasure to meet you at the airport at the baggage claim area.
5. I really appreciate a lot that you emailed me to inform me the flight information.
6. I would like to reserve a hotel room for you.
7. If you have any request, please do not hesitate to tell me via email or phone.
8. It is sunny/in rainy season/very warm/a bit chilly.
9. Best regards.
10. Yours sincerely …

- Teacher may point out some mistakes.

Reference：

From:	ericlee@ hotmail. com
To:	smithpark@ hotmail. com
Subject:	Welcome

Date: June 16，2010

Attachment:

Dear Mr. Park，

　　It's a great honor to get your email and we are looking forward to your visit. We are glad to know you are interested in our product. During your stay in China，we would show you around our company and plant.

　　I really appreciate a lot you emailed me to inform me the flight information. I am available to meet you at the airport at the baggage claim area. And I would like to reserve the hotel room for you. If you have any request for the hotel room，please do not hesitate to tell me via email or phone.

　　We are looking forward to your coming.

Best regards，
Yours sincerely，
Eric Lee

Step 3

Demonstrate how to track the flight information online.

Target：

Introduce how to use a certain website to track flight information orally.

Guidance：

- Suppose the client is coming. Eric is worried and asks for help.
- Eric is asking his colleague to explain to him how to track the flight information online.
- Suppose Ss are Eric's colleague.
- Ss are going to explain orally and show it online.
- Ss need to scan Article 1 once again.
- Ss had better work in pairs.
- Teacher should guide Ss to use the suggested expressions.
- 1 - 2 pairs can be invited to present their dialogue.

Reference：

A：Hi，Sarah，could you please do me a favor?

B：What's up，Eric?

A：You know，my first client is coming to visit our company. I have no experience picking clients up at the airport. What am I going to do? I mean I may miss him or be late if I can not track the flight information.

B：You would like to track the flight information，right?

A：Exactly.

B：Don't worry，Eric. I can show you a useful website.

A：Thanks. If you can demonstrate it to me，that would be a big favor.

任务过程控制关注点
Minefield

- 提醒学生要尽量理解和运用网站的语言。
- 提醒学生课后尽量上该网站实际演示。

Expressions Pool

1. Hi，... could you please do me a favor?
2. My client is coming. You know，it is my first time to pick up clients at the airport on my own. I am a bit worried.
3. Could you please give me some tips? Any good suggestions?
4. What's up?
5. Don't worry. It's a snack. I can show you a useful website. You can have a try.

B：All right. Come here. I can show you. Step 1, log onto the Internet and search for flightstats. com.

A：I can take notes.

B：Step 2, enter the flight details for the airline you wish to track. You can choose to enter the flight number, to and from airport names or a flight route. Step 3, enter the flight date and choose on arrival and click on the Search button. Step 4, review the flight status results. Here arrival information such as: airport name, actual time of departure, gate used, and any reported delays are included. That's all.

A：It is really useful. Thanks a lot.

B：Not a big deal. Good luck, Eric.

A：Thanks.

Step 4

Role-play of meeting at the airport and on the way to the hotel.

Target：
Know how to greet a client and have small talks with a client.

Guidance：
- Ss read the direction and try to understand the situation and role cards.
- Ss work in pairs.
- According to the role cards and situation, Ss can make a dialogue.
- Teacher should guide Ss to use the suggested expressions.
- 1 - 2 pairs can be invited to present their dialogues.

Reference：

A：Ah, Mr. Park, glad to meet you, I'm Eric Lee from ABC Textile Foreign Trade Company.

B：Glad to meet you too, Eric. It's very kind of you to meet me at the airport.

A：How was your flight, Mr. Park?

B：The flight was smooth and the service was satisfactory.

A：I'm glad to hear that. I hope you'll have a pleasant stay in China.

B：I'm sure I will.

A：Is this all your baggage?

B：Yes, it's all here.

A：Let me take this traveling bag for you if you do not mind.

B：Oh, please and thank you.

A：Let's go. This way, please. Our van is at the parking lot.

B：Okay.

A：Mr. Park, I have booked the hotel room for you. Shall we go to the hotel now or would you like to have something to eat?

B：I am fine now. I had some snacks on the plane. I think we can go to the hotel.

A：I see.

. . .

A：How do you like the weather here?

B：It is not bad.

A：Mr. Park, what do you like to do in your spare time?

B：I like doing some sports. Golf is my favorite.

A：That's great. Shanghai has some good golf courses. It will be our honor to

任务过程控制关注点
Minefield

- 提醒学生对话要自然,贴近实际。
- 提醒学生注意机场接机环境下两人均有点陌生,应非常礼貌,不应过于亲密。
- 提醒学生注意语言使用得当,但也不应害怕语言不丰富不敢开口讲。
- 提醒学生注意主题任务是"机场接待并在去酒店的路上进行简单对话",千万不要对话太多,导致客户厌烦。

Expressions Pool

1. Glad to meet you.
2. How was your journey?
3. I have booked a hotel room for you.
4. How do you like the weather here?
5. What would you like to do in your spare time?
6. It's so kind of you to come to meet me.
7. Can you tell me about any interesting places to visit?
8. I'd like to have a nap if you do not mind.
9. Thanks for your hospitality.

invite you to play golf.

B: Haha, thanks for your hospitality.

...

A: Mr. Park, here we are. Please take a rest in the room. What time shall I come to pick you up to the company?

B: Tomorrow morning 9 o'clock.

A: OK. See you tomorrow.

Step 5

Work out a reception plan for Mr. Park. Give reasons for your arrangements.

Target:

Be able to propose some activities to entertain a client.

Guidance:

- Ss read the direction and try to understand the situation and role cards.
- Ss work in pairs.
- According to the role cards and situation, Ss can make a dialogue. The dialogue should be focused on understanding the client's interests and giving suggestions.
- Teacher should guide Ss to use the suggested expressions.
- 1–2 pairs can be invited to present their dialogues.
- Ss should work out a reception plan by using a table.

Reference:

A: Good Morning. Mr. Park. Did you get enough rest last night?

B: Good Morning. I had a wonderful sleep. I guess I was a bit tired.

A: Well, Mr. Park, the general manager of our company has prepared a dinner in your honor at Hilton Hotel. I came here to invite you to attend the dinner on his behalf.

B: That's kind of him. So what time?

A: At 6:00 if it is convenient for you.

B: Sure. Please tell Mr. Zhang that I thank him for his invitation.

A: Yes. Then I might come to pick you up at 5 p.m., OK?

B: It's OK.

A: See you then.

B: Bye.

...

C: Good evening, Mr. Park. Glad to see you.

B: Good evening, Mr. Zhang. I really appreciate your preparing such a splendid dinner for me.

C: You are welcome. So, what kind of food would you like to have for dinner, Chinese food or Western food?

B: Chinese food. I am crazy about it.

A: Great. We will serve Chinese food.

B: Thanks. You are so nice.

A: Now I propose a toast to further development of our cooperation.

B: I propose a toast to the health of everyone here tonight and to the friendship. Cheers!

...

任务过程控制关注点
Minefield

- 提醒学生开拓思维。记忆 Warm-up 里认知到的关于商务招待活动的词汇,并在此任务中运用。
- 提醒学生对话要自然,贴近实际。
- 提醒学生注意语言使用得当,但也不应害怕语言不丰富不敢开口讲。
- 提醒学生对话要礼貌。
- 提醒学生对话的关键是了解客户需求和兴趣,并据此提出有关招待活动的建议。
- 提醒学生除了对话还要给出一张表格来显示会安排的活动及时间表。

Expressions Pool

1. Did you get enough rest?
2. Our manager would like to host a dinner at Hilton Hotel.
3. What do you like to do in your spare time, Mr. Park?
4. Would you like a foot massage for relaxing?
5. Karaoke is very popular in China. Would you like to have a try?
6. That's so kind of him.
7. Sounds interesting.
8. I'd like to have a try.
9. Thanks for your hospitality.

A：Mr. Park, I am wondering, what you would like to do in your spare time?

B：I like golf.

A：There are some golf courses here. We would like to invite you to play golf. How about tomorrow? It is going to be fine and we can play golf at the suburb.

B：I am excited. We can meet at the lobby of the hotel around 9 a.m.

A：Sure. And what activity would you like to take part in after dinner?

B：I have no idea.

A：If you do not mind, I can give you some suggestions. As a matter of fact, it will be our honor to entertain you after dinner.

B：Thanks for your hospitality.

A：Foot massage is popping up. It can help you relax after the long flight journey. Would you like to have a try, Mr. Park?

B：Sounds interesting. I'd like to have a try.

A：I see. I can make a reservation in foot massage center in this hotel.

B：Thanks.

A：My pleasure.

Activity	Time	Reason	Place
Dinner	5 pm	General manager's treat	Hilton Hotel
Foot massage	After dinner	To relax after the journey	Foot massage center in the Hilton Hotel
Play golf	9 am tomorrow	To satisfy Mr. Park's interests	Suburb

Step 6

After practicing all the tasks above, you may have interest in doing the followings after class.

A

Discuss the following questions：

1. What preparations should you make before meeting a client at the airport?

2. How can you make your client comfortable during the business reception?

B

Please make a drama according to the following situation.

Situation：An important client is going to visit your company. The manager asks one of his clerks to pick up the client at the airport.

Possible roles：manager, clerk, client, customer officer at the airport, van driver, hotel receptionist, etc.

Possible tasks：conversation between manager and clerk; conversation of greeting at the airport; conversation of the hotel; small talks.

Target：

Summarize what have been learned and apply them in practice.

Guidance：

● Ss are supposed to review what they have learned about business reception.

任务过程控制关注点
Minefield

● 提醒学生此任务属于后任务环节,应在课后自己操练。

● 提醒学生要将前面任务的语言进行积累。

● 提醒学生要勇于创新,并记录自己学习或表演的情况。

● 提醒学生重点应放在对商务接待这一主题进行语言演练及表演,而不要把重点放在道具准备等上。

- Ss are supposed to discuss freely.
- Teacher should encourage Ss to make the drama after class.
- Teacher should explain the direction clearly.

Action research
（教师自己的教学行动研究）

任务完成中的观察、反思（日志、随笔）	备忘

Language Points

Article 1

◆ (title) **How to *track* flights status**

track：to follow the course, to observe the changes, to chase or follow

[运用]　track flight status/laser/movement/rader/price...

e. g. This software can help to track the price changes.

[拓展]　*track* (*n.*) 轨道

This is a narrow running track.

keep track of sth. 追踪，记录

The professor will keep track of his students' attendance.

Article 2

◆ (line 2) ... **when your guest is *expected* to arrive ...**

expect：to anticipate, to suppose

[运用]　expect sb. to do sth., sb. be expected to do sth.

e. g. We expect our team to win the game.

She is expected to arrive in half an hour.

Article 3

◆ (line 1) ... ***impress* your client, it means ...**

impress：to have an effect on, to make an impression on

[运用]　impress sb., impress on sb. with sth.

e. g. The young chess player impressed the audience.

[拓展]　*impression* (*n.*) 印象

The teacher's words made a strong impression on me.

◆ (line 3) ... **when the plane *lands*, he has ...**

land：to come or touch the ground

[运用]　land safely, take off and land, land an airplane, landing time

e. g. Our plane is going to land. Please fasten your safety belt.

[拓展]　*land* (*n.*) 土地，陆地

Some animals live on land and some live in the sea.

They bought all the available land to make investment.

land→touch, arrive, descend

[仿写]　飞机安全地着陆在上海浦东国际机场。

◆ (line 14) ... **in airports across the *globe*.**

globe：the world, the earth

[运用]　across the globe, around the globe

e. g. Our company has over 500 franchises across the globe.

[拓展]　*global* (*a.*) 全球的

Global warming has become a common concern of all the human beings.

Competition becomes stronger with the development of the global economy.

globalization (*n.*) 全球化

The world is moving further toward multi-polarization and economic globalization.

[仿写]　这种疾病很快在全球范围内传播开来。

◆ (line 20) ... **the Executive lounge spa *served* 250 people ...**

serve：to provide service to sb., to supply, to cater

[运用]　serve tea, serve meal, serve as

e. g. This tea house serves black tea, green tea and others.

Sometimes Internet can serve as a personal assistant.

[拓展]　*service* (*n.*) 服务

Our restaurant is in service from 10 am to 9 pm.

[仿写]　这家理发店每天平均服务 10 名顾客。

◆ (line 21) ... **has driven the *rise* of ...**

rise：an increase

[运用]　rise of sth., a sharp rise, a steady rise, on the rise

e. g. The coming Christmas has driven a sharp rise of the sales in the shopping malls.

Prices were on the rise.

[拓展]　*rise* (*v.*) 上升

The sun is rising.

The unemployment rate has been rising during these two years because of the economic crisis.

rise◇fall, decrease

[仿写]　市场需求推动了房价的上升。

◆ (line 28) ... **they're *confined* to the airport**

confine：to keep, to limit, to restrict

[运用]　be confined to, confine sth. in a place

e. g. I was confined to my bed because of the disease.

[拓展]　*confined* (*a.*) 受限制的，封闭的

It is dangerous for miners to work in a confined space.

confinement (*n.*) 监禁

Some people think death is better than confinement.

〔仿写〕 减价销售（sales）只限于小件物品。

◆ （line 38） … chance to *recharge* their batteries.

recharge：to renew, to refresh one's energy

〔运用〕 recharge one's battery, relax and recharge, artificial recharge

e. g. You should recharge your battery with enough sleep.

〔拓展〕 recharge→revive, renew, reload

〔仿写〕 每天晚上我都给手机充电。

◆ （line 39） … airport spas *targeting* the business traveler …

target：to direct, to aim at

〔运用〕 target … market, target … consumers

e. g. Our products target the African market.

We need to target right employers if we want to be employed quickly.

〔拓展〕 *target* （*n.*） 目标

on target 一针见血

His criticism is on target. His colleagues have to make a new proposal.

〔仿写〕 童装应以母亲作为主要的营销目标，因为买什么童装是由母亲决定的。

◆ （line 44） … *emphasis* is on …

emphasis：the special importance

〔运用〕 emphasis on, place emphasis, lay emphasis, with emphasis

e. g. In order to make the guests more comfortable, more emphases should be placed on the facilities and service.

In his speech, he laid emphasis on cooperation between the two companies rather than competition.

〔拓展〕 *emphasize* （*v.*） 强调

Many parents emphasize the importance of education.

emphasis→stress

〔仿写〕 这家公司把重点放在新产品的研发上。

◆ （line 59） … is *likely* to be …

likely：possible, probable, tending

〔运用〕 be likely to, quite likely, as likely as not

e. g. She is not likely to come since it is almost midnight.

The pills are as likely as not they would kill me.

〔拓展〕 *likelihood* （*n.*） 可能性

There is no likelihood of his winning in this game.

likely◇unlikely

〔仿写〕 这部电影很有可能会获奖。

◆ （line 64） … another source of *competitive* advantage …

competitive：tending to be successful in rivalry

〔运用〕 competitive advantage, competitive product, competitive price, highly competitive

e. g. Our products are highly competitive due to the competitive prices.

〔拓展〕 *competition* （*n.*） 竞争

The competition for scholarship in colleges is very strong.

competitive→rival

〔仿写〕 职业资格证使他在求职中更有竞争力。

Translation of Texts

Text A

商务接待的好提示

Eric Lee 是 ABC 纺织品外贸公司的员工。他即将要做第一单生意。他的美国客户要来参观公司并做进一步的商务谈判。Eric 有点儿紧张。他想在接待时给他的客户留下一个好印象以便谈成生意。他的上司推荐给他三篇文章阅读以获得一些提示。

文章 1　如何追踪航班

去机场接客户，准时到达十分重要，但同时您可能担心航班信息会有所变更。现在，有了国际航班追踪器能够进行实时追踪。您可以根据机场名、航班号以及航线进行追踪。请根据以下提示追踪航班状态。

步骤 1. 访问网站：www. flightstats. com，进入"航班（Flight）"标签界面，点击"航班状态（Flight Status）"。

步骤 2. 输入您想查找的商业航空公司的航班信息。

步骤 3. 向下滚屏，点击"航班状态展开"以查找关于此航班的全部信息。

步骤 4. 查看飞行过程中的详细信息变更。

步骤 5.如果您想得到即时航班信息变更通知,请注册申请"航班警报器"。

文章 2　如何快速地接到您的客户

去机场前:

1. 了解您的客户计划到达机场时间。
2. 查看他所搭乘飞机的航空公司以及航班号,并将这些信息记录,随身携带。
3. 告诉客户您将去接机,在行李认领区碰头。
4. 查看航空公司网站,或在预计航班到达前一小时致电机场。

接机时:

1. 在航班到达时间前 15—30 分钟到机场。
2. 将车停在短期停车场。记好你停车的位置。
3. 在抵港班机的显示屏中查看航班状态以及行李认领区编号。
4. 根据标示抵达行李认领区。
5. 迎接客户,领取行李。
6. 回到车上。

文章 3　如何让您的客户在商务访问期间感觉舒适

对任何公司来说,接待客户的能力都是最受用的技能之一。如果你给客户留下了深刻的印象,就会带来更多的商机。诀窍在于:发现你的客户喜欢做什么,确保他们来访贵公司时过得愉快。做好准备工作,商务接待也能成为一大乐事。

请客户吃饭。请客人吃一顿丰盛的晚餐是招待客户的基本内容。

带客户参加休闲活动。招待客户打打高尔夫球或卡拉 OK。

带客户逛逛。

想一些富有创意的方式来招待他们。

Text B

机场新服务:高管商务 SPA

英国《金融时报》

在肖恩·哈灵顿(Séan Harrington)坐飞机出差前,他总要享受一次快速水疗(SPA)。飞机降落后,他会再做一个水疗,这回还加上一次按摩。这样一来,他就准备好了面对一天工作中要做的任何事情。他表示,用水疗放松自己,能够大大缓解商务旅行的

压力。他并非唯一喜欢在机场享受水疗放松休息服务的人。"长途旅行中,在同一个位置上坐很长时间会让任何人事后觉得浑身僵硬和疼痛,"Jaeger 的首席执行官贝琳达·厄尔(Belinda Earl)表示,"我认为,当你在目的地降落后做个按摩确实是个好主意:它会帮助你在连续开会的时候集中精力,熬过那些日子。"水疗正在全球范围内的机场涌现。"现在在世界上任何地方,你都能够走进一间贵宾休息室,找到一个能让你在抵达后精力充沛或者在登上午夜航班之前进行放松的水疗场所,"厄尔表示。

需求非常旺盛——哈灵顿称,在头一周,航空贵宾休息室每天接待 250 名顾客。安全措施的加强推动了机场水疗服务的兴起,因为人们抵达机场的时间提前了。尽管通过安检的时间有所增加,但商务旅客往往能够享受快速通道服务,因此有空余的时间来做按摩。他还指出,"长途旅客通常在换乘航班之间有空余时间,有时候甚至是几小时,这段时间里他们只能呆在机场"。

商务旅行已经不同于过去。航班的频率和成本意味着,在 4 天内先后飞往悉尼、雅加达、孟买和伦敦能够成为现实,即使这种旅途并不令人愉快。商务仓中的折叠床意味着,公司希望它们的员工在飞机上睡觉,然后从机场直接去办公室。疲惫不堪的高管似乎正在利用水疗这一难得的机会给自己充电。

盯住商务旅客的不仅仅是机场——酒店也正在加入这一行列。值得注意的是,商务水疗与传统水疗在两个主要方面有着不同。第一,商务旅客没有整天的时间闲逛,因此重点在于快速理疗,尤其是在机场。第二,传统水疗的主要客户是女性,而多数商务旅客都是男性。因此重点应放在按摩上而不是放在美容上。

一些人或许会认为,在商界,高管水疗按摩的增长就像卡布基诺咖啡上的泡沫。但在这个企业高管休息时间急剧减少的世界里,这种水疗服务很有意义。在开会前在笔记本电脑上疯狂地干几分钟活儿或者做个按摩,哪一种选择更有益呢? 此外,在飞机上睡觉之后,多数人看上去都十分糟糕,没有人希望在一项重要交易的谈判中看起来筋疲力尽。或许 15 分钟的水疗,是高管另一个竞争优势的来源。

Explain these words and expressions through their context or with the help of a dictionary.

1) land (Para. 1)   飞机着陆(v.)
e. g. The plane is going to land.

2) be confined to (Para. 2)   被限制在……地方
e. g. Some people's thoughts are confined to the old customs.

3) head straight to (Para. 3)   直接走到
e. g. It's possible to take this path to head straight to the sea.

4) counterpart (Para. 4)   对手,等同的对方(n.)
e. g. The sales manager called his counterpart in the other company.

5) respect (Para. 4)   在……方面(n.)
e. g. These two cities are quite similar in this respect.

6) pretty (Para. 5)   非常(adv.)
e. g. The earthquake was pretty horrible with so many victims homeless.

2

Match the words to their definitions.

 Key

1—D, 2—C, 3—B, 4—E, 5—A

3

Fill in the blanks with words from the list in Exercise 2.

 Key

1. Some illnesses are caused by <u>stress</u>.
2. He worries about the <u>frequency</u> of his wife's shopping for brand names.
3. She felt her body become <u>stiff</u> after listening to such a long report.
4. Many miners used to work in a <u>dreadful</u> situation.
5. It is cruel to <u>confine</u> a lark in a cage.

Reading Skills Exercises:

1

List the reasons for the rise of spa at the airport according to the article.

 Key

Sitting in the same position on long trips would make anyone feel stiff and achy. It's a really good idea to have a massage when you land.
Heightened security has driven the rise of the airport spa.
Stressed-out executives are seizing on spas as a much-needed chance to recharge their batteries.

Language practice

Vocabulary

1

Finish the list of nouns. Then complete the sentences that follow.

 Key

Verb	Noun
invest	investment
differ	difference
solve	solution
object	objection
survive	survivor, survival

1. I am afraid there is not much *difference* in their points of view.
2. I'm not sure if we can gain any profit from the *investment*.
3. There are only a few *survivors* from the air crash.
4. Nuclear is not the only *solution* to energy crisis.
5. There is no *objection*, so we will begin with the next project.

2

In the grid below, 10 words connected entertaining activities are hidden. Three have been found for you. Find the others.

 Key

ballet, skiing, drama, snooker, bar, tea, disco, golf, karaoke, skate.

3

Fill in the blanks with words from the above exercise.

 Key

1. In the UK, clerks like to hang out in a *bar* after work.
2. She used to be a famous *ballet* dancer.
3. His favorite sport in winter is *skiing*.

4. In Japan, China and Korea *karaoke* is very popular. Many people like singing.
5. Two *golf* courses are available nearby.
6. *Disco* is usually noisy.
7. Chinese people have a long history of drinking *tea*.
8. Ding Jun-hui is a good *snooker* player.
9. In winter, many people *skate* on the lake.
10. We are moved by the *drama*.

Translation

Translate English into Chinese and underline the pattern. Study the pattern. Then translate the Chinese into English by using the pattern. Please do the followings according to the example.

 Key

1. It costs four times as much to gain a new client as it costs to keep an old one.
   主要句型：花在……方面的钱是花在……的……倍。
   中文翻译：花在获得一个新客户上的钱是花在保留一个老客户上的四倍。
   花在买衣服上的钱是花在买书上的两倍。
   English translation：It costs twice as much to buy clothes as it costs to buy books.
2. I would like to take this opportunity to invite you to a cocktail party this evening.
   主要句型：借此机会，我想邀请您……
   中文翻译：借此机会，我想邀请您参加今晚的鸡尾酒会。
   借此机会，我们想邀请您和您夫人去听今晚的音乐会。
   English translation：I would like to take this opportunity to invite you and your wife to the concert this evening.
3. Please let us know if you can make the trip.
   主要句型：请告知我们您是否……
   中文翻译：请告知我们您是否能来。
   请告知我们您是否能参加明天的会议。
   English translation：Please let us know if you can attend tomorrow's meeting.
4. I should be cheerful if you could come to take part in the event.

主要句型：您如果能来……那就叫人太高兴了。

中文翻译：您如果能来参加这个活动那就叫人太高兴了。

您能来参观我们的公司真叫人高兴。

English translation：I should be cheerful if you could come to visit our company.

Grammar

Grammar Exercises

Study the models and rearrange the following words into a correct sentence by using the same tense as the model. Please do the following according to the example.

 Key

1. Demand is becoming high now.
2. A boy was hit by a car on this street last week.
3. Great changes have taken place since 1978.
4. Tom had collected a thousand stamps by the end of last month.
5. They will have been married for twenty years by next year.

Listing

1

Work with your partner to fill in the blanks, using the words in the box. Listen and check your answers, and then follow the recording.

 Script

1. Our plane has <u>landed</u> at Shanghai Pudong International Airport. The <u>local</u> time is 10:30 a. m.
2. For your <u>safety</u>, please stay in your seat until the plane has come to a complete stop.
3. If I'm not <u>mistaken</u>, you must be Miss Smith from America.
4. I'm <u>delighted</u> to meet you and let me introduce myself.
5. The flight was <u>smooth</u> and the service was satisfactory.
6. Shall we go to the <u>van</u> now?
7. Is this all your <u>baggage</u>? Let me take this traveling bag for you.
8. Your temperature is normal. Everything is OK. You may go through <u>customs</u> now.
9. Welcome to Shanghai. Your passport, visa and customs <u>declaration form</u>, please.
10. I do feel a little tired, and maybe it is because of the <u>jet lag</u>.

2

Listen to the conversation and answer the following questions.

 Script

A：Ah, Mr. Johnson, glad to meet you, I'm Mike Li from Shanghai Times Garments Import & Export Corporation.

B：Glad to meet you too, Mr. Li. It's very kind of you to meet me at the airport. The airport is very nice.

A：How was your flight, Mr. Johnson?

B：The flight was smooth and the service was satisfactory.

A：I'm glad to hear that. I hope you'll have a pleasant stay in China.

B：I'm sure I will.

A：Shall we go to the parking lot now?

B：Thank you very much.

A：Is this all your baggage?

B：Yes, it's all here.

A：Let me take this traveling bag for you.

B：Oh, thank you.

A：Let's go. This way, please.

Key

1. Mr. Johnson.
2. The flight was smooth.
3. Shanghai Times Garments Import & Export Corporation.
4. The parking lot.
5. Very nice.

3

Listen to the conversation. In which order do you hear these sentences?

 Script

A: Mr. Johnson, you must be very tired after the long flight. Please sit down and have a short rest.

B: Thank you very much. It's very kind of you to meet me. I do feel a little tired. Maybe it is because of the jet lag. I'll be well after a short rest.

A: Would you like a cup of coffee or tea?

B: No, thank you. Chinese tea is famous all over the world. I have just had a cup of tea on the plane. It tasted good.

A: Mr. Johnson, our car is waiting outside. I'll drive you to the hotel. I hope you'll have a good rest there and recover from the jet lag soon.

B: Nothing to worry about. I'll be good as new soon.

 Key

(2) It's very kind of you to meet me.
(6) I'll drive you to the hotel.
(5) Would you like a cup of coffee or tea?
(3) Maybe it is because of the jet lag.
(1) Mr. Johnson, you must be very tired after the long flight.
(4) I'll be well after a short rest.

4

Your company is going to invite Mr. Johnson for dinner. Fill in the form after listening.

 Script

A: Good morning, Mr. Johnson. Glad to see you again.

B: Good morning. Glad to see you, too.

A: So, did you sleep well?

B: Oh, yes. Thank you for everything.

A: My pleasure. Mr. Tang, you know, our general manager, has prepared a dinner in your honor. I came here to invite you.

B: It's very kind of him. What time will it be?

A: At 7 p.m. Is it okay for you?

B: Sure.

A: What kind of food would you like to have? Chinese food or western food?

B: Chinese food, of course.

A: Is there anything you would not like to have?

B: As a matter of fact, I don't like spicy food. But chicken is my favorite.

A: I see. Then I might come to pick you up at 6 p.m., Ok?

B: It sounds good.

A: See you then.

B: Bye.

Key

Host's name	Mr. Tang
Guest's name	Mr. Johnson
Food style	Chinese food
Dishes which will not be ordered	Spicy food
Dishes which should be ordered	Chicken

Speaking

1

Role-play a conversation according to the following situation. After the practice, change roles.

Role Cards

Role A: Eric who is going to make recommendation on what specialty to buy.

Role B: Mr. Park who is asking for Eric's suggestions.

Flow Chart

Eric	Mr. Park
Greetings.	Greetings. Ask for recommendation on gifts.
Ask who the gifts are for.	Tell Eric the usage of the gifts.
Ask what Mr. Park would like to buy, food or clothes.	Tell him your preference.
Tell Mr. Park your recommendation.	Show your interest and ask where you can buy it.
Explain the place in details.	Show your appreciation.
Show that you are glad to help.	

Suggested Words and Expressions

Eric	Mr. Park
I think . . . is a good choice. In my opinion, I think something useful/practical/nice is the best. What kind of things are you looking for? What would you like to buy/see? Do you need anything particular? Who do you need to buy for? I've got just the place for . . . I know a great place/spot for . . .	Do you have any good recommendation? I'd like to buy some of your local specialties. I'd like to bring something back as a souvenir. I want to buy something for . . . I'd like to bring something to . . . Would you tell me where I can get/buy . . . ?

Reference:

A: Hello, Mr. Park. How is your feeling after these days in Shanghai?

B: Terrific! Shanghai is a nice place. The beautiful scenery impresses me so much. Thank you for your considerate arrangement and your company.

A: That's my pleasure. Well, what do you want to do next?

B: Before I end up this trip, I'd like to buy some specialties to bring back as presents. Do you have any good recommendation?

A: Yes, of course. Well, could you tell me first to whom you'd give away your presents?

B: OK, I'd like to bring something mainly to my wife.

A: I see. So in my opinion, I think the silk product is a better choice. China has a world-wide fame of home of silk.

B: That is really a great idea! My wife must be happy to have a silk coat.

A: Besides silk coat, there are many other silk products like silk gown, silk scarf and silk handkerchief etc. that you can choose to buy for your families.

B: Fantastic! So would you tell me where we can get some authentic silk products?

A: Sure. I've got just a place for silk shopping. The Shanghai Story is the best place for you. I think you can certainly select your favorites.

B: That's very nice of you to give me so much advice and recommendation. And I wonder if you could company me to go shopping in your spare time.

A: I'd like to. It's only 3 o'clock and quite early for the dinner. So why not go shopping right now?

B: Good! I can't wait to be there.

2

Work with your partner to make up a dialogue involving the following situation.

Role Cards

Role A: Eric who is coming to the airport to see off Mr. Park.

Role B: Mr. Park who is flying back and showing his appreciation.

Flow Chart

Eric		Mr. Park
Time to say goodbye.	→	Show your appreciation.
Express the pity time flies. Remind the happy days.	→	Express the same pity.
Express your desire to see him again.	→	Ask him to express your thanks to Mr. Zhang. And thank Eric for showing you around the city.
Express it's your honor.	→	Express you are happy about the trip.
Say goodbye. And wish him to have a nice trip.	→	Say goodbye.

Suggested Words and Expressions

Eric	Mr. Park
The time has come to say goodbye.	I have had a delightful time.
Here is your ticket.	I really appreciate you spending time showing me around the city.
It's my honor.	Thank you for your warm hospitality.
Have a nice trip.	
We are looking forward to your visit again.	

Reference:

A: Now you are to board the plane. Here we are saying good-bye.

B: It's very nice of you to see me off. I really had a delightful stay here. The time has come to say goodbye.

A: How time flies! You've been in China for nearly twenty days. It seems as if it were only yesterday that I met you at the airport. And now you are leaving.

B: Yeah, it's been a most wonderful experience for me. I wish I could stay a little longer, but I have lots to do back home, you know.

A: That's true. I hope to see you again soon.

B: I hope so. Don't forget to drop in on me if you and Mr. Zhang are ever in America.

A: Okay.

B: Thank you for your warm reception and hospitality. I really appreciate you spending time showing me around the city.

A: It has been my honor.

B: I'm sorry I couldn't find time to say good-bye to Mr. Zhang. Will you be kind enough to say thanks to him again for me?

A: Certainly. I'd be glad to.

B: Thank you very much for everything you've done for me. I shall cherish this trip. Let's keep in touch and look forward to next cooperation.

A: Sure. We look forward to your visit again. Here is your ticket. Have a nice trip. Good-bye.

B: Thanks. Good-bye.

Writing

1

Improve the following sentences.

 Guidance:

Teacher should point out that Ss may make the similar mistakes.

 Key

1. In order to celebrate our <u>company cooperate</u> (*companies' cooperation*), we are having a party this evening.
2. We would like <u>invite</u> (*to invite*) you to a party.
3. Our manager is going to host a dinner for you <u>participate</u> (*to participate*).
4. There is no dress code <u>demand</u> (*to demand*) you.
5. We will <u>honor</u> (*be honored*) if you present.

2

Please write an email to invite your client to take part in an entertaining event you have arranged. You can refer to the following sample.

 Guidance:

Teacher should ask Ss to read the sample email and find out the keys to write an email. If possible, invite 1 − 2 Ss to explain the underlined sentences in the sample email. Teacher encourages Ss to write an email according to the given situation. Invite 2 − 3 Ss to read their emails.

Reference:

To: johnson7657@ hotmail. com

Cc:

Subject: Cocktail party invitation

Dear Mr. Johnson,
To wish a successful cooperation between our two companies, we would like to invite you to join us in a cocktail party at 7:30 pm on Sep. 19 in Four Season Dining Hall, Four Season Hotel.
Please feel free to bring another person with you as our guest if you would like to join us. We will be honored if you can come. Please let us know.
Best regards,
Paul Tang
General manager
Shanghai ABC Silk Garments Company
Email: paultang@ abc. com

Learning for fun

Listen to the story and then retell it in class.
Omitted.

Unit 2   Fashion

Objectives

- **Career skills**
  Knowing some famous brands; dressing for different occasions; providing good customer service in a fashion store; writing an invitation card.

- **Reading**
  1. Scanning/skimming
  2. Reading for general information
  3. Looking for supporting details

- **Writing**
  1. General writing: sentence types
  2. Practical writing: invitation card

- **Listening**
  1. Listening for key words
  2. Listening for general information and details
  3. Listening for note-taking

- **Speaking**
  1. Talking about styles
  2. Shopping and bargaining

- **Language focus**:

Key words and phrases

brand occasion garment wear dress
fashion style outfit survey
recommend fitting room discount
stylish mixed preppie jeans
practical classic blazer dress code
domestic copycat rival sportswear
approve oppose

Teaching Arrangement

Warm-up & Unit task (Text A)
1) Time schedule: 2 periods
2) Suggested lesson structure
   Warm-up: 10 – 15 minutes
   Text A: 10 – 15 minutes
   Unit task steps 1 – 2 (pre-task):
   10 – 15 minutes
   Unit task steps 3 – 6 (while-task):
   30 – 45 minutes

Reading (text B)
1) Time schedule: 1 period
2) Suggested lesson structure
   Language points: 20 – 25 minutes
   Language practice: 20 – 25 minutes

Listening
1) Time schedule: 1 period
2) Suggested lesson structure
   Listening exercise 1: 10 minutes
   Listening exercise 2: 10 minutes
   Listening exercise 3: 10 minutes
   Listening exercise 4: 15 minutes

Speaking & Writing
1) Time schedule: 1 period
2) Suggested lesson structure
   Speaking: 20 – 25 minutes
   Writing: 20 minutes

Teaching Procedures

Warm-up

Do you know any famous brands of garments?
Please fill in the blanks of the following table.

Target:

Ss can know some names and logos of some famous fashion brands. Here more menswear are shown to draw boys' attention.

Guidance:

- Ss read the direction.
- Ss fill in the gaps of the table.
- Teacher may invite 3 − 4 Ss to call out the answers.
- Ss are encouraged to show their preferences.

Reference:

Logo	Brand	Nationality	Main product
LeVi's	Levi's	U. S. A	Jeans
dunhill	Alfred Dunhill	England	Knightsbridge Menswear /Suits
JACK JONES	Jack Jones	Denmark	Casual Menswear
Goldlion	Goldlion	China (Hong Kong)	Formal Menswear
Giorgio Armani GA	Giorgio Armani	Italy	High-class Formal Menswear
adidas	Adidas	Germany	Sportswear

2

How will you dress to suit different occasions?

A

Please match the following garments to each picture.

B

Disscuss in groups of three. Choose the right garments to fit to different occasions.

Target:

Ss can review some words on fashion which they have learned before. Then Ss can try to express their ideas on the different dressing styles for different occasions.

Guidance:

- Ss read the direction of Section A.
- Ss match the words to pictures.
- Teacher helps to check the answer.
- Divide Ss into groups of three. If it is a large class, each group may have more Ss.
- Ss read the direction of Section B.
- Ss read the different occasions and discuss what dressing style will fit.
- Ss read the sample and try to imitate the language so that they can express their ideas.
- Teacher may invite 2 groups to express their ideas.
- The teacher may help to give some tips and explain some difficult language points.

 Key

C	orange T-shirt	G	denim/skirt
E	coat	D	pink dress
B	striped blouse	H	jeans
A	a black suit	F	white trousers

Reference:

I plan to wear a black suit with the striped blouse, since it is my first day working in the office. I want to show others that I am professional, so I think I should be dressed in a formal style. A pair of black high-heels is a good match for the suit. On the business trip, simple and convenient clothes are a great choice. How I am dressing is a part of the company's image. Therefore, a coat and jeans will help a lot. If I am invited to a party, it will be suitable to wear a one-piece dress. So I am going to pick the pink dress from my closet. On Sunday's beach, an orange T-shirt and a denim can make out a casual feeling for myself and goes well with the relaxing background.

Tips

Having your own dressing style is very important and fitting in the dress code in the place where you are working is also very important.

Professional dressing code tends to be formal style.

Clerks tend to be dressed in a simple and comfortable style when they are on business trips.

People tend to choose casual style when they are hanging out with friends.

Unit task

Read Text A and practice some real tasks on the topic of fashion.

 Task Map(任务导航)

本单元任务要求学生围绕时尚这一话题下可能涉及的任务进行具体实践,通过模拟情景进行模拟实践,巩固学生用英语查阅信息、汇报、建议、提问与回答等能力。

本单元设置了一个情景:一个新毕业生 Lily Zhou 由学校推荐到全球知名的时装零售店工作,工作的具体岗位是时装销售顾问。在此前提下,本单元设计了一系列任务。就业是一个双向的选择,所以一方面 Lily 需要了解该公司的情况,另一方面她也需要知道该公司提供给她的工作岗位职责是什么。然后用市场调研作为一种手段使任务步骤间有一个过渡。之后成为销售顾问后把任务转到中心场景即销售卖场里,任务就设定为用来介绍时装的价格、款式、尺码等较为简单的工作。进而,该任务的设置继续发展为更为高级的时装销售人员较为重要的工作,即针对不同的客户需求推荐不同的风格及搭配。

本单元任务分为 6 个步骤,第一个步骤是学生模拟成情景设定中的角色,听取该公司人事部门主管阐述公司整体情况;第二个步骤是学生模拟身份,通过上官方网站来了解岗位职责;第三个步骤是学生模拟身份,做一份服装行业需要的调研,这个步骤是一个过渡步骤;第四个步骤是写出调研报告;第五个步骤是主任务环节,情景模拟,在卖场帮客人拿衣试衣,主要包含基本的服装店会话;第六个步骤是情景模拟,是本单元的主任务,配合时尚话题,要求学生模拟身份,根据不同的客人的要求为他们选择搭配衣服。同时该步骤设定的客人身份比较多,课堂内完成几项之余学生还可在课外完成其他几项。

本单元任务的安排主要根据活动过程顺序来设定,每一任务为后续的步骤做基础。

Process Break-down

Pre-task:

Step 1   Listen and sort out information.

Ss listen and take notes. Fill in the blanks. It is the background information for the following steps. Also, the information itself is also a piece of fashion news to Ss.

Step 2   Understand the responsibility of the position.

Ss watch a video and read the text. Figure out the responsibility of the job.

While-task:

Step 3   Do a survey

A: Ss describe their classmates' dressing style.

B: Ss are making a survey. They are going to ask others to finish questionnaires.

Step 4   Ss analyze data collected from the above step. They write a report by following the sample.

Step 5　Role play selling items to a customer at the store.

Ss can make a conversation according to the role cards and flow chart. In order to practice, the Ss work in pairs and switch turns.

Step 6　Provide more professional customer service on the selling floor.

Ss should choose 2 - 3 customers. With tips of Text A, Ss should describe different styles for different customers. It is the main step.

While-task：

Step 6　Concerning more than 3 situations are offered in this step, the situations which cannot be covered in class can be regarded as post task.

Step 1

Listen and sort out information.

任务过程控制关注点
Minefield

Target：

Know some information for the following steps.

- 提醒学生快速阅读已给信息。
- 提醒学生听力需要全神贯注。
- 提醒学生注意复合式的听力题型。

Guidance：

- Ss read Text A.
- Ss listen to what the director is saying about the H&M.
- Fill in the blanks.
- Invite 1 - 2 Ss to present the answers.
- Teacher can do a little explanation afterwards.
- It is read only once.

- 提醒学生要养成听的习惯，不要害怕失败。
- 提醒学生这则听力本身也是一则时尚信息。

Key

H&M was established in Sweden in 1947 by Erling Persson. We now sell clothes and cosmetics in around 2,000 stores around the world. H&M offers fashion and quality at the best price. H&M offers fashion for women, men, teenagers and children. The collections are created centrally by around 100 designers. H&M also sells own-brand cosmetics, accessories and footwear. The stores are refreshed daily with new fashion items. H&M has about 16 production offices around the world, mainly in Asia and Europe. H&M employs about 76,000 people.

---- **Expressions Pool** ----

1. ... was established ...
2. We sell ...
3. It has ... stores.
4. We offer fashion and quality.

Step 2

Understand the responsibility of the position.

任务过程控制关注点
Minefield

Lily is watching a video, in which a sales adviser called Anta is describing her work.

Target：

Sort out the information and know what a sales adviser does in the daily work.

- 提醒学生不要被生词限制住，阅读时需要利用上下文猜测关键词，非关键词可以忽略。阅读也应引入常识。
- 提醒学生快速阅读时应采用查读法。
- 提醒学生这个步骤的任务是为接下来需要完成的实际任务提供理论依据。

● 提醒学生观看 Video 时要关注
语言。

Guidance：

● Suppose Ss are Lily.
● Ss watch video.
● Invite 1 − 2 Ss to present their answer.

Refercence：

A sales adviser should <u>provide excellent customer service on the selling floor, in the fitting room and at the cash registers.</u>
<u>Handle garments that arrive daily: unload trucks, open and unpack the merchandise.</u>
<u>Stock and replace merchandise on the selling floor.</u>
<u>Keep the sales and service areas tidy and well-maintained.</u>
<u>Stay informed about promotions and sales activities.</u>
Anta's description：
(Omitted. This part is meant to let students get the main idea of Anta's description, not to pinpoint any exact words.)

 Script

I love the clothes and the fashion. I moved to New York and I was a fashion major. So, that was one of the first places I came shopping at. And it was really exciting and upbeat, and . . . So I'm like . . . I would love to work here.
"I only have a 2 or a 6. You wanna try the 6? Or the 2? Actually, you're tiny. "
The best thing working in retail is the freedom of not having micro-management, being up on fashion, working with friendly people, exciting people. I would say that's the best.
"How are you doing? That looks really cute. Do you need new sizes or anything?"
"I think I'm gonna end up getting this one in the other color. It's like a pinkish color. "
"OK. I could definitely go find it for you. The same size?"
"Yeah. "
We get the truck every day. So we're constantly getting in new shipments. So basically, it's running out clothes, maintaining your section, running from the fitting room, um . . . garment care, standards. Just a constant cycle about running the clothes back out to the floor, replenishing the floor, giving great customers service, making the store look good and meeting new people, giving the whole vibe of H&M.
"It's really . . . Anyway you wear . . . I think people put it on the side and then just will put . . . cover over one eye. "
It is a very busy job. I mean you have your ups and your downs. But when it's up, it's very busy.
"I can help the following guest. "
"Did you find everything OK?"
"Do you like darker colors? Or lighter colors?"
People always ask："What should I wear for this?" "Do you have anything that's like this?" Every day I would say I'd get somebody like that whether it's for business, or party, or a luncheon, or anything. The way I take initiative is just communicating to my management about what's going on. In my section, what I see that needs to be moved around or what needs to be pushed or I could let them know that it's not doing very well. It's very hands-on, and, and, your department, so you kinda take control.

" — These scarves aren't selling very well. So I was thinking of putting them so — , maybe somewhere in this A area so we can push them out. I was gonna just maybe fold a few down in the same area or hang them on a spigot over here. "

A perfect day at H&M is making our goal — everything selling out. That would be a perfect day. But it's not always perfect. So . . . But I would say it's perfect when you . . . when you're happy. And . . . I am. So, I would say a lot of . . . I have a lot of perfect days at work.

Step 3

Do a survey.

A

Describe a classmate's dressing style.

Target：

Know how to describe others' dressing style.

Guidance：

- Suppose Ss are Lily and her classmates.
- Observe classmates' dressing style.
- Describe a classmate's dressing style.
- Teacher should guide Ss to use the suggested expressions.
- 1 - 2 Ss can be invited to present their description.

B

Ask ten classmates of yours to finish the following questionnaire. Collect ten finished questionnaires.

Target：

Introduce questionnaires as a main method to make a survey.

Guidance：

- Suppose Ss are Lily and her classmates.
- Raise your requirement politely so that others would like to answer your questions.
- Distribute the questionnaire to the classmate who is willing to do one.
- Ask them to answer questions.
- Collect at least 10 questionnaires.
- Teacher should guide Ss to pay attention how to design a questionnaire.

Step 4

Write a survey report.

Target：

Know how to write a survey report.

Guidance：

- Ss read the direction and try to understand the situation.
- Read the sample.

任务过程控制关注点
Minefield

- 提醒学生要尽量理解和运用描述他人着装风格的表达方法。
- 提醒学生问卷的形式和关键词句。
- 请别人帮你完成问卷需要礼貌。

Expressions Pool

1. Could you please help me to finish a questionnaire? It may take you several minutes.
2. I am from . . . company.
3. The purpose of the survey is to . . . .
4. Thanks for your time.

任务过程控制关注点
Minefield

- 提醒学生写调查结果报告之前一定要有一定数量的数据。
- 提醒学生调查结果报告必须真实反映调查的数据。
- 提醒学生注意调查报告的撰写规律。
- 提醒学生勇于尝试。

------- Expressions Pool -------

1. I have made a survey about . . . among . . .
2. According to my data, . . . would like to choose . . . , because . . . .
3. It shows/reviews/tells us that . . . .
4. . . . account for 20%.
5. The major factor affecting people when they are going to . . . is . . . .
6. the majority, only a few . . .

- Ss figure out the outline of a survey report.
- Teacher should guide Ss to use the suggested expressions.
- Ss write their survey report according to the data they have collected.
- 1 - 2 Ss may be asked to present their reports.

Reference :

I surveyed 10 classmates about their dressing preferences. According to my survey, college students like a casual style in their daily life. Most of them like loose dress, since it looks casual and it is comfortable. They do know many brands. However, they think they cannot afford many of them. Therefore price and style should be the two major factors when they make decisions. Sportswear is their good choice. 90% of classmates I surveyed would like to choose sportswear in whatever season. 10% think that tank-top is not a good choice even in summer because they prefer more traditional dressing style.

Step 5

Role-play a conversation of selling items to customers at a store.

任务过程控制关注点
Minefield

- 提醒学生开拓思维。把关于服饰的词汇记忆起来并在此任务中运用。
- 提醒学生对话要自然，贴近实际。
- 提醒学生注意语言使用得当，但也不应害怕语言不丰富不敢开口讲。
- 提醒学生对话要礼貌。
- 提醒学生对话的关键是如何在服装专卖店与顾客会话。

Target :

Know how to sell items to customers.

Guidance :

- Ss read the direction and try to understand the situation and role cards.
- Work in pairs.
- According to the role cards and situation, Ss can make a dialogue. The dialogue should be focused on talking about style, size and prices.
- Teacher should guide Ss to use the suggested expressions.
- 1 - 2 pairs can be invited to present their dialogue.

	Sales assistant	Customer
About price range	What kind of price range do you have in mind? What is the maximum price you have in mind?	Up to about . . . I don't really care. No more than . . .
About pattern & color	I think the color suits you well. This is the hottest style in this season. I think this pattern is well-suited for this shirt. It sure looks good on you.	What is the hottest style this summer? I'd like to see some new arrivals. Can you pick me one that goes well with this jacket?
About size	I think it's a little too small for you. I think this size will give you a better fit. Shall I take your measurements? I will go and check our stock.	Do you have a larger one? You do seem to have my size on the shelf. Do you think it will fit me? It's about . . .
About price	I am sorry but we cannot give you any discount. Our best offer for today is 25% off. We can give you 30% off for cash. I am sorry that's the best price. Thanks, but we cannot take tips.	Can you give me a discount? Can I get it cheaper if I pay in cash? Can you take a little more off? Keep the change.

Reference：

A：Welcome. What can I do for you？

B：I am looking for a tennis skirt. Do you have any new arrivals？

A：Sure. This way. The tennis skirts are on this shelf. All of them are made of 100% cotton. Please take your time.

B：Thanks. But could you please tell me what color is the hottest this summer？

A：White is the classy and red is popular.

B：Can I try them both？

A：Sure. The fitting room is this way.

B：Thanks.

. . .

B：Which one looks better？

A：I think the red one suits you better. But I think it's a little bigger. It looks loose. I can get you a smaller one.

B：Thank you.

A：Here you are. Try it on, please.

B：It is better, and how much is it？

A：It is 280 *yuan*.

B：It's a little bit expensive. Can I have a discount？

A：Sorry, it's a new arrival, so we cannot offer any discount.

B：I see. Anyway, I will take it. I like it.

A：Thanks. It surely goes well with your figure. Please come to the cashier.

B：Thanks for your help.

A：Enjoy your shopping.

---- Expressions Pool ----

1. What can I do for you?
2. What kind of price range do you prefer?
3. I am sorry, but we can't make any reduction.
4. We have some clothes on discount.
5. I will take it.
6. Can I try it on?
7. The fitting room is this way.
8. I am sorry but you cannot try on more than 3 items.
9. We'd appreciate it very much if you could bear in mind that because of the nature of the merchandise, we can neither exchange your purchase nor give you a refund.

Step 6

Provide more professional customer service on the selling floor.

任务过程控制关注点
Minefield

Target：

Know how to match items to suit different requirements or styles of different customers.

Guidance：

- Ss read the direction and try to understand the situation.
- Ss read the tips from the Text A.
- According to different requirements of different customers, Ss can make a decision to choose what to match. What they can match have been shown in pictures.
- Teacher should guide Ss to use the suggested expressions.
- 2 – 3 Ss can be invited to present their choices.

- 提醒学生认知不同人的着装风格。
- 提醒学生注意积累表达着装风格的词汇和表达方法。
- 提醒学生该任务还可以扩展为和别人讨论着装风格的话题。
- 提醒学生该任务应以时装风格是否与场景吻合,不强调标新立异、奇装异服。
- 提醒学生参考步骤2中的视频获得一些灵感。

Reference：

1. *Gossip Girl* shows us many stylish girls. You've got the right choice. Could you please look at these two pictures? Our designer's inspiration is actually from the hot drama. We call it as "New York City Girl". The fashion style's major factor is that two styles are mixed together, for example, sportswear and high-heels, or preppy blouse and cool blazer.

2. Miss, you are quite fit. Therefore, I think simple styles will suit you well. Since jeans are your favorite. How about a white T-shirt and jeans? They are perfect match and you will have a simple and timeless style.

3. Miss, you are quite in. Actually, this year, many fashion designers do think practical is fashion. Therefore we have many choices. But I think the material and color are the most important factors. I recommend clear color and soft material. And you know what, this season you can even kick the uncomfortable high-heels. Would you please come here? I will show you some hot items.

4. Congratulations. You two look so sweet. In this season many items do fit the happiest bride. Please look at these two pictures. We can find that it is a fairytale style. The designer would like to use soft chiffon to make a romantic feeling. As for the color, a pure color such as white or black is a good choice. In addition, dresses with cute fabric flowers are also hot.

5. Sir, it's my pleasure to introduce the hottest style this season. Actually as you can see, many suits still have the classic style. But what makes the suits not stiff and more stylish is two elements: colorful scarves and wrinkled material. If you do not like the scarves, a hat is also a hottest combination. Andy just bought a hat in our store days before. You know, the relaxed and traveler's look is really in.

6. You guys are going hiking? It is really a season to get refreshed in the nature. Lucky you. And I think nowadays, young guys do want to look stylish. Sportswear should be stylish and no longer stiff. How about these picks? They are new arrivals. A simple but stylish Tee with shorts should be a good match. If you think it is a bit simple, a mix with a cardigan will be really in. Do not forget sports shoes with bright color.

Action research
（教师自己的教学行动研究）

任务完成中的观察、反思（日志、随笔） 备忘

Language Points

Text A • • • • • • • • • • • • • • • • • •

◆ (**line 1**) **Not all of us are fashionably** *inclined*, . . .

inclined: having a natural ability in a specified subject

[运用]　be . . . inclined

e. g. John was musically inclined and he finally became a musician.

[拓展]　*be inclined to do sth.* 有某种倾向;很有可能做某事

Jane is inclined to be lazy.

He is inclined to be late for work when it's cold outside.

◆ (**line 7**) . . . **everyone can** *spot* **a fashion disaster** . . .

spot: to pick out, to catch sight of, to recognize, to discover

[运用]　spot sb. , spot sth.

e. g. He spotted his wife in the crowd.

She couldn't spot the difference between the two pictures.

[拓展]　*spot* (*n.*) 斑点,污渍;地点

There are several spots of mud on her skirt.

Shall we go out this weekend? I've found a nice picnic spot.

◆ (**line 21**) . . . **get out there and** *forge* **your own style!**

forge: to create by means of much hard work

[运用]　forge a treaty, forge a relationship

e. g. Each country needs to forge its own economic development strategy.

[拓展]　*forge* (*v.*) 伪造

The politician was forced to forge a signature.

Text B • • • • • • • • • • • • • • • • • •

◆ (**line 5**) . . . **need only take a** *stroll* **down** . . .

stroll: a slow, leisurely walk

[运用]　take a stroll

e. g. This couple used to take a troll after dinner.

[拓展]　*stroll* (*v.*) 散步

[仿写]　雨停了,我们出去散个步吧。

◆ (**line 18**) . . . **in a** *reversal* **of the natural order of things**, . . .

reversal: making sth. the opposite of what it was; turning around

[运用]　a . . . reversal, a reversal of . . .

e. g. His luck suffered a cruel reversal when he was thirty years old.

[拓展]　*reverse* (*v.*) 使(某物)反转,将(某物)翻转

Choices made today may be impossible to reverse in the future.

[仿写]　请把你的衣领翻过来。

◆ (**line 34**) . . . **it costs a** *fraction* **of the price** . . .

fraction: small part, bit, amount or proportion (of sth.)

[运用]　a fraction (of sth.)

e. g. Could you move a fraction closer?

[拓展]　*fractional* (*adj.*) 微小的;支离破碎的

The candidate has only a fractional share of vote.

[仿写]　这只是整个计划的一小部分。

◆ (**line 37**) **The role that** *imitation* **played** . . .

imitation: the act of imitating

[运用]　by imitation

e. g. We can learn to pronounce a word by imitation.

[拓展]　*imitate* (*v.*)

He amused his friends by imitating the teacher.

[仿写]　她擅长模仿鸟叫。

◆ (**line 64**) **Their** *ascent* **up the valuc chain** . . .

ascent: the act of ascending

[运用]　begin one's ascent, a slow/gradual/rapid ascent

e. g. He called back as he began his ascent.

[拓展]　*ascend* (*v.*) 上升;攀登

The stairs in the old castle ascend in a graceful curve.

[仿写]　他们在攀登途中遇到了困难。

Translation of Texts

Text A

周丽丽即将从学校毕业。学校就业服务中心推荐她到 H&M，一家时装零售店，做一名时装销售顾问。她的主要工作职责主要包含以下几点：

- 在销售区、试衣间和收银台提供卓越的顾客服务。
- 处理每天到货的服装：帮助货车卸货，并拆封商品。
- 负责销售区的货品存放和补货。
- 保持销售区和服务区整洁有序。
- 及时掌握主题营销活动及促销活动的信息。

现在她要阅读一篇文章为自己的工作做好准备。

如何发现最新的时尚潮流

我们大家并不是人人都是时尚的，因此我的这篇文章就是来帮助你找到自己的风格。你就可以避免因为自己判断失误而看起来很难看，也没必要完全照抄别人的风格。你只需照着不同的媒介给你的启发，把这些启发运用到自己身上，找到符合自己性格的风格。现在我就来教你几招如何马上发现最潮的时装吧。

第一步　观察别人

到人群中去挑那些穿得很难看的人，我相信你立马可以挑出来。从自己身边经过的人如果穿得很糟糕很难看的话，我们每个人都会一眼就发现了。为了调查到我们身边的时尚，观察别人是最省钱、最简单，也是最不会有什么坏处的方法。

第二步　杂志

我们知道现在大多数杂志都已经变成垃圾。比起时装，杂志更关心什么是健康的生活方式之类的事。但是杂志还是会告诉你每季里你该穿的颜色和款式，还会告诉你到哪里能买到这些东西。你所选的杂志会决定你的风格。*Vogue* 这本杂志是把时装当作艺术的，所以这本杂志里多数的服装都不适合我们大多数日常的穿着风格。如果你要实用点的时装，那就看看 *Marie Claire* 或者 *Jane*。这两本杂志介绍的衣服相对比较平民化，价钱也更便宜些，这两本杂志还可以作为指导你如何进行混搭。

第三步　打开电视

看看类似于"时装急救"或是"什么不该穿"这样的电视节目。信息量很大。

第四步　上网

寻找时装是永远没有终点的。在你追求寻找时装的时候，你读了这篇文章，那才只是一个开端。在世界各国有成千上万的时装网站可以帮助你找到自己的风格。马上尽情地享受全世界为你准备的时装盛宴吧，那样你就可以创造出自己的风格。

Text B

中国本土服装品牌正在崛起

中国本土消费品牌日益崛起，对外国名牌构成挑战，已经成为中国工业发展的一个明显趋势。任何怀疑这一点的人，只要去福建省的一个小城市晋江的大街上走一走，就会深有感触。

在一段典型的百十米长的街道两侧，有 34 家出售各种本土品牌产品的商店。向耐克（Nike）和阿迪达斯（Adidas）（据信，两家公司今年的在华销售额可能都在 10 亿美元左右）发起挑战的，是安踏（Anta）、361 度、李宁（Li Ning）、星泉（Xingquan）、贵人鸟（K-Bird）、德尔惠（Deerway）和特步（Xtep）等本土竞争对手。七匹狼（Septwolves）、利郎（Lilanz）、宏兴百货（Hongxing Baihuo）、365＋1、雅仕（Yashi）和卡宾（Cabeen）则把目标瞄准了乔治·阿玛尼（Giorgio Armani）、雨果博斯（Hugo Boss）和杰尼亚（Ermenegildo Zegna）等品牌。

这些名称也许听起来并不耳熟，甚至很怪异。但现实是，事物的自然秩序正在逆转：小鱼开始吃大鱼了。那些十多年前从西方品牌持有者手中承接外包制造业务的中国公司，如今纷纷成功推出了自己的品牌产品。通常情况下，它们所销售产品的质量与它们过去为外国大牌制造的产品并没有什么差别。

"它的面料主要是山羊绒和少许羊毛，与阿玛尼外套完全一样，"一名利郎专卖店的店员指着一件剪裁时髦的灰色外套说。经营这家专卖店的是晋江本土公司中国利郎（China Lilang），于今年 11 月在香港上市，融资 10.6 亿港元（合 1.37 亿美元）。

"但你可以从价签上看到，它的售价仅是阿玛尼的一个零头，"她补充道，"别人看不到商标，所以看起来就和穿着阿玛尼一样。"

不少晋江公司并不讳言模仿在企业发展中扮演

的角色。七匹狼是一家在深圳上市的晋江公司,《21世纪经济报道》(*21st Century Business Herald*)曾援引该公司董事长周少雄的话称,他的公司先是模仿外国品牌,接着学会了如何自我创新。该报称,七匹狼发展初期曾模仿过法国鳄鱼(Lacoste),但如今,当周少雄在香港逛购物中心时,他对 Zara 和 H&M 更感兴趣。

七匹狼如今是如此成功,以至于催生了一整批狼的模仿者。在晋江市中心的大街上,可以看到诸如与狼共舞(Dancing Wolves)、狼道(Wolf Zone)和狼的诱惑(Temptation of Wolves)等名称的商店,彼此相隔仅几米远。到了一定阶段,这些年轻的仿冒者可能会侵蚀正牌公司的品牌价值,但就目前而言,七匹狼看起来是安全的。该公司今年以来的销售额较 2008 年翻番,使它得以扩大在全国各地的专卖店网络。

同样成功的还有不少总部位于晋江的运动服饰制造商,比如安踏、特步、匹克和 361 度。它们都从外国品牌的代工厂起家,但如今都凭自身实力获得了国际认可,正从耐克和阿迪达斯那里赢得中国市场份额。赞助美国国家篮球协会(NBA)球星的决定,加快了它们向价值链上游迈进的步伐。NBA 在中国广受欢迎,部分原因是因为有中国球员姚明和易建联的参与。

Explain these words and expressions through their context or with the help of a dictionary.

1. boomerang (title)(澳大利亚土著的)飞去来器;(比喻)自食其果(*v.*)
e. g. The rapid currency rise is threatening to boomerang on New York's real estate industries.

2. outlandish (Para. 3)陌生的(*adj.*)
e. g. What she wears is rather outlandish.

3. indistinguishable (Para. 3)无法区别的(*adj.*)
e. g. Its color makes the bird indistinguishable from the tree it rests on.

4. innovate (Para. 6)创新(*v.*)
e. g. Our company is well-prepared to innovate in order to progress.

5. copycat (Para. 7)盲目模仿者(*n.*)
e. g. She is a copycat who follows her sister's lead in everything.

6. erode (Para. 7)侵蚀(*v.*)
e. g. We should prevent the rights of the individual from being eroded.

Reading Skills Exercises:

1

Please fill in the blanks by using the tips.

 Key

As we can see, many domestic brands are rising these years, such as Li Ning, Xingquan, K-bird, Xtep, Steptwolves, Lilanz, Yashi, etc. (listing some brands). The Chinese companies are now successfully having their own branded products. Often, the products that they sell are similar to those they used to make for the foreign brands. However, the price is much lower. Take Lilanz as an example, it is made mostly of cashmere and a little wool, exactly like an Armani coat, but it costs much less than Armani (using the example of Lilanz from the text). Many Chinese companies first imitated foreign brands. Now we are glad to see some changes. Chinese brands learned how to innovate themselves (by Zhou Shaoxiong, Chairman of Septwolves).

2

Match the words to their translation.

 Key

1－E, 2－C, 3－B, 4－A, 5－D

Language practice

Vocabulary

1

Choose the correct word order.

 Key

1. a traditional Japanese   2. the annual California state budget   3. a preliminary police investigation   4. a north London house

2

Pattern substitution pratice.

 Key

1. Dutch-born;   2. Stanford-educated;
3. ground-launched

Translation

Translate the following Chinese sentences into English by putting the given words and expressions into right order.

 Key

1. Domestic branded goods are not inferior to foreign ones.
2. Arriving in Shanghai, you should take a stroll down Nanjing Road.
3. Li Ning is a local Guangzhou company.
4. This is a Beijing-based company.
5. Adidas is an internationally-recognised company.

Grammar

Grammar Exercise
1 B   2 D   3 C   4 C   5 B

Listening 🎧

1

Work with your partner to fill in the blanks using the words in the box. Listen and check your answers, and then follow the recording.

 Script

1. You've got to know how to wear skinny jeans and a jacket, and then put a bow tie with it.
2. The one place you might see a bow tie in a professional environment is on an elderly, well-dressed partner.
3. Her waist has reduced from 25 to 20 inches.
4. She wears a jacket with a high waist.
5. The dress perfectly set off the seventeen-inch waist.
6. He wears a fur- collared jacket.
7. A tight blazer sets off her curves.
8. This color will never go out of fashion.
9. I can not find a pair of shoes in my size.
10. The skirt is made out of natural fibres.

2

Fill in the form after listening.

 Key

1. a pair of trousers
2. 20 inches
3. blue
4. 268 yuan

 Script

A: What can I do for you?
B: I want to buy a pair of trousers.
A: This way please.
B: This blue pair looks beautiful. Can I try them on?
A: What waist size do you want?
B: 20 inches.
A: Wait a moment.
A: Here you are. Try them on please.
B: They are too tight.
A: Try this pair please.
B: They fit well. How much are they?

A: 268 yuan.

B: OK, I'll take them.

3

Listen to the conversation. In which order do you hear these sentences?

 Key

> (4) When will you make sales promotons?
> (3) Can you give a 20 percent discount?
> (5) We will call you if we do.
> (1) How much is this pair of shoes?
> (2) 278 yuan.

 Script

A: How much is this pair of shoes?

B: 278 yuan.

A: Can you give a 20 percent discount?

B: Sorry, you know the prices in the franchise will not be discounted except during the promotion.

A: When will you make sales promotions?

B: We will call you if we do.

B: Thank you very much.

4

Listen to the conversation and answer the following questions.

 Key

> 1. West Beijing Road
> 2. Line 4
> 3. A pair of branded shoes
> 4. Domestic brands
> 5. Tom doesn't know.

 Script

A: Tom, I want to buy a pair of brand name shoes, can you tell me where I can buy them?

B: No problem. I have ever been to several West Beijing Road-based franchise stores such as Anta, Xtep, Peak, 361° and Adidas.

A: Which number bus should I take?

B: You can take Line 4. What brands do you prefer, domestic or foreign?

A: Domestic brand name products. They are as good as foreign brand name products in quality and style.

B: I think so. And they are also cheaper.

A: What color is in fashion this year?

B: I am not sure. But I think white never goes out of fashion.

A: Thank you!

B: You are welcome.

Speaking

1

Role-play a conversation according to the given situations. After the practice, change roles.

Role A: Approves of young girls wearing low-slung skirts and navel-baring tank tops.

Role B: Opposes.

Flow chart for arguments.

Role A	Role B
State that the concept of dressing style needs to be changed.	Explain that they are living in a conventional society.
Express the desire of leading fashion.	Accept the concept of being fashionable but worry about acceptability.
Explain the society needs new ideas. So does fashion.	Do not agree. State that school girls are not allowed to wear in a sexy way.
State that school girls should show their advantages: cool, sexy.	Against. Believe that blind pursuit of fashion will corrupt values and boost materialism.
Explain that individuality is encouraged by the current society.	Against. Explain that too much personality may bring disorder to school.
Express disagreement and close the conversation.	

Suggested Words and Expressions

Role A	Role B
There is no single sign of fashion. We're supposed to lead the fashion. Get out of the box! Why hide yourself under the boring sportswear? Obviously, we can't reach an agreement on this topic.	I don't think this dressing style is suitable. We have to consider its acceptability. It's just not right. Don't get too far away.

Reference:

A: Look at our campus. There is no single sign of fashion. The style and the concept need to be changed. Young girls like us should wear low-slung skirts and navel-baring tank tops in this hot summer.

B: Is it necessary? China is a traditional country. We're all living in this conventional society. I don't think this dressing style is suitable.

A: Come on, young girl! We're supposed to lead the fashion.

B: Fashion is good. But we have to consider its acceptability. Look, we're students, not the super stars and professional fashion makers.

A: Old school. Get out of the box! The society needs new ideas. Girls need new looks.

B: Think about our identity. School girls should not be allowed to wear low-slung skirts and navel-baring tank tops. It's just not right.

A: School girls should show their advantages. Look at you, you are typically cool and sexy. Why hide yourself under the boring sportswear?

B: Not true. The most important thing lies in how we behave rather than how we look. The blind pursuit of fashion and beauty will corrupt values and boost materialism.

A: I don't think so. The whole society is encouraging people to show their personality and individuality.

B: Well. Don't get too far away. Too much personality means irresponsibility. It can bring disorder to school's daily running.

A: Obviously, we can't reach an agreement on this topic.

2

Work in groups of three. Work with your group members to make up dialogues involving the following situation.

Your friends want to buy a navel-baring tank top, but she worries a little. She hopes that you can go with her to buy one.

Role A: you want to buy a navel-baring tank top, but you are a little worried. You hope your friend can go with you.

Role B: you will encourage your friend to buy a tank top and help her to buy at a low price.

Role C: you are the shop assistant who wants to sell a tank top. You have a listed price and a lowest price. You wouldn't sell the item below your lowest price.

Flow chart

Role A	Role B	Role C
Ask where to buy.	Suggest a franchise store.	
(at the store)		Greetings. Ask what the customers need.
Tell the assistant what you need.		Introduce the items on sale.
Ask if they have tank tops.		Ask what style they like.
	Make some suggestion to your friend.	Encourage A to try on different items.
Ask if there is a discount.		Explain. Try not to lower your price too easily.
		State your best price.
Make a deal.	Help your friend to knock down the price.	

Suggested Words and Expressions

Role A	Role B	Role C
Where can I find something good? We want to buy a tank top. Do you have navel-baring ones? Where is the fitting room? What do you think? I can get it with a discount, right? Let's make it a deal!	I know a nice franchise store on West Beijing Road. We can take Line 4. It is only twenty minutes' ride. Let's check it out. Hey, what about this one? Try it on. You look great. It's too pricey. How could this small piece cost so much!	We have some clothes on discount these days. We have many different styles. Just try them on if you like. 20% off is already low price. Look, the quality and design are worth the price. What I am offering is a knock-down price.

Reference:

A: Hey, I want to get myself some clothes. Where can I find something good?

B: I know a nice franchise store on West Beijing Road.

A: Sounds good. How far is it?

B: We can take Line 4. It is only 20 minutes' ride. Let's check it out.

(20 minutes later)

B: Here we are!

C: Welcome! What can I do for you?

A: My friend and I want to buy some nice pieces of clothes for the coming season.

C: You've got the right place! We have some clothes on discount these days.

B: See. I said it was a nice store.

A: Great! We want to buy a tank top. Do you have navel-baring ones?

C: Of course. We have many different styles and just try them on if you like.

B: Hey, what about this one? Try it on.

A: Alright. Where is the fitting room?

C: This way, please.

(a few seconds later)

A: What do you think?

B: You look great.

C: Yes! It matches you perfectly. This piece goes well with your figure. And the color makes you sparkle.

B: Let me see. RMB 500 yuan? It's too pricey.

A: I can get it with a discount, right?

C: Yes. But this line of clothes is new arrival. 20% off is already low price.

B: Come on. Make it lower. How could this small piece cost so much!

C: Well. I can offer you another 10% of discount. Look, the quality and design are worth the price. What I am offering is a knock-down price.

A: I don't think it's reasonable.

B: Me either. Give me your lowest price. My friend loves this one. Just tell us.

C: 300. That's my best price.

B: 250?

C: No way. 275. Final offer.

A: Let's make it a deal!

Writing

Please write an invitation card.

Target: This part aims at helping the Ss learn how to write an invitation card.

Guidance: The form of invitation needs to be emphasized.

Reference:

Honorable Ms. Lily Zhou

You are invited to join us in the fashion party

On Friday, the eleventh of October

At 8:00 p.m.

39 Queen Boulevard, Hong Kong

Unit 3   Advertising

Objectives

- **Career skills**

  Designing a job advertisement; designing an advertising campaign for a product.

- **Reading**

  1. Scanning.
  2. Reading for main idea(s).
  3. Looking for topic sentence and supporting details.
  4. Guessing word meaning from context.

- **Writing**

  Practical writing: Designing a poster.

- **Listening**

  1. Identifying the speaker's tone of voice: agree or disagree.
  2. Listening for key words and numbers.
  3. Listening for general information and details.

- **Speaking**

  1. Discussing how to make an ad for room renting.
  2. Talking with a client about an advertising campaign.

- **Language focus**

  Key words and phrases

  advertisements   selling point   slogan
  job advertisement   campaign   method   advantage
  disadvantage   rent-a-room ad   TV ad
  stimulate   commercial   appeal to

Teaching Arrangement

Warm-up & Unit task (Text A)
1) Time schedule: 2 periods
2) Suggested lesson structure
   Warm-up: 10 - 15 minutes
   Text A: 10 - 15 minutes
   Unit task steps 1 - 2 (pre-task): 10 - 15 minutes
   Unit task steps 3 - 4 (while-task): 15 - 20 minutes
   Unit task steps 5 - 6 (while-/post-task): 25 - 30 minutes

Reading (Text B)
1) Time schedule: 1 period
2) Suggested lesson structure
   Language points: 20 - 25 minutes
   Language practice: 20 - 25 minutes

Listening
1) Time schedule: 1 period
2) Suggested lesson structure
   Listening exercise 1: 10 minutes
   Listening exercise 2: 10 minutes
   Listening exercise 3: 10 minutes
   Listening exercise 4: 10 minutes

Speaking & Writing
1) Time schedule: 1 period
2) Suggested lesson structure
   Speaking: 20 - 25 minutes
   Writing: 20 minutes

Teaching Procedures

Warm-up

Look at the following pictures. These are advertisements placed in our daily life. Try to find out what product is sold and what selling point is stressed on in each advertisement.

Target:

Ss brainstorm what products are sold and what selling points are shown in the different advertisements.

Guidance:

- Ss read Warm-up Task1.
- Ss discuss what they have seen in the advertisements.
- Ask Ss to read the sample.
- Invite 3 Ss to present their answers.

Reference:

Tire is sold in Picture 2. The selling point is that the tire runs smooth and steady even on snowy roads.

Rubber gloves are sold in Picture 3. The selling point is that the rubber gloves do not slip.

Shaving blade is sold in Picture 4. The selling point is that the blade is super sharp.

Read and appreciate the following advertising slogans of some famous brands. Discuss with your partner and exchange what you know about the brands.

Target:

Ss can learn and appreciate the advertising slogans of some famous brands in this task.

Guidance:

- Ss read Warm-up Task 2.
- Ss discuss and exchange what they know about the brands.
- Invite 2 - 3 Ss to introduce what they know about the brands.
- Ss work in groups translating the advertising slogans into Chinese.
- Invite 2 - 3 Ss to present their answers.

Reference:

- 有路就有**丰田车**。(套用谚语 Where there is a will, there is a way.)
- **钻石**恒久远,一颗永流传。(De Beers(**戴比尔斯**)钻戒广告采用夸张手法,暗示爱情的永恒,富有诗意,充满浪漫。)
- 要醒神,喝**七喜**。(简单传神,英文表达很押韵。)
- **苹果电脑**,不同凡"想"。(将"不同凡响"替换一字,一语双关。)

- 和我不一样,我的**劳力士手表**从不需要休息。(运用拟人手法,凸显产品卓越品质。)

Background Information:

The First 5 World-Famous Advertising Firms:

Omnicom Group 奥姆尼康(美国)

IPG/ Interpublic Group(美国)

WPP(英国)

Publics 阳狮集团(法国)

电通(日本)

The First 5 Well-Known Advertisers:

1. 威廉・伯恩巴克(William Bernbach,1911 – 1982):DDB 广告公司的创始人之一。
2. 小马里恩・哈珀(Marion Harper Jr. 1916 – 1989):缔造 IPG(英特帕布利克集团),并开创广告传播集团先河的哈珀大帝,美国广告界 20 世纪最富有创新王国的缔造者。
3. 李奥・贝纳(Leo Burnett,1891 – 1971):李奥・贝纳广告公司的创始人。
4. 大卫・奥格威(David Ogilvy,1911 – 1989):奥美广告公司,广告之父,发展了艾伯特・拉斯克的"平面推销术"的理论,留下了许多令人难忘的创意。
5. 罗瑟・瑞夫斯(Rosser Reeves,1910 – 1984):特德・贝茨广告公司,提出"USP 理论"的第一人。

Unit task

Read the advertisements in Text A and practice a series of real tasks of designing advertisements.

 Task Map(任务导航)

广告是因为某种特定的需要,通过一定的媒体形式向公众传递信息的宣传手段。广告从目的上进行分类可以有多种形式,而且各种广告的文本和表现形式都不一样。随着业务发展,公司常常需要借助报纸、网络等媒体手段登载招聘广告。招聘广告不仅仅要讲清楚需招聘人员的职位、职责、素质要求;同时,招聘广告也是一个窗口,让应聘者了解招聘公司的基本情况等。商业广告则主要侧重在表现形式上如何对其产品进行宣传包装。

本单元结合 Text A 的选文,假定情景,把这些广告作为某假定的广告公司的作品。并在此基础上设定情景,要求学生模拟身份为该公司设计一则招聘广告和一项商业广告活动。通过完成一系列的真实工作任务,认识各种不同的分类广告,了解广告文案的特点,熟悉招聘广告的内容构成、形式、习惯表达等,以及初步了解商业广告宣传活动的形式和表达方法。

本单元任务分为 6 个步骤,学生在假定情景中以模拟的广告公司职员的身份完成两项广告设计的工作。第一个步骤让学生认识各种不同的分类广告,了解广告文案的特点;第二个步骤让学生熟悉招聘广告中关于素质要求、职责等方面的常用表达方式;第三个步骤让学生知道广告中需要告知应聘者哪些公司信息。第四个步骤让学生认识招聘广告由哪5个部分构成,并能据此对 Text A 中的招聘广告范文进行结构解剖,找出这5个部分;第五个步骤为主任务,通过完成前几个任务的知识积累,让学生针对某公司设计一则招聘广告;第六个步骤是主任务,因为给学生的选择余地较大,所以也有部分可以作为课后任务进行操作,其中心是让学生针对某一指定产品进行广告宣传活动的设计。每一任务为后续的步骤做基础。

Process Break-down

Pre-task:

Step1 Read the three classified advertisements and get background information.
Ss get the general idea of the classification of different advertisements.

While-task:

Step2 Choose appropriate English for an English job advertisement.
Ss learn the right way to express the responsibility and requirements of a job.

Step3 Fill in the chart with related information.
Ss read a name card and sort out some information.

Step4 Read Advertisement 1 again in Text A, and then match the subtitles with corresponding information.

Step5 Ss de a job advertisement for AQG Company on their own based on all the above information. Ss are expected to fill in the blanks from 1 - 15.
Ss should be encouraged to finish the main task and to pay attention to the text of the job advertisement.

Step 6 Ss de an advertising campaign to advertise a product.
With some tips, Ss should choose one way to design the campaign. It is the main step.

Post-task:

Step 6 Concerning more than 2 ways are offered in this step, what cannot be covered in class can be regarded as post task.

Step 1

任务过程控制关注点
Minefield

● 提醒学生不要被生词限制住,阅读时引入常识。
● 提醒学生在练习中有意识地使用不同的表达方式。

Read the three classified advertisements and get background information for the following real tasks.

Target:

Get to know three different kinds of classified advertisements as well as the features of a job advertisement.

Guidance:

● Ss work in groups of three, each reading one of the three ads by themselves.
● After reading, Ss can exchange ideas.
● Invite 1 - 2 Ss to present their answers.
● Teacher can do a little explanation afterwards.

Reference：

A

Advertisement 1 is <u>a job advertisement</u>.

Advertisement 2 is <u>a math tutor service advertisement</u>.

Advertisement 3 is <u>a vehicle for sale advertisement</u>.

B

I think a job advertisement should <u>be short, terse and pithy（informative/read like a friendly and sincere letter）</u>...

In my opinion, a job advertisement is generally composed of <u>5 parts</u>, including <u>Position, Qualifications and skills required, Contact information, Company introduction, and Job description.</u>

So far as I'm concerned, people usually place a job advertisement on <u>newspapers, magazines, or the Internet, etc.</u>

Step 2

Choose appropriate English for an English job advertisement.

任务过程控制关注点
Minefield

Target：

Get to know the different expressions. During this step, Ss can also discuss different ways to express the same meaning.

Guidance：

- Finishing Step 1, Ss have already known what a job advertisement is like.
- Ss work in pairs, matching the English translation to the Chinese version.
- Invite 3 Ss to present their answers.
- Teacher can do a little explanation afterwards.

● 提醒学生开拓思维。看到左栏中的中文后，不要急于到右栏寻找答案。让学生开展头脑风暴，自己探讨英文表达方式。
● 引导学生思考：招聘广告中关于应聘者能力素质、职责等方面的要求还有哪些？

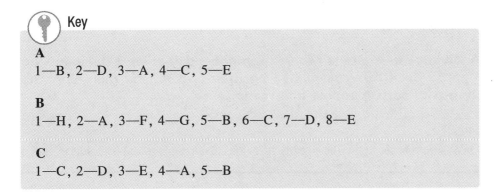

Key

A

1—B, 2—D, 3—A, 4—C, 5—E

B

1—H, 2—A, 3—F, 4—G, 5—B, 6—C, 7—D, 8—E

C

1—C, 2—D, 3—E, 4—A, 5—B

Step 3

A job advertisement should present some basic company-related information. The following chart may help the interviewees know about the company-AQG. Please fill in the blanks with information related by referring to the name card of managing director of AQG.

任务过程控制关注点
Minefield

● 提醒学生讨论要围绕任务主题。
● 提醒学生合理分工，考虑各人不同的英语能力水平。

Target：

Get to know what kinds of company-related information are needed in a job advertisement.

Guidance:

- Read the chart and judge what company-related information is missing.
- Read the name card of the managing director of AQG.
- Find the information that is missing in the chart.
- Fill in the chart with information related.
- Invite 2 Ss to present their answers.
- 4 Ss work in a group, role-playing as if one is answering what others ask about the company.
- Teacher can do a little explanation afterwards.

🔑 Key

Name of the company	AQ Electric Suzhou Co., Ltd
Address of the company	No. 66 Yinyan Rd, Suzhou New District, 215151 Suzhou, P. R. China
Contact number of the company	Telephone: +86(0)512 - 66169999 ext. 8111 Mobile: +86(0)13913578882 Fax: +86(0)512 - 66513292 E-mail: andreas. bjor@ aqg. se
Website of the company	www. aqg. se
Contact person	Andreas Bjork
Working hours	Monday-Friday 8:30a. m. - 5:30p. m.
Company profile(概况)	A leading company in electronics in the East of China
Years of being in business	10⁺ years

Step 4

任务过程控制关注点
Minefield

- 提醒学生注意快速阅读中寻找细节信息点的技巧。
- 提醒学生注意招聘广告的 5 个组成部分的先后顺序。

A job advertisement is generally composed of at least the following 5 parts. Read Advertisement 1 again in Text A, and then fill in the form with corresponding information.

Target:

Make sure that Ss know the 5 parts of a job advertisement and are able to judge them.

Guidance:

- Teacher asks Ss what 5 parts are indispensable in a job advertisement.
- Ss read the job advertisement in Text A and judge the 5 parts.
- Ss sort out corresponding information.
- Ss work in pairs and exchange their ideas.
- Invite 2 Ss to present their answers.
- Teacher can do a little explanation afterwards.

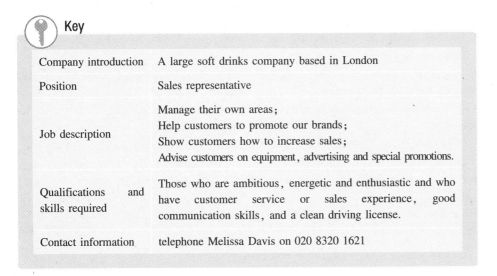

Company introduction	A large soft drinks company based in London
Position	Sales representative
Job description	Manage their own areas; Help customers to promote our brands; Show customers how to increase sales; Advise customers on equipment, advertising and special promotions.
Qualifications and skills required	Those who are ambitious, energetic and enthusiastic and who have customer service or sales experience, good communication skills, and a clean driving license.
Contact information	telephone Melissa Davis on 020 8320 1621

Step 5

Design a job advertisement for AQG Company on your own based on all the above information. You are expected to fill in the blanks 1 – 15 and name the subtitles for each part (A – E) in the job ad referring to Step 4.

 Key

1. Suzhou   2. leading   3. electronics   4. personal assistant
5. Meeting minutes taking
6. Work schedule setting
7. Business negotiations interpreting
8. healthy and ambitious
9. fluent in spoken and written English
10. 3⁺ years' corresponding work experience
11. Good organization and interpersonal skills
12. andreas. bjor@ aqg. se   13. Andreas Bjork   14. +86(0)13913578882
15. www. aqg. se
A. company introduction   B. Position   C. Job description
D. Qualifications and skills required   E. contact information

Step 6

Design an advertising campaign for a product.

Target:

Ss can try to write a slogan for a product and choose one medium to advertise the product.

Guidance:

- Ss work in groups of 5 or more.
- Ss read the situation. Teacher explains that an advertising campaign requires Ss to choose a medium to advertise a product.
- Ss read the Advertisement 3 from Text A. Teacher guides Ss to fill in the form

任务过程控制关注点
Minefield

- 提醒学生开拓思维。回忆自身经历,有没有在英文报纸或网络上看到一些公司的招聘广告?它们通常由哪些内容组成? 具体到职责描述和应聘者能力素质要求等方面,通常有什么样的普遍要求?
- 提醒学生换位思考。作为招聘方,你想传达的公司形象是什么样的? 想避免的信息有哪些?

in order to figure out the selling points of the product.

- Teacher guides Ss to read the Career Focus. Ss work in groups to create a slogan to advertise the product.
- Teacher explains about three methods of advertising campaign according to the tips.
- If Ss choose radio, they should pay attention to the slogan, the text and how to read it.
- If Ss choose TV, they should use a story to advertise the product. They can create characters and plots concerning the product.
- If Ss choose a billboard, they should make sure it is eye-catching.

Key

A:

Name of the product	Kubota compact utility vehicle
The selling points	Start quicker, run quieter, stop smoother; Comfort, technology and refinements of a larger utility vehicle

Reference:

B: Kubota compact utility vehicle, carry the world on!
Kubota, compact size, competitive power!
Kubota, your good assistant.
Kubota, starts quicker, runs quieter, stops smoother.

C: Radio: Kubota compact utility vehicle comes with great power. Are you in trouble, my fellow labor worker? You are going to be saved! Choose Kubota, choose an easier life. Kutoba can start quicker, run quieter and stop smoother.

TV: A farmer was working with a clumsy shovel in the field under the burning sun. He sweated a lot and hardly opened the eyes. The farmer straightened his back and looked around the vast field he was standing on. He dropped that tool and took a long sigh. Suddenly, Kubota compact utility vehicle moved toward him from the other side at a high speed. A friend of the farmer drove the vehicle with great joy. He said, "We are saved!" The farmer didn't look upset anymore. He smiled at the camera with a thumb-up.

Billboard:

Starts quicker
Runs quieter
Stops smoother

Kubota
THX-1136

Your good assistant

Action research
（教师自己的教学行动研究）

任务完成中的观察、反思（日志、随笔）　　　　　　　　　备忘

Language Points

Text A • • • • • • • • • • • • • • • •

Advertisement 1

◆ (line 2) **Last year we increased our sales by 15% and *launched* several new products.**

launch：(a company) makes sth. available to the public.

e. g. The powerful allies helped the company launch a "low-cost" network computer.

［运用］ launch into (a speech, task, or fight)：to enthusiastically start sth.

e. g. The CEO launched into a speech about the importance of new projects.

［拓展］ *launch* (*n*.)：推出

e. g. The company's spending has also risen following the launch of a new project.

Advertisement 2

◆ (line 1) **ADVANCED math skills, patient, professionally trained, experienced *private* tutor.**

private：belonging only to you

e. g. They want more state control over private property.

［运用］ private life/thoughts/feelings/places/companies, etc.

e. g. I've always kept my private and professional life separate.

［拓展］ *privacy* (*n*.)：隐私；私人空间

e. g. He resented the publication of this book, which he saw as an embarrassing invasion of his privacy.

Advertisement 3

◆ (line 2) ***Available* in Kubota orange and blue.**

available：sth. that you can find or obtain.

e. g. This store has about 500 copies of the book available for purchase.

［运用］ available resources/information/opportunities/options, etc.

e. g. The available resources we can provide are listed as follows.

［拓展］ *availability* (*n*.) 可获得性

e. g. The easy availability of guns.

Text B • • • • • • • • • • • • • • • •

◆ (line 9) **... increase your sex *appeal* if you use ...**

appeal：(*n*.) a quality that people find attractive or intersecting.

e. g. Its new title was meant to give the product greater public appeal.

［运用］ sex/public appeal

e. g. Ads that promise to increase your sex appeal if you use a certain product are very common.

［拓展］ *appeal*：(*v*.) 吸引

e. g. On the other hand, the idea appealed to me.

［仿写］ 他的建议对我没有吸引力。

◆ (line 25) **... young people's desire to *conform*.**

conform：to be of required type or quality of sth. such as a law, social norms or someone's wishes.

［运用］ conform to

e. g. The lamp has been designed to conform to new safety standards.

［拓展］ *conformity*：(*n*.) 随大流

e. g. Excessive conformity is usually caused by fear of disapproval.

［仿写］ 这个产品的性能与广告上所说的一致。

◆ (line 36) **... whether they are getting *solid* value for their dollars ...**

solid：being useful and reliable.

［运用］ solid advice/performance

e. g. The organization provides the company with solid advice on a wide range of subjects.

［拓展］ *solidly* (*adv*.) 坚定地；连续地

e. g. People who had worked solidly since Christmas enjoyed the chance of a Friday off.

［仿写］ 我不相信传闻(rumor)，我只相信确凿的证据。

◆ (line 44) **... *stimulates* demand ...**

stimulate：to encourage sth. to begin or develop further.

e. g. America's priority is rightly to stimulate economy.

［运用］ stimulate production/demand/competition/consumption

e. g. Product promotion can stimulate consumption.

［拓展］ *stimulative* (*a*.) 刺激性的

e. g. It's possible that a tax cut might have some stimulative effect.

［仿写］ 他被对手的挑战刺激了。

◆ (line 53) **... try to make their *commercials* creative.**

commercial：an advertisement that is broadcast on television or radio.

［运用］ TV commercials/radio commercials

e. g. Turn off the channel — there are too many TV

commercials.

［拓展］ *commercial*（*a.*）商业（化）的

e. g. Shanghai is a major center of commercial activities in China.

There were no commercial radio stations until 1920.

［仿写］ 很多人感到现在的艺术都太商业化了。

◆（**line 64**）... *violate* the rules of ...

violate：to break an agreement, law, promise, or standard.

［运用］ violate rights/rules/the Constitution/law

e. g. They went to prison because they violated the law.

［拓展］ *violation*（*n.*）违反

e. g. To deprive the boy of his education is a violation of state law.

［仿写］ 违反规定就要受到惩罚。

◆（**line 67**）... are influenced by ads and often buy on *impulse*, ...

impulse：a sudden desire to do sth.

e. g. Unable to resist the impulse, he glanced at the sea again.

［运用］ on impulse：凭一时冲动

e. g. Sean is a fast thinker, and he acts on impulse.

［拓展］ *impulsive*：（*a.*）易冲动的

e. g. He is too impulsive to be a responsible mayor.

［仿写］ 她突然有一种想逃走的冲动。

Translation of Texts

Text A

Advertisement 1

你想成功吗？
还不快来应聘 IBI 公司销售代表！

底薪£30,000 + 公务车 + 福利

我们是一家大型软饮料公司,总部位于伦敦。去年我们公司的销售额增长了15%,同时还推出了好几款新产品。目前,我们公司为发展壮大营销力量,向全国各地有经验的销售代表提供工作机会。我们的销售代表们管理各自的服务区域,帮助客户推广品牌,向客户展示如何提高销售额,并就有关设备、广告、促销等问题给客户提出建议。

如果您

- 有抱负
- 有活力
- 有热情

并具备

- 客服或销售经验
- 良好沟通能力
- 无不良记录的驾驶证

我们欢迎您前来应聘。

一经录用,我们将提供优厚的薪资、公司福利,以及激励计划。

欲知详情,欢迎来电垂询 Melissa Davis,联系电话:020 8320 1621

Advertisement 2

提供数学家教

现有数学水平高、耐心、经专业训练、有经验的家教。如被指导者努力,保证有所提高。各种层次教学都有,价格实惠。

联系电话:28277546

Advertisement 3

小巨人

*RTV*500

启动快捷
运转无声
刹车平稳

新款 Kubota RTV500 小型多用途车拥有大型多用途车所具备的舒适度、新技术及改进工艺。Kubota RTV500 橙色和蓝色两款有现货供应。四轮驱动的 Kubota RTV500 适用于上班或外出驾游。详情垂询 Kubota 各地门店经销商,欢迎试驾。

地址：北卡莱罗纳州东门罗（邮编28112）

74 号 3144 号高速 布鲁克斯经销公司

联系电话：704－233－4242

营业时间：周一～周五 7：30—17：30；

周六 8：00—12：00

KUBOTA

www. kubota. com

Text B

广告——是利是弊？

广告的目的无非是为了卖出商品。这就意味着广告商将竭尽全力让你想要某种东西——他的商品——无论你需要与否。换句话说，登广告的人在为他的产品制造需求。别忘了，如果你不了解一件东西，你自然不会去买。

先让我们来看看广告商是如何吸引年轻消费者的。

如果我们使用了某种产品定会魅力大增，这样的广告随处可见。几乎所有的产品都会使用这一招。广告商让你相信如果你吃、嚼、喝、穿或用他们的产品，你将会更时尚、更受欢迎。对青年人来说，约会十分重要，所以他们必须让自己装扮宜人，体味清新，掩盖皮肤的缺陷，发型恰到好处。广告就会告诉你怎样使用一种特别的发胶来让年轻的先生女士们对彼此更具吸引力。当然，也有提醒你去除口臭、体臭的广告。调查报告显示针对年轻人的化妆品每年的销售额高达 100 亿美金，这并不令人吃惊。

广告商也迎合年轻人的趋众心理。年轻人喜欢把自己看成是"我行我素"很有个性的人，但是这只说对了一半。看看你周围的同龄人的发型和着装吧。你们相同的东西可能很多，只不过你不愿意承认而已。而且，广告商也迎合年轻人追崇时尚的愿望，迎合他们骄傲和嫉妒的心理。

广告商也让他们的年轻消费者知道商品的价格以及能得到的售后服务，因为消费者感兴趣于他们所买的东西是否物有所值。

这时你可能想知道广告到底是好是坏。实际上，两者兼而有之。为了帮助你确认，以下分别列出了广告之利弊。

广告之利

1. **刺激需求** 需求促进销售，从而扩大生产。而生产规模的扩大则会保持较高的就业率。

2. **广布信息** 消费者通过广告了解已上市的新产品的信息。

3. **刺激竞争** 生产商不得不保持警觉，因为消费者会随时了解新品牌及其价格。

4. **提供娱乐** 大多数情况下，广告商会尽力使他们的广告充满创意又妙趣横生。有些人甚至喜欢看这些电视商业广告。

广告之弊

1. **有时误导公众** 有些广告故意耍滑头，实质就是欺骗公众。有些广告让演员扮成医生促销保健产品，这相对更容易误导观众相信他们所看到的。

2. **常常滥用语言** 有些广告很愚蠢或毫无意义，甚至还违背预言规则滥用语言。

3. **鼓励冲动购物** 消费者受广告影响常常凭一时冲动购物，没有事先计划。他们常常购买那些他们并不需要的东西，也没有买到最合算的东西。

4. **提高商品价格** 登广告要花钱。而产品的广告成本也加在了消费者的开支成本上了。

Explain these words and expressions through their context or with the help of a dictionary.

1) solid (Para. 5) 扎实的，可靠的（*adj.*）
e. g. His proposal seems a solid plan to me.

2) stimulate (Para. 7) 刺激（*v.*）
e. g. A cut in interest rate should help stimulate economic recovery.

3) commercial (Para. 10) 商业广告（*n.*）
e. g. The government launched a campaign of TV commercials and leaflets.

4) violate (Para. 12) 违反，破坏（*v.*）
e. g. They violated the ceasefire agreement.

Reading Skills Exercises：

1

Mark each of the following statements True（T）or False（F）.

Key

1—T，2—F，3—T，4—F，5—F

2

Match the words to their definitions.

 Key

1—C, 2—D, 3—A, 4—B

Language practice

Vocabulary

1

Fill in the blank in each sentence with an appropriate form of the given word.

 Key

1—employer/employees, 2—encouragement, 3—destruction, 4—shortage, 5—assistant

(**Note**: the various suffixes of noun)

2

Fill in each blank with one of the two words from each pair and note the difference of meaning between them.

 Key

1—live, 2—general/common, 3—tiny, 4—ill, 5—regular

3

Complete each of the following sentences with a proper word from the box, change the form where necessary.

 Key

1 — blemishes, 2 — appeal to, 3 — solid, 4 — conform, 5 — are on our toes

Translation

Put the following Chinese sentences into English by using the given words. Part of the sentences has been given.

 Key

1. Anyone <u>who violates the traffic regulations</u> will be punished.

2. Pop songs about love and life <u>appeal to young college students very much</u>.
3. <u>Consumers often buy on impulse</u> what they do not need.
4. Increasing violence at the campus <u>warns educators of the serious mental problem</u> of some students.
5. All policemen have to keep <u>on their toes with the coming of Washington summit</u>.

Grammar

(**Note**: Teachers may deal with the summary chart of modals selectively. In other words, teachers may choose to explain some of them depending on the overall level of students)

Grammar Exercise:

Rewrite these sentences using an appropriate modal listed below to replace the words in italics.

should	have to	mustn't	don't have to

Example: If you want your website to be effective, *it is necessary to* work on it all the time.

If you want your website to be effective, <u>you have to work on it all the time.</u>

1 It is a good idea for online retailers to dispatch orders quickly.

Online retailers <u>should dispatch orders quickly.</u>

2 One of the good things about their websites is that it is not necessary to register.

One of the good things about their websites is that you <u>don't have to register.</u>

3 It is a good idea to put your logo on every page of your site.

You <u>should put your logo on every page of your site.</u>

4 If you order before March 15, there's no obligation for you to pay until July.

If you order before March 15, you <u>don't have to pay</u>

until July.

5 This deal is very important for all of us, so no mistakes please!

This deal is very important, so we <u>mustn't make any mistakes</u>!

Listening

1

Work with your partner to fill in the blanks using the words in the box. Listen and check your answers, and then follow the recording.

 Key

1. agencies,   2. recommend,   3. magazine,
4. rent,   5. launched,   6. commercial,
7. billboard, 8. classified,
9. second-hand, 10. unique

 Script:

1. Many of the <u>agencies</u> advertise in the "Help Wanted" sections of the daily papers.
2. Businesses have considerable freedom to advertise and <u>recommend</u> pesticides to the farmer.
3. A company may advertise its products by means of newspapers, <u>magazines</u>, and television.
4. If you <u>rent</u> that apartment, will you stay there for a long time?
5. This camera is newly <u>launched</u> to meet the needs of professional photographers.
6. They receive a mass of order after the TV <u>commercial</u>.
7. Haier erected a <u>billboard</u> in a shopping district of Tokyo to show its determination to reach Japanese marketplace.
8. You should check the employment office and the <u>classified</u> ads for job openings.
9. It's a <u>second-hand</u> pick-up but still running with great performance.
10. I'd like to stress on the <u>unique</u> selling point of my apartment in the advertisement.

2

Listen to the dialogues, paying attention to the ways people agree and disagree with the opinions expressed. Decide whether the second speaker agrees or disagrees with the first speaker and tick the right box.

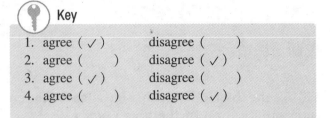

	Key		
1.	agree (✓)	disagree ( )
2.	agree ( )	disagree (✓)
3.	agree (✓)	disagree ( )
4.	agree ( )	disagree (✓)

 Script:

1. — Do you think we should put an ad in the newspaper to sell our apartment?
   — Sure, why not?
2. — There'll be a volleyball match between Cuba and Russia on Channel 5.
   — Are you absolutely sure?
3. — The idea of the Nike commercial appeals to me very much.
   — You said it.
4. — Didn't you think the movie we saw last night was a waste of time and money?
   — I wouldn't say that.

3

Listen to the dialogue three times and fill in the blanks with the missing information.

Key

Roommates wanted

<u>Female</u> roommate wanted for pleasant, sunny two-bedroom apartment on <u>Fifth</u> Avenue, three blocks from campus. Share <u>rent</u> and utilities. Available <u>September 1</u>. Call Maggie at <u>5556792</u> between 5 and 9 p. m.

 Script:

Placing an Ad

(Ring . . . Ring . . . sound of phone being picked up)

John: Hello, Campus Daily, advertising department. This is John speaking.

Maggie: Hi. I'm calling to place an ad.

John: Sure. Under what classification?

Maggie: Well, I'd like it in the "Roommates wanted" section.

John: All right. And how would you like it to read?

Maggie: It should read "Female roommate wanted for pleasant, sunny two-bedroom apartment on Fifth Avenue, three blocks from campus. Share rent and utilities. Available September first. Call between 5 and 9 p. m. and ask for Maggie.

John: Uh Huh. You'll want your telephone number on it, right?

Maggie: Oh sure. Thanks for reminding me. It's 555 – 6792.

John: And how long do you want it to run?

Maggie: For a week. I guess. How much would that be?

John: Let's see — it's $10 a week per line. Your ad will take up three lines, so that's $30.

Maggie: All right.

4

Listen to the passage and then mark each of the following statements True (T) or False (F).

 Key

1. F 2. T 3. F 4. F

 Script:

Different Kinds of Advertising

Advertising is an important part of marketing. Very few companies are able to sell a product without advertising. There are many different kinds of advertising, such as: newspaper advertising, radio advertising, magazine advertising, television advertising and promotion, etc . . . . The simplest is called promotion. That is to say, some booklets are handed to people in the street or are mailed to them so that people get latest information about the products. Newspaper advertising is the cheapest kind, while television advertising is the most expensive.

Television advertising can usually be very successful because it can reach a large audience. Small companies often find it too expensive to afford it, so they often use newspapers to advertise.

Speaking

1

Role-play a conversation according to the following situations. After the practice, change roles.

Role Cards

Role A: Maggie has a room to rent. She is asking her friend to give her some advice on how to write an ad so that she can rent her room more effectively.

Role B: Julie, Maggie's good friend. She has experience to rent spare rooms to others via writing good ads. She is now giving advice to Maggie.

Flow chart

Maggie	Julie
Greet and express your depression.	Greet and ask what happened.
Explain and ask for help.	Show your willingness to offer help.
Tell your friend that you have already advertised it on a student newspaper but it did not work.	Suggest that Maggie should write a room for rent ad by herself.
Show you agreement and ask for advice.	Advise on making a list of terms of the rental such as the charge, the length of the lease, the facilities, and special terms on smoking and pets, as well as a list of benefits of the rental.
Tell Julie the benefits of your rental.	Advise on where your friend can place her ad.
Show your gratitude and express your anxiety to write the ad soon.	Show your good wish.

Suggested Words and Expressions

Maggie	Julie
Hey, I am a bit worried. I am trying to rent my spare room, but ... I tried ... , but it didn't work. That's exactly what I am thinking about. I do need your help/advice. Yes. You are absolutely right. Let me take notes. My apartment is in a good neighborhood. Furthermore, it is ... walk to ... Hang on. What about this line? Thanks. You've done a great favor. I am about to write it. I will let you know what is going on.	What's up? Have you ever tried ... ? Why not write a room for rent ad by yourself. In order to find a high-quality tenant, you will need to write an effective room for rent ad. Make a list of the terms of your rental. How much rent will you charge? How long of a lease will you require? What facilities are included? How large is the room? Is there a private bathroom for the tenant? What about smoking and pets? When is the rental available? You also need to list the benefits of your rental. For example ... Internet and local newspapers should be good choices for you to place the ad. Good luck. And let me know the latest news.

Reference:

A: Hey, Julie. Do you have a minute? I am so bothered.

B: Sure. Maggie. What's up?

A: You know it is really hard to find a nice part-time. And I need to pay my bills. So I want to rent my spare room.

B: Have you advertised it for rent?

A: Yes, I tried the campus newspaper, but it didn't work. I have waited for a week, but no one contacted me to rent it. I just called the students newspaper and let them advertise it.

B: Why not write a room for rent ad by yourself and place it?

A: Actually that's exactly what I am thinking about. And I need your advice. I know you have experience in writing such kind of stuff.

B: I am glad to help. Listen. In order to find a high-quality tenant, you will need to write an effective room for rent ad. First, you should make a list of the terms of your rental. How much rent will you charge? How long of a lease will you require? What facilities are included? How large is the room? Is there a private bathroom for the tenant? What about smoking and pets? When is the rental available?

A: Yes. You are absolutely right. Let me take notes. These are really important terms.

B: You also need to list the benefits of your rental. That is to say, what makes it a great place to live?

A: Yes, my place is in a nice neighborhood. It is a 5-minute walk to campus from the apartment. I will provide private bath. Hang on. What about this line? "A 5-minute walk to campus from this bedroom and private bath for rent means you'll never be late to class again."

B: Great. And do not forget to place your ad online and on the local newspaper.

A: Thanks, Julie. You've done a great help. I am about to write the ad and place it.

B: You are welcome. Good luck. Let me know the latest news.

A: Sure. I will call you ASAP.

2

Work with your partner to make up a dialogue involving the following situation.

Role Cards

Role A: Bob, who is an advertising agent and is receiving a client. Bob should pay attention to the client's needs, such as the product, the brand image, the target consumers and so on.

Role B: Sam Wang, who is the marketing director of a local auto dealer. He is asking Bob to make a TV advertisement for a newly-launched brand. He should state out some factors such as brand image, target consumers so that the advertising agent knows how to create an ad.

Flow Chart

Bob	Mr. Wang
Greetings and self-introduction.	Greetings and self-introduction.
Ask what service Mr. Wang needs.	Show the purpose of your visit.
Tell Mr. Wang that your advertising agency's strength. Ask what product will be advertised.	Tell Bob your company's product and preference.
Ask about the main goal of the advertisement.	Show the main goal.
Ask about the brand image.	Explain the brand image.
Ask Mr. Wang what target consumers the product is going to aim at.	Tell Bob about the target consumer.
Ask Mr. Wang whether a pop star is needed or not.	Express your attitude.
Show your passion to make the advertisement.	Wish a good cooperation. Say goodbye.
See your client off.	

Suggested Words and Expressions

Bob	Mr. Wang
I am an advertising agent. What can I do for you? We specialize in designing and making TV commercial ads. What is the main goal you want to achieve with this advertisement? What kind of image would you like to develop? What target consumers would you like to aim at? You aim at mid-range market and high-end market, right? Do you want a pop star in the advertisement? It is our honor to design the ad for your company. I will work on it soon and let you know.	I am Sam Wang from Coruscant Auto Sales. Here is my name card. We are looking for someone to design and make an ad. TV ad is our preference. We want to promote a newly-launched car. The brand is Magotan. We'd like to introduce the brand to the local market and raise consumers' awareness on the new product. We want to create a successful and smart image. Successful businessmen and well-educated people will be our target consumer. Yes. We hope consumers recognize that our product is the symbol of their social status and high quality life. It depends on the idea of the ad. Great. Please let me know your idea soon. Then we will discuss other details such as charge and time. I am looking forward to a good cooperation.

Reference:

A: Good afternoon. My name is Bob Lee, advertising agent. Please take a seat. Here is my name card. What can I do for you?

B: Good afternoon. I am Sam Wang from Coruscant Auto Sales. Here is my name card. Our company is looking for someone to design and make a TV commercial advertisement for our product.

A: You've come to the right place. Our agency specializes in designing and making TV advertisement. Mr. Wang, what product do you want to promote?

B: We want to promote a newly-launched car. The brand is Magotan.

A: What is the main goal you want to achieve with this advertisement?

B: We'd like to introduce the brand to the local market and raise consumers' awareness on the new product.

A: What kind of image would you like to develop?

B: We want to create a successful and smart image.

A: What target consumers would you like to aim at?

B: Actually we want to have a wide range of target consumers. But successful businessmen especially executives and well-educated people would be our most important target consumers.

A: They should be successful and smart, aren't they?

B: You're right.

A: I see. You aim at mid-range market and high-end market, right?

B: Yes, we hope consumers recognize that our product is the symbol of their social status and high quality life.

A: Do you want a famous person or a pop star in the advertisement?

B: It depends on the idea of the ad.

A: OK, Mr. Wang, it is our honor to design the ad for your company. I will work on it soon with my team members and let you know our ideas. Mr. Wang, if your company needs us to present our idea of the ad, please inform me of the time and place. We will get ready.

B: Great. Please let me know your idea soon. Then we will discuss other details such as charge and time. I am looking forward to a good cooperation. All right, Mr. Lee, it is really nice talking to you. See you soon then.

A: Mr. Wang, nice talking to you too. See you next time. Let's keep in touch.

Writing

Please design a poster. It can be a film poster, or a sales poster, and even a football match poster. You can refer to the following sample.

Reference：

（omitted）

 Guidance：

Teacher should ask Ss to read the sample poster and find out the keys to design and write a poster. If possible, invite 1 – 2 Ss to explain the keys such as *what*, *where*, *when*, *and how attractive*. Teacher encourages Ss to write a poster.

Learning for fun

Watch the TV commercials and have fun. （视频见教学光盘）

1. 可口可乐广告
2. 百威啤酒广告
3. 保时捷轿车广告
4. 耐克广告
5. 李宁广告

Unit 4　Finance

Teaching Arrangement

Warm-up & Unit task（Text A）
1）Time schedule：2 periods
2）Suggested lesson structure
　　Warm-up：10 – 15 minutes
　　Text A：10 – 15 minutes
　　Unit task steps 1（pre-task）：
　　10 – 15 minutes
　　Unit task steps 2 – 5（while-task）：
　　45 – 60 minutes

Reading（text B）
1）Time schedule：1 period
2）Suggested lesson structure
　　Language points：20 – 25 minutes
　　Language practice：20 – 25 minutes

Listening
1）Time schedule：1 period
2）Suggested lesson structure
　　Listening exercise 1：10 minutes
　　Listening exercise 2：15 minutes
　　Listening exercise 3：15 minutes
　　Listening exercise 4：15 minutes

Speaking &Writing
1）Time schedule：1 period
2）Suggested lesson structure
　　Speaking：20 – 25 minutes
　　Writing：20 minutes

Objective

- **Career skills**
Use and explain how to use an ATM；ask and answer questions in an interview；describe a person's appearance；write a bank deposit receipt.

- **Reading**
1. Reading for main idea(s)
2. Skimming/Scanning
3. Reading for key word spotting
4. Reading for finding out the cause
5. Reading for guessing word meaning from context

- **Writing**
1. General writing：practice sentence patterns
2. Practical writing：bank deposit receipt

- **Listening**
1. Listening for key words
2. Listening for general information and details
3. Listening for note-taking

- **Speaking**
1. Opening a savings account
2. Reporting loss of a passbook

- **Language focus：**

Key words and phrases
bank　stock　economy　recession　transaction ATM　PIN　cash　deposit　withdraw　process witness　suspect　excess　receipt　money barter　mortgage　passbook

Teaching Procedures

Warm-up

Look at the following pictures, discuss them with your partner and write down at least one word about the content of each picture.

Target:

Ss understand the meaning of each picture and brainstorm the relevant financial items.

Guidance:

- Ss read Warm-up 1.
- Ask Ss to discuss with their partners.
- Ask Ss to write down the name of each picture according to the request.
- Invite 1 − 2 Ss to present their answers on behalf of their partners.
- Encourage Ss to express their understandings of these items.

Key

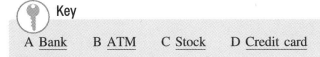

A Bank   B ATM   C Stock   D Credit card

Background Information

- ATM

  An automated teller machine (ATM) or automatic banking machine (ABM) is a computerized telecommunications device that provides the clients of a financial institution with access to financial transactions in a public space without the need for a cashier, human clerk or bank teller. On most modern ATMs, the customer is identified by inserting a plastic ATM card with a magnetic stripe or a plastic smart card with a chip that contains a unique card number and some security information such as an expiration date or CVVC (CVV). Authentication is provided by the customer entering a personal identification number (PIN).

- Stock

  The stock or capital stock of a business entity represents the original capital paid into or invested in the business by its founders. It serves as a security for the creditors of a business since it cannot be withdrawn to the detriment of the creditors. Stock is distinct from the property and the assets of a business which may fluctuate in quantity and value.

- Debit card

  A debit card (also known as a bank card or check card) is a plastic card that provides an alternative payment method to cash when making purchases. Functionally, it can be called an electronic cheque, as the funds are withdrawn directly from either the bank account, or from the remaining balance on the card. In some cases, the cards are designed exclusively for use on the Internet, and so there is no physical card.

- Credit card

  A credit card is part of a system of payments named after the small plastic card issued to users of the system. It is a card entitling its holder to buy goods and services based on the holder's promise to pay for these goods and services. The issuer of the card grants a line of credit to the consumer (or the user) from which the user can borrow money for payment to a merchant or as a cash advance to the user.

- Sub-prime mortgage crisis

The subprime mortgage crisis is an ongoing real estate crisis and financial crisis triggered by a dramatic rise in mortgage delinquencies and foreclosures in the United States, with major adverse consequences for banks and financial markets around the globe. The crisis, which has its roots in the closing years of the 20th century, became apparent in 2007 and has exposed pervasive weaknesses in financial industry regulation and the global financial system.

--- Expressions Pool ---

Financial items：
share, stock holder, bull/ bear market, bond, recession, inflation, recovery, interest, mortgage, foreign currency, exchange rate, stock market ...

Sentence pattern：
I guess ... because it is ... I would not like to ... because it is ... This must be ... for it is ... It cannot be ... because of ...

Match the money with the right country or region.

Target：
Ss can realize whether they are familiar with currencies. Ss can obtain some knowledge of foreign currencies.

Guidance：
- Ss read Warm-up 2.
- Ask Ss to write down their answers.
- Invite 1 - 2 student to present their results.
- The teacher may prepare some different notes and show them to Ss.
- Teacher explains the symbols and histories of these currencies.

🔑 **Key**

1. Euro　2. American dollar　3. Japanese Yen　4. Rouble
5. British Pound

Unit task

Read Text A and practice some real tasks on the topic of finance.

 Task Map(任务导航)

　　"金融"对于广大学生而言只是一个模糊的概念,在学生的层面,跟"金融"最亲密的接触就是发生在银行这一环境中。不过学生对于经济大环境是好是坏也有一定的了解和判断。本单元任务以生活化的角度来展开对"金融"这一话题的讨论,将活动场景搬到银行,开展环环相扣的任务型学习活动。

　　特此要求学生围绕"金融"可能涉及的任务进行具体实践,通过模拟情景进行模拟实践,巩固学生用英语询问、介绍、建议、描述、提问与回答等能力。

　　本单元任务分为6个步骤,第一个步骤让学生通过阅读课文,匹配ATM机使用的相关英文表达法及使用程序的陈述;第二个步骤让学生通过角色扮演,能够以对话、提问回答的形式来口头表述如何使用ATM机;第三个步骤为主任务,设置特殊情节——"抢劫",要求学生扮演目击者和警察的角色,完成描述人物及事件的任务;第四个步骤与第三步紧密联系,要求扮演警察的学生通过记录"目击者"口述的信息,完成事件概括与嫌犯侧写;第五个步骤也是主任务,学生完成记录单后,对于嫌犯的样貌特征进行口头报告;第六个步骤要求学生扮演"罪犯"和"记者",阅读课文,收集有关金融危机与就业危机的信息,模拟一次对"罪犯"的采访。

任务的安排主要根据事情发展顺序来设定,每一任务为后续的步骤做基础。

Process Break-down

Pre-task：

Step 1　A：Translate Chinese ATM instructions into English.

　　　　B：Known how to withdraw money from ATMs.

While-task：

Step 2　Pair work：Explain how to use an ATM.

Step 3　Role play：Conduct a police interview.

Step 4　Practical writing：Forms of interrogation.

Step 5　Retelling：What do the suspects look like.

Step 6　Role play：Interview criminals.

Step 1

Read the following instructions for ATM and get information for the following tasks.

A

Write down the English counterparts of the following Chinese phrases about ATM-operating.

Target：

Recognize the official term for items and actions involving the use of ATMs.

Guidance：

- Ss read the instruction by themselves and get to know the official terms for items and actions involving the use of ATMs.
- During this step, Ss can connect the English term with the common sense and actual experience of using ATMs in daily life. So that Ss can figure out and master the English correspondents.
- Invite 1 – 2 Ss to present their answers.
- Teacher can do a little explanation afterwards.

任务过程控制关注点
Minefield

- 提醒学生不要被生词限制住,阅读时引入常识。
- 提醒学生在练习中有意识地进行题目与原文的比对,从而了解原本陌生的表达方式。

Key

Insert the card	Enter your PIN	Select a language
Confirm	Select a transaction	Deposit money
Withdraw money	Take the receipt	Take your card

B

How to withdraw money from ATMs.

The following are steps involved in withdrawing money from ATMs. Please put them into the right order.

Target:

Know how to withdraw money from ATMs.

Guidance:

- Ss read the instruction and compare the order with the given statements or terms.
- Ss need to put the expressions into the right order according to the content in the instruction.
- Invite 1 – 2 Ss to present the answers.
- Teacher can do a little explanation afterwards.

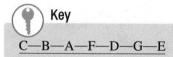 **Key**

C—B—A—F—D—G—E

Step 2

任务过程控制关注点
Minefield

- 提醒学生开拓思维,联系大学新生的身份和经历,合理设置会话情境与情节。
- 提醒学生换位思考。当我们已经得知如何操作 ATM 机时容易忽略很多细节的解释,但我们置身解说者 Tom 的角度上时,必须要把每一步骤解释清晰,并且要强调注意事项;同时扮演 Jack 的学生更要主动发问求教。
- 提醒学生善用已知的表达法。为求信息明朗,要用简单句和简易词来说明。

Explain how to use an ATM.

Suppose you are Tom. Your partner Jack needs to withdraw some money from an ATM, but he is new to it. Talk with him and tell him how to operate an ATM to withdraw money with the information you have got from Step 1.

Target:

Practice instructing a person to operate ATMs.

Guidance:

- Finishing Step 1, Ss have already known how to name the items and actions involving the use of ATMs and the steps to withdraw money successfully.
- Ss need to play a certain role with one partner as Tom & Jack. Tom is supposed to tell Jack how to operate an ATM. Useful expressions are listed.
- Invite 2 Ss to present their answer and the teacher needs to check whether they have mastered well.
- Teacher should guide Ss to use the suggested expressions.
- 1 – 2 pairs can be invited to present their dialogue.

Expressions Pool

Tom：
1. Hi, Jack! You look rather anxious. What's up?
2. Oh, I see. What about using an ATM?
3. Well, don't worry. Actually, it's a piece of cake.
4. First … Then … After that … Next … Finally …
5. You are very welcome.

Jack：
1. Well, just now I went to the campus bank to withdraw some money, but it was crowded with students.
2. One of the clerks asked me to go there again tomorrow, but I have to pay my tuition fee this afternoon.
3. I have no idea how to operate one at all. Any suggestions?
4. Yes, I think I can. Thank you very much.

Step 3

Role-play a police interview.

Right after Jack withdrew money, two men stopped him with a knife and robbed him. Suppose you are a policeman who is in charge of this case. Ask your partner, as the assumed witness, a couple of questions relevant to the suspects.

Target：
Inquire and describe an event which happened in the circumstance of ATMs.

Guidance：
- Work in pairs by playing roles of the witness and the policeman.
- Ss need to think and prepare independently, avoiding the situation that Ss co-design every sentence and Q&A cycle.
- The student playing witness needs to picture the whole "robbery" and the image of criminals in mind with the help of some written notes by himself.
- The student playing policeman needs to write down every possible question that can lead to the truth.
- The pair of Ss talk to each other by putting forward and answering questions.
- Meanwhile, the student playing policeman needs to take notes of the description of the event and people involved so that Step 4 can be done successfully.
- Teacher should guide Ss to use the suggested expressions.
- 1 - 2 groups will give an oral presentation of their conversation.

Reference：
A：The Policeman   B：The Witness
A：Excuse me, Sir. I'm a policeman and I'm here to investigate the bank robbery. I was told that you saw the suspects last morning, is that true?
B：Yes, that's true. I passed by the bank shortly before the robbery happened and saw two suspicious people looking around and whispering.
A：What time did you see them? Can you still remember?
B：Yes, at about 10:30 - 10:40 in the morning.
A：What were you doing at that time?
B：I was on my way to my little son's school. I went there to send him an umbrella, for it was going to rain.
A：I see. May I ask you several questions about the suspects? I need your help

任务过程控制关注点
Minefield

- 提醒学生一切安排都要合理,而非一味地制造戏剧效果。
- 提醒学生运用一切知识和资讯,将"笔录"做得尽可能仔细、专业。
- 提醒学生同时完成下一步骤的任务。扮演目击证人的学生要做到发音清晰,逻辑明确;扮演警察的学生要合理提问,记录有效信息。

Expressions Pool

Words：investigate; the bank robbery; suspects; pass by the bank; tall/short/in medium height; thin/fat; young/old/middle-aged; pullover/raincoat/sweater/uniform; scar/mole/tattoo;

Sentences：
1. What time did you see them?
2. May I ask you several questions about the suspects?
3. Could you describe to me their appearances?

（续表）

4. Do you think you can recognize them when you see them again?
5. If you promise what you've just said is true, please sign your name here.
6. Contact with me at × × × × × if you think of something new.

very much, actually.

B： OK, I would be glad to be of any help and I will tell you every detail I know.

A： Very good. What did they look like?

B： One is tall and thin and the other is medium height.

A： How old are they?

B： . . .

A： Are they men or women?

B： . . .

A： What clothes did they wear?

B： . . .

A： Could you describe to me their appearances?

B： . . .

A： Did you hear what they say?

B： . . .

A： Could you tell where they are from by their accents?

B： . . .

A： Do you think you can recognize them when you see them again?

B： . . .

A： Do you know anything else about them?

B： . . .

A： If you promise what you've just said is true, please sign your name here.

B： . . .

A： Contact me at 2965280 if you think of something new.

B： Sure, I will.

A： Thanks a lot, bye.

B： Bye-bye.

Step 4

任务过程控制关注点
Minefield

- 提醒学生在开始"做笔录"前充分想象并勾勒事件可能的经过和嫌犯的形象。
- 提醒学生可以先将能够想到的描述人物的词汇短语——列举，在听记过程中可以提高效率。
- 提醒学生在完成对话后相互核对信息，查看笔录是否与目击者的证词匹配。

Fill in a form of interrogation.

Ss are supposed to be policemen and witnesses. The policemen will take some notes.

Target：

Take notes and fill in the form.

Guidance：

- This step is actually simultaneously processed with Step 3.
- The student playing policeman needs to write down every possible question that can lead to the truth.
- The pair of Ss talk to each other by putting forward and answering questions. Meanwhile, the student playing policeman needs to take notes of the description of the event and people involved.
- Fill in the form of description.
- The 2 Ss in the pair check the information with each other.

------ Expressions Pool ------

1. She/He has short hair/medium length hair/long hair/long wavy dark hair/long and straight hair/short and curly hair.
2. She/He is dressed in a light brown suit and a red tie.

Step 5

Retell the looks of the suspects.

Ss are supposed to portray the two suspects with the help of the information in the form above and describe the portraits to other policemen.

任务过程控制关注点
Minefield

- 提醒学生使用已经记录下来的信息进行描述。
- 提醒学生注意语言、语气。这是在警员会议的场合进行嫌犯侧写的报告，所以语言应客观，语气语调沉着冷静。

Target：

Practice how to describe a person by information given.

Guidance：

- Ss describe the two suspects with the help of the information in the form.
- Teacher should guide Ss to use the suggested expressions.
- 1 - 2 students can be invited to present their portraits.
- If time permits, teacher can ask several Ss to draft the portrait on the blackboard while some student is describing a suspect. By doing so, Ss can get a direct feedback from classmate fellows and a moment of fun at the same time.

Reference：

Good morning everyone! I had a fruitful talk with one of the witnesses this morning. According to what they said to me, two men suspects were involved in this serious bank robbery. Based on the information they provided, I portrayed the bank robbers. Please look at the screen now and I will describe to you the suspects in detail so that we can know more about them and take effective measures to arrest them as soon as we can.

The first ...

And the second ...

At last, I strongly advise that the two portraits be copied and put up in public places as soon as possible. I have every good reason to believe that, with our joint effort, this case will surely be solved in the not too distant future.

—— Expressions Pool ——

1. I had a fruitful talk with one of the witnesses.
2. Based on the information they provided, I portrayed the bank robbers.
3. The first ... And the second ...
4. At last, I strongly advise that ...
5. I believe that, with our effort, this case will surely be solved.

Step 6

Role-play an interview with the criminals.

Several days later, the criminals were arrested by the police and put into prison. To the astonishment of all people, they are both graduates who have just left college. Suppose you are a newspaper reporter and interview them. Try to find out their hidden motivation to commit such a crime under the circumstance mentioned in Text A.

任务过程控制关注点
Minefield

- 提醒学生对话要自然，贴近实际，同时合理想象。
- 提醒学生语言使用得当，但也不应害怕语言不丰富不敢开口讲。
- 提醒学生阅读 Text A，以此作为案件发生的经济背景，并从中提炼词汇句子来解释"犯罪动机"。
- 提醒学生此段对话属于新闻采访，注意语言的情绪和提问的技巧与专业。

Target：

Talk about how the economic downturn affected people's life by doing an interview.

Guidance：

- Ss read Text A, paying attention to the expressions related with economic crisis and employment issues.

- 2 Ss co-work by playing roles as reporter and criminal. An interview will be conducted between the pair.
- The student playing reporter needs to ask about the legal awareness of the criminal, the motive or the reason by raising objective questions.
- The student playing criminal needs to refer to the content in Text A and explain the helpless situation he/she met at that time with showing regrets.
- Teacher should guide Ss to use the suggested expressions.
- 1 – 2 pairs can be invited to present their dialogue.

-------- **Expressions Pool** --------

1. Do you know it's illegal to rob a bank?
2. Why did you break the law?
3. Do you have a job? / Weren't you employed?
4. Are you feeling regretted now?
5. What would you do if you were meeting another chance?
6. I didn't have enough money to support my life. / I was jobless.
7. My company went bankruptcy because of the global economic crisis.

Reference：

Reporter：As college graduates, do you know it's illegal to rob a bank?

Criminals：Yes, we know that clearly.

Reporter：Then, why did you break the law?

Criminals：Because we didn't have enough money to survive the world.

Reporter：Why? Weren't you employed?

Criminal：Yes, we were both once employed. But five months ago our company went bankruptcy because of the global economic crisis, so we both lost our jobs.

Reporter：Is robbery the only way to earn money? Aren't there any better ways to earn a decent life?

Criminals：There surely are. But money is easy to spend and hard to earn. It seems that we'll never get enough money to spend.

Reporter：Are you feeling regretted now?

Criminals：Yes, very. But it is too late.

Reporter：At this time, what do you want to say most to people of your age?

Criminals：Do not learn from us. Earn money in legal ways, otherwise you will suffer too much.

Action research
（教师自己的教学行动研究）

任务完成中的观察、反思（日志、随笔）	备忘

Language Points

Text A

Passage 1

◆ （title） ***Recession*** **Easing，but Many Americans Still Afraid to Spend**

recession：a period of reduced economic activity

［运用］　in/during/from/out of/after/through recession
suffer/face/fight/endure/experience/defeat/
keep recession

e. g.　Manufacturing has been in recession for six months at least.
Both economies have suffered grievously from recession.

［拓展］　*recession*（*n.*）撤退
The recession of the army from the war was significant to the whole situation.

◆ （title） **Recession *Easing*，but Many Americans Still Afraid to Spend**

ease：to lessen pain or discomfort

［运用］　ease up/down/off, take ease

e. g. Ease up, Alva! I was only going to the john.

［拓展］　*ease*（*n.*）安心，悠闲
Hick was softened up with alarming ease by Marv Hughes.
at ease，*of ease* 舒适，安逸
Alfred shrugged, and seemed for the moment somewhat less at ease.

◆ （line 4） ... **investors feel more sure about signs of economic *recovery* ...**

recovery：return to an original state

［运用］　recovery from/after ...

e. g.　I see no prospect to his recovery from the disease

［拓展］　*recovery*（*n.*）重获，复得
The owner has offered a reward for the recovery of the stolen goods.

◆ （line 6） ... **to *lift* the world's largest economy ...**

lift：to give temporary assistance

［运用］　lift up ...

e. g.　The child is lifting up his voice. Go and have a look.

［拓展］　*lift*（*n.*）免费搭车，搭便车；鼓舞，振奋
Can you give me a lift to the subway station?
我可以搭你的便车到地铁站吗？
Her spirits lifted after she heard the news.
听到消息以后她的精神振作起来。

◆ （line 42） ... **the main opposition party in the *lead* ...**

lead：an advantage held by a competitor in a race；a position of leadership

［运用］　in the lead/take the lead ...

e. g.　And Africans are in the lead in peace processes in both places.
We were just waiting for someone to take the lead.

［拓展］　*lead*（*n.*）主角，主要演员；领导，榜样
He's playing the lead in the new play.
他在这出新剧中担任主角。
He is one of leads we should learn.
他是我们应该学习的榜样之一。

Text B

◆ （line 2） **The *appearance* of money plays ...**

appearance→coming, arrival, rise

［运用］　the sudden appearance of ...

e. g.　The sudden appearance of a policeman caused the thief to run away.

［拓展］　*appearance*（*n.*）外观，外貌
She was a young woman of good appearance.
To all appearances, it had been a normal day.
appear（*v.*）看上去好像，似乎
The old man appears to be in good health.

［仿写］　为了让项目顺利通过,他亲自出面参与会议。（appearance）

◆ （line 3） ... **in the *process* of social development.**

process：a series of actions of a development

［运用］　be in the process of doing something；in process of time

e. g.　The bridge is in the process of being built.
In process of time, Rome became a great empire by conquest.

［拓展］　*process*（*vt.*）加工，处理
How fast does the computer process the data?

［仿写］　随着时间的推移,货币的形态发生了变化。（process）

◆ （line 6） ... **caused by the *excess* of food.**

excess：a quantity that is greater than required

［运用］　in excess of；an excess of

e. g.　After a few months, his apartment was sold in excess of 20 million.
An excess of fat in one's diet can lead to heart

disease.

［拓展］ *excessive*（*adj.*）过度的，过分的

She takes an excessive interest in clothes.

［仿写］ 她坚持叫他不要喝过了量。（process）

◆（line 12）... *consumption* by the family naturally prompted them ...

consumption：the act of consuming something

［运用］ consumption of ...

e. g. Consumption of oil has declined in recent years.

［拓展］ consume（*v.*）消耗，消费

Arguing about details consumed many hours of the committee's valuable time.

The fire soon consumed the wooden buildings.

［仿写］ 英国人每年消费大量的茶叶。

◆（line 15）... these exchanges were conducted by means of *barter* ...

barter：exchange goods without involving money

［运用］ on a barter basis

e. g. They have arranged food imports on a barter basis.

［拓展］ barter（*v.*）作物物交换，以货换货

The mountaineers bartered between each other.

［仿写］ 他们用农产品交换机器。

◆（line 16）... they were strictly limited both in *volume* and speed ...

volume：the property of something that is great in magnitude

［运用］ in volume

e. g. We do see an increase in volume, as you mentioned, in the traffic.

［拓展］ *volume*（*n.*）卷，册；体积；容积

For that article he has worked over some 30 volumes of Chinese history.

It is popular with housewives because of small volume, and convenient installation and maintenance.

［仿写］ 价格根据体积大小而定。

◆（line 37）The *adoption* of money in place of barter ...

adoption：the act of accepting with approval

［运用］ adoption of ...

e. g. He was pleased by the adoption of a little girl.

［拓展］ adopt（*v.*）采用，正式接受，收养

The factories have adopted the newest modern technology.

Different schools will adopt different solutions.

［仿写］ 他去法国后，很快就接受了法国的生活方式。

◆（line 47）The possibility to *convert* the fruits of one's labor into money ...

convert：to change the nature, purpose, or function of something

［运用］ convert ... into ...

e. g. It causes you to convert calories into fat.

［拓展］ convert（*n.*）改变宗教（或信仰、观点）的人；皈依者

Listen to him now as he tells us how and why he became a convert.

［仿写］ 他很早就皈依佛门。

◆（line 42）... speed，and *efficiency* of transactions ...

efficiency：the quality of work, effectiveness

［运用］ improve efficiency，at peak efficiency

e. g. The efficiency can be improved by downsizing staff of the factory.

This machine is working at peak efficiency.

［拓展］ efficient（*adj.*）有能力的，效率高的

Teachers use efficient teaching aides to better achieve their goal.

［仿写］ 在技术限制下，生产效率无法提高。

◆（line 58）... with the increasing size and *density* of urban populations ...

density：the amount per unit size

［运用］ density of ...

e. g. The density of population in this city is very high.

［拓展］ dense（*adj.*）密集的，愚钝的

The ship ran down a fishing-boat during the dense fog.

One or two of the students in my class are a bit dense.

［仿写］ 密林掩护了游击队员的行动。

Translation of Texts

Text A

经济衰退正在减轻，但许多美国人仍然不敢消费

这周，股票价格坐上了过山车，跌一天，涨一天。专家称这种局面可能会一直持续到投资者对经济恢复信号感到更加肯定。

有些投资者担心美国人不会采取足够的措施来让这个世界上最大的经济体走出经济低谷。现在是返校的季节，但全国零售商联合会称，与校园相关的销售跟去年比下滑了。

（某位）母亲：“我不想花超过 20 美元买个背包。”

民众消费占美国经济活动的 70%，但消费者信心（指数），即对国民经济信任的测量指标，在这个月意外下跌。在经历了二战以来最久的经济衰退之后，大批民众都对消费感到不安。

（某位）妇女：“我情况还好，但仍觉得自己可能随时会失去工作，仍没有确切的安全性。这就是为什么我会更多关注。”

尽管速度变慢，但工作岗位一直在消失，处于失去房子危险之中的美国人达到了破记录的数量。轻松轻松（就能）贷款的日子已经过去。财政部称，接受政府援助的银行，他们的贷款持续第 15 个月下滑。

然而，有些经济学家称，在经济（活动）中，有其他一些信号显示，经济衰退已经结束，或即将结束。下面的问题是：经济恢复会有多快或多慢？

日本的经济衰退也可能正在结束。日本是世界第二大经济体。（日本）官方本周报告称，在 4—6 月份期间，日本国内总产值增长了 9‰。这是 15 个月以来，日本经济的首次增长。

但有人担心日本和美国可能面临“二次下滑”经济衰退。这是指一段时期的增长之后，紧跟着另一次衰退。日本将在 8 月 30 日举行全国大选。公众民意调查显示，主要的反对党处于领先地位。

在欧洲，上周的报告显示其最大经济体德国，以及法国历时一年的经济衰退正在减轻。在 4—6 月份期间，这两个国家都有 3‰的增长。对 16 个使用欧元的国家来说，这个消息加大了（经济）早日恢复的希望。

然而，国际货币基金组织的首席经济学家（Olivier Blanchard）称，世界经济危机的影响将同时破坏未来几年的（市场）供应和需求。Olivier Blanchard 称，即使在恢复之后，全球经济产量也不能达到这次经济危机之前的水平。

Text B

货币在社会发展中的作用

货币是过去五千年来人类最伟大的发明。货币的出现在社会发展进程中起着很重要的作用。

剩余的食物交换使货币的创造成为可能。然而在简单的交易过程中货币其实是不需要的。在早期简单的经济条件下，绝大多数的产品和服务都是以家庭为单位生产的，一些必要的产品交换就是以物物交换的形式完成的。早期农民有能力生产比自己家庭所消费的更多的粮食，自然会促使他们用剩余产品换回其他商品或服务。由于这些交换是以物物交换的方式，交易的数量和速度都受到很大的限制。易货交易要求买卖双方都想要对方所拥有的剩余产品。物物交换还受空间上的限制。由于长距离运输产品需要艰辛的体力劳动，易货交易主要是在有限的地理区域进行。许多产品由于易腐烂的性质也限制了易货交易。生产者不鼓励生产超出他们期待的更多用于消费或者同他人进行交换的产品，以免在此期间造成产品变质。

贸易的发展使货币的产生成为一种必然。随着分工的细化，不仅仅是生产得到了改善和促进，物物交换的形式也不再满足贸易的需求。因此货币就作为一种交易的中介诞生了。货币的最早形式之一是在古巴比伦由政府粮库签发的储存粮食的收条。

货币的使用以相似的方式逐渐从一个国家传播到另一个国家。货币的采用对早期物物交换的社会具有深远的影响，也极大地促进了社会的变革和扩张。城镇化的进程使人们接触越来越频繁，货币使人们交易的数量、规模、速度和效率大大地增加了，

甚至远距离的交易也增多了。货币把人们的劳动成果变成钱的功能意味着这些劳动成果可以无条件的储存起来,这克服了时间的限制,也激发了人们的劳动积极性。这种将实际货物转换成方便携带的货币的能力克服了空间差别对人们生活的影响,这使得人们在大范围地理区域内进行贸易成为可能。货币还能够对产品和服务提供普遍的估价标准。货币排除了易货贸易方式下的双方相互需求的一致性,使得更大数量的交易成为可能。同时,货币的方便携带和大数量的结算加速了商品交换的速度。由于货币的使用和城市人口密度和规模的扩大,交易速度和交易量也不断增加,对社会发展的影响成指数关系增长。

就货币发展的历史而言,有各种各样的东西在不同时期不同地区充当着货币的角色。牛、贝壳、珠子,烟草叶和其他比如说铁、铜、银子、金子之类的金属,这些都曾被作为货币使用进行交易。由于大量金属货币非常重也不方便,现在很多政府都发行纸币。每个政府决定自己的货币单位和价值标准。无论货币是由什么材料做的,其主要功能就是作为交易的媒介,以此证明并推动着社会的发展。

Explain these words and expressions through their context or with the help of a dictionary.

1. decay (Para. 2) *v.* 腐烂,衰败

e.g. Leaves which fall to the ground decay and become part of the soil.

2. medium (Para. 3) *n.* 媒介

e.g. Air is a medium for sound.

3. adoption (Para. 4) *n.* 采用

e.g. I argued him into the adoption of the plan.

4. overcome (Para. 4) *v.* 克服

e.g. There is no difficulty we cannot overcome.

5. valuation (Para. 5) *n.* 估价

e.g. He set a high valuation on the painting.

Reading Skills Exercises:

1

Read Text B and answer the following questions.

 Key

1. How could people buy things before money appeared?
   People could exchange things by means of bartering.
2. What're the disadvantages of barter?
   Barter could be limited by space, time, volume, and the nature of products.
3. What was the earliest form of money in the ancient Babylon?
   One of the earliest forms of money was the receipt issued for grain deposits at government warehouses in ancient Babylon.
4. What're the advantages of money over bartering?
   Money increased the number, speed, and efficiency of transactions, even over long distances. It could overcome the limitation of time and space.
5. Could you please tell your class the impact of money on the development of society? (Omitted)

2

Match the words to their meanings.

 Key

1—D, 2—C, 3—A, 4—B, 5—E

3

Fill in the blanks with words from the list in Exercise 2, make some changes if necessary.

 Key

1. This food will decay rapidly on contact with air.
   这种食物一接触到空气即迅速变坏。
2. He always deposits half of his salary in the bank. 他总是把一半薪金存入银行。

3. A noise <u>prompted</u> the guard go back and investigate. 一阵声响促使警卫走回去察看。

4. He wanted to <u>convert</u> his dollars into Japanese yen. 他想将美元换成日币。

5. The <u>excessive</u> use of power leads to tyranny. 滥用权力将导致暴政。

Language practice

Vocabulary

1

Give the correct form of the following words according to the requirements. Then complete the sentences that follow.

commercial	*n.* commerce
appear	*n.* appearance
invent	*n.* invention
create	*n.* creation
excess	*a.* excessive

1. In human history, cultural exchange began with the very <u>creation</u> of culture.

2. The <u>invention</u> of paper was a great contribution to human civilization.

3. She was a young woman of good <u>appearance</u>.

4. After a few months' negotiation with the buyer, his apartment was sold in <u>excess</u> of 20,000 yuan.

5. <u>Commerical</u> television is an effective medium for advertising.

2

Learn how to describe trends in English by doing the following exercises.

A What kind of movement do the symbols below describe? Match them to the words. Then compare your answers with a partner. (Use some words more than once.)

A: decline, decrease, fall
B: double
C: increase, gain, rise, improve
D: halve
E: level off
F: peak
G: plummet
H: recover
I: rocket
J: triple

B Use the correct form of the words above to fill in the blanks.

1. Unemployment <u>fell/declined/decreased</u> by 1.5

million last year. It <u>fell/declined/decreased</u> from 4.5 million to 3 million. It has already <u>fallen/declined/decreased</u> by half a million this year, to 2.5 million this month.

2. Inflation <u>fell/declined/decreased</u> by 4% in ten years: it was 5% in 1991, but it <u>rose/increased/gained</u> from 6% in 1992 to 9% in 1999. In 2001 it <u>rose/increased/gained</u> further by 3% and at the end of the year it was 4%.

Translation

Put the following Chinese sentences into English by using the given words. Part of the sentences has been given.

 Keys

1. The firm <u>is now in the process of</u> combination.

2. He <u>made the black record disappear not by means of</u> schemes, but <u>by means of</u> a clever trick.

3. Professor Smith's new book <u>prompts students' interest in his course.</u>

4. We'll soon <u>convert him to our thinking.</u>

5. I <u>deposited the money I had left</u> from my trip.

Grammar

Grammar Exercises:

1

Choose the correct answer to complete the following sentences.

 Key

1. A 2. B 3. C 4. D 5. B 6. B 7. B
8. A 9. B 10. A

2

Correct the ten sentences that use the wrong form of verb.

1. Your family is (are) very kind. I'll never forget the favor you've done me.
2. When and where to build the new school haven't (hasn't) been decided.
3. Three quarters of the land is covered with green grass while the rest are (is) covered with pine trees.
4. Not even one of the hundred students who took the test have (has) passed.
5. On each side of the street stands (stand) a lot of trees.
6. There seem (seems) to be a knife and fork on the table.
7. The students in our school each has (have) known the meaning of WTO.
8. The number of people who own cars are (is) increasing.
9. Such people as he is (are) to be punished.
10. It were (was) Tom and John who played a trick on the old man.

Listening 🎧

1

Work with your partner to fill in the blanks using the words in the box. Listen and check your answers, and then follow the recording.

 Script

1. The total value of bad loans fell to 1.28 _trillion_ yuan ($160.6 billion) by the end of June.
2. We trade with people in all countries on the basis of _equality_ and mutual benefit.
3. There has been a _slowdown_ in the wool trade with you.
4. Wow, you _fixed_ my computer in less than 10 minutes. You're super.
5. The new owner of the company is not very popular but he is able to _deliver_ the goods.
6. The value of the stock has begun to _bottom_ out and should soon begin to increase in value.
7. We must begin to stop spending money in a _wasteful_ manner.
8. The car salesman gave us a _hard sell_ so we decided to go to another dealer.
9. The company began to _go into red_ when the price of oil began to rise rapidly.
10. We were unable to get the new product off the _ground_ (投放市场) and will have to wait until next year.

2

Listen to the conversation and answer the following questions.

 Script

June Richmond is having trouble working the ATM at the Higashi Bank. She must ask one of the clerks for help.

A: Excuse me, but I seem to be having trouble with this ATM. My card is stuck and nothing came out!

B: Well. Let me see if I can help you. Did you enter the correct PIN number?

A: Yes, I am sure I did. I use my birth date as my PIN number. It's easy to remember it that way.

B: Well, everything seems to be in order. The screen is asking you to enter your PIN again. Maybe you've entered the wrong PIN.

A: No, I don't think so. You try it. My PIN is 0315. I was born on March 15.

B: Well, I entered that number, but the screen is asking you to enter the PIN one more time. Are you sure you're using the correct PIN?

A: Yes, I'm sure! I use my birth date as the PIN of my account, and my husband uses his birth date as the PIN of his account.

B: Well, whose card are you using? Did you, somehow, take your husband's card by mistake?

A: There was no mistake! I took his card because he wanted me to get some money from his account. I have my card here in my purse.

B: But ma'am. If you're using your husband's card to take money, you must use his PIN.

A: Aha ha, I mixed them up. Thank you!

 Key

1. The bank clerk.
2. No.

3. Her husband's card.
4. In her purse.
5. Yes, of course.

3

Listen to the conversation again. Fill in the blanks with the words you hear.

 Key

1. Well. Let me see if I can help you. Did you enter the correct <u>PIN</u> number?
2. I am sure I did. I use my birth <u>date</u> as my PIN number. It's easy to <u>remember</u> it that way.
3. Well, everything seems to be in <u>order</u>. The <u>screen</u> is asking you to enter your PIN again.
4. Yes, I'm <u>sure</u>! I use my birth date as the PIN of my account, and my husband uses his birth date as the PIN of his <u>account</u> .
5. There was no <u>mistake</u>! I took his card because he wanted me to get some money from his account. I have my card here in my <u>purse</u>.

4

Al and Virginia Baxter are talking to their banker, Tony Flora, about a housing loan. Fill in the form after listening.

 Script

A – Al Baxter   F – Tony Flora   V – Virginia Baxter
A: We'd like to get some information about mortgage loans, Mr. Flora. We'd like to buy a house.

F: Well, Mr. Baxter, we generally lend 80% of the bank's appraised value on 30-35-year mortgages if the house is less than 10 years old.
V: Oh, it's almost a brand-new house. I think it was built two years ago.
A: Yes, it's a real good deal. The price is just right.
F: Bank appraisals are usually slightly lower than the actual market prices, Mr. Baxter, so you'll have to figure on at least at a 25%−28% down payment.
A: Yes, we planned on that.
V: What's the interest rate on mortgage loans?
F: It fluctuates a little depending on the various factors in the loan, but around 8.75% for longtime clients.
A: Well, we've been banking here since we got married 8 years ago, Mr. Flora, so I guess we qualify.
F: Yes, you certainly do, Mr. Baxter. Let's fill out this application, so we can get started on the paperwork. It takes some time to complete a mortgage loan transaction.

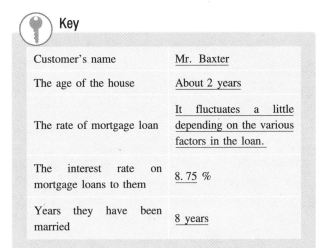 Key

Customer's name	<u>Mr. Baxter</u>
The age of the house	<u>About 2 years</u>
The rate of mortgage loan	<u>It fluctuates a little depending on the various factors in the loan.</u>
The interest rate on mortgage loans to them	<u>8.75</u> %
Years they have been married	<u>8 years</u>

Speaking

1

Role-play a conversation according to the following situation. After the practice, change roles.

Situation:
June Richmond is asking a clerk at the Bank of China about opening a savings account. The clerk is explaining to her.

Role Cards
Role A: The bank clerk
Role B: Mrs. Richmond

Flow Chart

The bank clerk	Mrs. Richmond
Greetings.	Greetings. Ask to open a savings account.
Say that she can open an account in her name only or a joint account with her husband.	Ask him about the interest.
Say they pay the highest interest rate permitted.	Ask if it is difficult to open an account.
Tell her it is easy. Ask her to fill out a table.	Ask what the use of ... (table) is.
Give her some advice.	Show her thankfulness.

Suggested Words and Expressions

The bank clerk	Mrs. Richmond
May I help you, sir/madam? I'd be happy to help you. You may ... All that's necessary is to ... ... is enough to ... It is my pleasure to ...	I'd like to ... Can you give me some information? Is it difficult to ... ? What else should I provide? Which kind of form should I fill in? I really appreciate the effort ...

Reference

C – Clerk   R – Mrs. Richmond

C: May I help you, ma'am?

R: Yes, please. I'd like to open a savings account. Can you give me some information?

C: Yes, I'd be happy to help you. We call our regular savings account plain passbook savings. You may open an account in your name only, or a joint account with your husband. You may make deposits or withdrawals at any time.

R: Do I earn interest on the account?

C: Yes, we pay the highest interest rate permitted for commercial banks. We credit the earned interest to your account automatically every quarter.

R: Is it difficult to open an account?

C: No, Ma'am, not at all. All that should be done is to fill out this form, give your signatures and make your initial deposit. Even a dollar is enough to open the account.

R: Let's see. You want my name, address, occupation, date of birth and Social Security number.

C: Yes.

R: I see. Well, let me fill this out and I'll open an account.

2

Work with you arter to make up a dialogue involving the following situation.

Situation:

The other day, Mrs. Richmond has lost her saving passbook.
She asks the clerk to help her.

Role Cards:

Role A: The bank clerk

Role B: Mrs. Richmond

Flow Chart

The clerk	Mrs. Richmond
Greet.	Ask for help and explain the situation.
Suggest a solution.	Enquire the procedure.
Ask the necessary information.	
Check the ID card.	
Ask Mrs. Richmond to fill in an form.	Fill out the form and hand it to the clerk.
Tell Mrs. Richmond what she should do next.	Express gratitude and say goodbye.
Wish her a good day.	

Suggested Words and Expressions

The clerk	Mrs. Richmond
Is there anything I can help you? I'm sorry to hear ... That'll do. Please fill out the application form.	I lost my passbook ... What should I do? Let me think it over. It's very kind of you. Thank you for your effort.

Reference

A: Excuse me. I lost my passbook this morning. What should I do?

B: I'm sorry to hear that. But you can report it lost.

A: What's the procedure?

B: Please tell me the account name and number, maturity, amount and code number if you have that information.

A: Let me think it over. Oh ... , it's a one-year fixed deposit with 1,500 USD in it. No code number and the account name is Jim Brown. Is that all right?

B: That'll do. Now show me your ID card, please.

A: Here you are.

B: Please fill out the application form. Please come to renew your passbook or get your money in seven days.

A: It's very kind of you.

B: You're welcome.

Writing

1

Please fill out an application for a personal sole account of HSBC according to the given information.

Target:

Fill out an application form for a personal sole account.

 Guidance:

Ss read the direction, the situation and the given information.

Teacher guides Ss to fill out the form.

Teacher may invite 2 Ss to give their answers.

Key

Title: Sir
Full first name(s): Gao
Surname: Qi
Sex: Male
Marital status: Married
Date of birth: 17 - January - 1971
Employment status: Employed
No. of dependants: 1
Daytime telephone number: 00852 - 2824 - 6111
Evening telephone: (none)
Mobile telephone number: (none)
Email address: gqhk@ gmail. com
Confirm email address: gqhk@ gmail. com
Post code: 00852
House/Flat no. or name: 15-B of Garden Mansion
Date moved to this address: 8 - April - 2010

Learning for fun

(Omitted)

2
Please fill out the above form again according to your own personal information.
(Omitted)

Unit 5   Expo

Objective

- **Career skills**

  Applying to attend Canton Fair especially as exhibitor; writing a company's profile, making a brochure for the company.

- **Reading**
  1. Reading for main idea(s)
  2. Skimming/Scanning
  3. Reading for general information and details
  4. Reading for guessing word meaning from context

- **Writing**
  1. General writing: practice sentence patterns
  2. Practical writing: poster

- **Listening**
  1. Listening for key words
  2. Listening for general information and details
  3. Listening for note-taking
  4. Listening for identifying procedure

- **Speaking**
  1. Receiving a visitor at the booth of a trade fair
  2. Introducing a product to a visitor at a trade fair

- **Language focus**

  ### Key words and phrases

  fair   expo   booth   brochure   profile
  Canton Fair   exhibitor   exhibit   phase
  stand application   impression   theme
  variety   invest   expect   represent   book
  greet   introduce   poster

Teaching Arrangement

Warm-up & Unit task (Text A)
1) Time schedule: 2 periods
2) Suggested lesson structure
   Warm-up: 10 – 15 minutes
   Text A: 10 – 15 minutes
   Unit task step 1 (pre-task): 10 – 15 minutes
   Unit task steps 2 – 4 (while-task): 30 – 40 minutes
   Unit task step 5 should be completed after class
   Unit task step 6 (post-task): 10 – 15 minutes (preparation should be completed after class. The performance can be shown on class.)

Reading (Text B)
1) Time schedule: 1 period
2) Suggested lesson structure
   Language points: 20 – 25 minutes
   Language practice: 20 – 25 minutes

Listening
1) Time schedule: 1 period
2) Suggested lesson structure
   Listening exercise 1: 10 minutes
   Listening exercise 2: 15 minutes
   Listening exercise 3: 15 minutes
   Listening exercise 4: 15 minutes

Speaking & Writing
1) Time schedule: 1 period
2) Suggested lesson structure
   Speaking: 20 – 25 minutes
   Writing: 20 minutes

Teaching Procedures

Warm-up

Match the list of international fairs with their Chinese versions.

Target:

Ss can have some rough ideas about fairs. If possible, Ss can learn some relevant words like expo, fair, trade fair, commodity fair.

Guidance:
- Ss read Warm-up 1.
- Ask Ss to match the list of fairs to the Chinese versions.
- Invite 1 − 2 Ss to present their answers.
- Ask 1 − 2 Ss to say whatever they know about any of the fair. Ss can speak Chinese.
- Ask 1 − 2 Ss to add other fairs if they know any. Ss can speak Chinese.

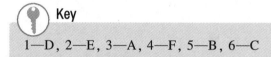

Key

1—D, 2—E, 3—A, 4—F, 5—B, 6—C

Background Information

```
························ What is a trade fair/expo? ························

    A trade fair is an exhibition organized so that companies in a specific
industry can show and demonstrate their new products and services.
Attending trade fairs can be an excellent way to test and open up domestic
and foreign markets. An ideal trade fair can help exhibitors or buyers to
see and compare new and relevant products or services, find new
suppliers, encounter new ideas and innovative companies, get up to date
with new technologies and make contact with other people in their area of
business.
    Expo includes trade fairs and other exhibitions to show great ideas or
technologies. Expo is usually sponsored by government or even a country.
• 1851 London Great Exhibition is regarded as the first Expo.
```

Match the Chinese translation to the English expressions.

Target:

Ss can do some preparation work in English before attending a trade fair. Ss can learn some skills which may benefit their career.

Guidance:
- Ss read Warm-up 2.

- Ask Ss to discuss in pairs.
- Ask 1 - 2 Ss to give the answers.
- Teacher may help to explain some difficult language points.

Key

1—B, 2—G, 3—C, 4—I, 5—F, 6—D, 7—E, 8—H, 9—A

③

Rank the above situations from Step 1 to Step 9 if your company is going to attend a trade fair.

Target:

Ss can know the steps before attending a trade fair. And Ss can make an action plan for doing all the preparations.

Guidance:

- Ss read Warm-up 3.
- Ask Ss to discuss in pairs.
- Ask 1 - 2 Ss to give the answers.
- If possible, Ss should explain reasons.

Key

Step 1	Step 2	Step 3	Step 4	Step 5	Step 6	Step 7	Step 8	Step 9
G	D	B	A	I	C	H	E	F

--- Expressions Pool ---

Words: the fair, trade fair, exhibition, expo, brochure, sample, booth
Sentence pattern:
I know something about London Great Exhibition. It should be the first expo. At that time many handcrafts with some creative ideas were exhibited.
In my opinion, the nine steps should be ranked like this: Step 1 G ... I think applying for visa takes time, so this step should be done in advance.

Unit task

Read Text A and practice a series of real tasks of attending trade fairs supposing that you are a clerk in a company and you are going to apply to attend the Canton Fair.

☞ **Task Map(任务导航)**

商展会是现代商务不可缺少的一个重要环节。商展参加者一般有两类身份：参展商和采购商。对于参展商,商展是参展企业的重要营销活动,更是企业向世界展示其产品和服务并开拓市场的重要活动。本单元任务的重点放在模拟参展商进行实践。

特此要求学生围绕参加广交会特别是参展前期的准备工作中可能涉及的任务进行具体实践,通过模拟情景进行模拟实践,巩固学生用英语查询、阅读、填申请表、制作文字材料等能力。

本单元任务分为6个步骤,第一个步骤让学生通过阅读了解广交会的信息和注意事项;第二个步骤是对照广交会的阶段要求核对相关产品的参展时间;第三个步骤是主任务之一,学生模拟身份,假定自己工作的公司要以参展商的身份去参加广交会,为了让采购商可以更方便了解公司,特准备公司简介；第四个步骤是主任务之一，模拟身份，模拟情景，根据以上公司简介的信息来填写申请展位的申请表；第五个步骤是主任务，需学生课后完成实物：模拟身份，模拟情景，根据以上公司简介的信息来制作展会宣传资料；第六个步骤是后任务环节，供学生课后讨论和演练。主要是针对商展的各项任务的典型注意事项进行复习性质的思考。另外还创造了一个在商展会上接待客户的情景剧表演的初步剧本。

本单元任务的安排是把 106 届广交会作为即将开始的广交会，以此作为任务实践的大背景。另外，本单元任务主要根据活动的顺序来设定，每一任务为后续的步骤做基础。

Process Break-down

Pre-task：

Step 1   A Ss practice reading so that Ss can scan for some information about Canton Fair and learn about it.

B Ss need to get important details about the 106th Session of Canton Fair.

While-task：

Step 2   Different exhibits are arranged at different dates. Ss should read and understand the chart in the text. Ss sort out the exhibits. It is important, if the company is going to attend Canton Fair, because the dates are related to flight tickets' and hotel rooms' reservation.

Step 3   Ss choose one product from the above step as the company's main product. Write a company's profile.

Step 4   Ss fill in the Stand Application. The company's information and products should be elicited from the above step.

Step 5   Ss work out a brochure for the company. It can be a group work. Each group makes one brochure after class.

Post-task：

Step 6   Ask Ss to discuss questions and make a drama after class concerning the topic of trade fair.

Step 1

任务过程控制关注点
Minefield

- 提醒学生不要被生词限制住，阅读时需要利用上下文猜测关键词，非关键词可以忽略。阅读也应引入常识。
- 提醒学生阅读摘录信息时应采用查读法。
- 提醒学生这个步骤的任务是为接下来需要完成的实际任务提供理论依据。
- 提醒学生个别信息在文章中并没有给出需上网查询。

Read Text A and get background information for the following real tasks.

A

Please collect information about Canton Fair and prepare for the following questions.

Target：

Know about Canton Fair.

Guidance：

- Brainstorm：What do you know about Canton Fair? Try to answer questions before reading.
- Ss are asked to read Text A.

- Ss are asked to list some key words.
- Some questions are not answered in the text. Ss should be encouraged to consult on the Internet.
- Invite 6 Ss to present their answers.
- Teacher can do a little explanation afterwards.

 Key

1. Canton Fair is held every half of a year.
2. and Oct. 15 to Nov. 4, 2009.
3. 15 days.
4. Different exhibits (9 sections). Machinery, vehicles, household items, personal care products, clothes, home textile . . .
5. About 15,000.
6. About 16,000. From all over the world, esp. European countries, America and other Asian countries.

--- **Expressions Pool** ---

1. Canton Fair is held every half a year.
2. Nine sections of commodities are exhibited.
3. It usually lasts half a month.

B

Elicit the information about the 106th Session of China Import and Export Fair and complete the following blanks.

Target:

Get important details about the 106th Session of Canton Fair.

Guidance:

- Ss scan Text A.
- Fill in the blanks according to the text.
- Invite 1 − 2 Ss to present their answers.
- Teacher can do a little explanation afterwards.

Key

name of the fair	the 106th Session of China Import and Export Fair
dates	October 15 to November 4, 2009
venue	China Import and Export Fair Complex
stand rate for raw space	3,000 RMB per sqm
stand rate for standard stand	30,000 RMB (9 sqm with standard facilities)
deadline for application	August 21, 2009

Step 2

Allocate the following products to specific phase of the 106th Session of China Import and Export Fair.

任务过程控制关注点
Minefield

Target:

Understand the chart about exhibition dates and identify different exhibits.

- 提醒学生阅读查找信息应用查读法。
- 提醒学生把产品归类。

- 提醒学生给出答案时应给出解释。
- 提醒学生要尽量拓宽广交会的背景阅读。

Guidance：

- Different exhibits are arranged at different dates. Ss should read and understand the chart in the text.
- Ss sort out the exhibits on the basis of recognizing the listed commodities.
- Ss should identify each item into a certain section of exhibits.
- Ss allocate different products to specific phase according to the text.
- Teacher should explain that it is important because the dates are related to flight tickets' and hotel rooms' reservation.
- Invite 1－2 Ss to present their answers. They had better give their supporting details.

Expressions Pool

Words：
A. laptop computer 笔记本
B. silk garment 丝绸服装
C. silverware 银制餐具
D. couch 沙发
E. bed sheet 床单
F. heater 取暖器
G. digger 挖土机
H. juice extractor 榨汁机

Sentence patterns：I think laptop should be exhibited during Phase 1, because it belongs to computer, which is arranged to be exhibited during Phase 1.

 Key

Phase 1   A F G H
Phase 2   C D
Phase 3   B E

Step 3

任务过程控制关注点
Minefield

- 提醒学生要尽量理解和运用公司简章的语言，并且发挥一定的想象力，设定公司的信息。
- 提醒学生自己写，然后在同类产品的小组中进行比较。
- 提醒学生简章是在商展会上用的，尽量要有一句话表明公司希望借此商展诚迎各方贵客。

Choose one product from the above step as your company's main product. Write a company's profile. You can imitate the sample, especially the underlined expressions.

Target：

Know how to write a company's profile if the company is going to attend a trade fair.

Guidance：

- Choose one product from the above step. Teacher may help to divide Ss into 9 groups. Each group chooses one product. Suppose the company mainly produces this product and is going to attend Canton Fair.
- Brainstorm：what facts should be included in a profile?
- Study the sample.
- Write the profile. Each student should write one profile.
- Compare their written profiles in the group.
- Teacher should guide Ss to use the suggested expressions.
- 1－2 Ss can be invited to read their profiles.

Expressions Pool

1. Our company was established in 1990.
2. The company is located in . . .
3. The company is a main skincare producer in Asian market.
4. The company specializes in/ deals in . . .
5. The company has a total capacity of . . . one year.
6. The products are mainly exported to . . .
7. Our product is noted for . . .
8. We take the opportunity of the trade fair to welcome customers from all over the world.

Step 4

Suppose your company is going to attend the 106th Session of China Import and Export Fair as exhibitor. You are asked to fill in the Stand Application. The company's informatopm and products should be elicited from the above step.

Target：
Know how to fill in a stand application in English.

Guidance：
- Ss scan some related information from the text quickly.
- Having finished the last two steps, each student has already chosen the product and written a company's profile. The information should be used in this step.
- The contact persons can be Ss themselves.
- Fill the application.
- Teacher should guide Ss to use the information.
- 1－2 Ss can be invited to present their applications.

Reference：
Information of the Exhibitor
Company Name（in English）：<u>ABC</u>
Company Name（in Chinese）：<u>爱山</u>
Address（in English）：<u>Chuangye Road No. 112, Industry Park, Huzhou City, Zhejiang Province, China, 313000</u>
Address（in Chinese）：<u>中国浙江省湖州市工业园创业路 112 号, 313000</u>
City/Postcode：<u>313000</u>   Country/Region：<u>China</u>
Contact Person：<u>Helen Chen</u>   ☐ Mr. ☑ Ms. Position：<u>Marketing Manager</u>
Telephone：<u>13567676767</u>   Fax：<u>057221567777</u>
E-mail：<u>helen112@ hotmail. com</u>   Website：<u>www. abcsilkgarment. com</u>
Stand Application

Type	Stand	Price	×	Qty/Area	=	Stand Fee
1	Standard stand（3M ×3M）	￥30,000 × (75%) per stand		2 Stand(s)		￥60,000
2	Raw space（set up by exhibitors, minimum 18 M²）	￥3,000 × (75%) per M²		M²		

Expressions Pool

Words：
stand, booth, apply for, application, address, contact person, fax, standard stand, raw space, stand fee, profile, specilize in
Sentence：
1. Raw space：3,000 RMB per sqm
2. Standard stand：30,000 RMB（9 sqm with standard facilities）
3. The Canton Fair will offer free stands or 25% discount to overseas exhibitors in order to support the overseas enterprises to participate.

Step 5

Design a brochure for your company. The brochure should include the company's profile and the main products' description with a price list.

Target:

Be able to work in team to design a brochure.

Guidance:

● Ss read the direction and try to understand it.

● Work in group. The group members have been identified during Step 3.

● Ss should work out the elements of a good brochure.

● The brochure should be made and printed.

● Teacher should guide Ss to finish this step after class.

● The brochures should be posted as a decoration to the classroom.

Expressions Pool

1. How to write a profile? (from Step 3)
2. How to describe a product?

Appearance: It is fashionable. It is ... meters high/wide/long.

It comes in 2 colors.

It arrives in new model.

It has a bigger screen.

Material: It is made of ... The material is natural and green.

Function: It is multifunctional. It can be used to ...

Special feature: It's the latest model. It has much more internal memory.

3. Price list:

Description	**Women's Sleeveless Shirt** round neck top with pleat		
Material	100% Bamboo fiber		
Color	White A61 − 55		Beige A61 − 56
Quantity(pcs)	300	500	1000 +
Unit Price	US $8. 80	US $8. 40	US $8. 00

Step 6

After practicing all the tasks above, you may have interest in doing the followings after class.

A

Discuss the following questions:

1. What preparations should you make before attending a trade fair?
2. How to make a good impression on the visitors?

B

Please make a drama according to the following situation.

Situation:

A foreign client, Mr. Park, visits ABC Company's booth. Mr. Park is interested in two products. ABC Company's salesperson is offering services and introducing products.

Possible roles:

Mr. Park, Salesperson of ABC Company

Possible tasks:

Greetings; self introduction; appreciation on the booth; interests in the products; introduction of the products, ect.

Target:

Summarize what have been learned and apply them in practice.

Guidance:

- Ss are supposed to review what they have learned about attending trade fair.
- Ss are supposed to discuss freely.
- Teacher should encourage Ss to make the drama after class.
- Teacher should explain the direction clearly.

---------------------------- **Expressions Pool** ----------------------------

The drama should be focused on the situation and topic.

Greetings, general information, products description should be included.

Greetings

Sales representative	Visitor
Hello, my name is . . . , I am with . . . , welcome to our booth. How should I address you? Good morning, can I help you in any way? Is there anything I can do for you? Sure, I am glad to. We've got some samples here. If you come this way, I will show them to you. What about having a look at these samples first?	Hello, nice to meet you. My name is . . . , and I'm interested in your . . . Good morning. Can you tell me something about your products? Yes, I'd like to know something about your . . .

General information

Sales representative	Visitor
Here is the introductory brochure of our company and main products. Would you like a packet of our promotional literature? Our company specializes in . . . , such as . . . We have been dealing with . . . It is a leading company/large-scale supplier of . . . We have achieved great success in . . . Our goods are well received in . . . These patterns are popular in the international market/among . . . It's the best seller.	Are these samples all made of . . . ? Are these your company's main products? Could I have a look at . . . ? Oh, really? How long have you been doing . . . ? Sounds very impressive. Oh, that's wonderful. Maybe there's something that we can work on together.

（续表）

Sales representative	Visitor
Our . . . are well known for their fine quality and fashionable design. We look forward to . . . at the global level/on a global basis.	

Product description

Sales representative	Visitor
This is our latest catalogue/price list. You'll surely find something interesting in it. We have a wide range of products. May I know what particular items you are interested in? Firstly . . . , secondly . . . , and thirdly . . . It is . . . times faster/slower/bigger/smaller than . . . It is this year's latest design. It's sold remarkably fast/well received . . . I think it will also find a good market in your area. You can see they are good in material, fashionable in design and superb in workmanship. They are available in all sizes from S to XL. The material is absolutely of excellent quality. We can change our design to meet customers' needs/exact specifications.	I am particularly interested in your range of . . . What features/characters does it have . . . That's very special/marvelous/terrific . . . It feels/looks/smells . . . I think these patterns are quite good. They look pretty. How many colors does it have? How many sizes is it available in? Can you process according to supplied samples? Is it possible that you make the goods according to the patterns we provide?

Action research
（教师自己的教学行动研究）

任务完成中的观察、反思（日志、随笔） 备忘

Language Points

Text A ● ● ● ● ● ● ● ● ● ● ● ●

◆（line4）... complete exhibit *variety*, the biggest ...

variety：a collection of things, group

［运用］ a variety of

e. g. This operation system is useful in a variety of situations.

［拓展］ *various*（*a.*）不同的, 各种各样的 various ways/colors/courses

There are various ways to solve the problem.

◆（line7）... Canton Fair was *initiated* from ...

initiate：begin, originate

［运用］ initiate an action/a project/a plan

e. g. This term, we will initiate a new teaching plan to boost students' motivation.

［拓展］ *initiative*（*n.*）主动性, 首创精神 on one's own initiative

You must make a reasonable decision on your own initiative.

initiator（*n.*）创始人, 发起人 play the role of an initiator, an initiator in art

The U. S. is the earliest initiator of advertising education in the world.

◆（line14）... foreign *invested* enterprises, ...

invest：to lay out money with the expectation of profit

［运用］ invest in a project/real estate/the factory

e. g. He showed good judgment in deciding not to invest in the project.

［拓展］ *investor*（*n.*）投资者 overseas/domestic investor

An unfavorable policy allowance may keep the overseas investors out.

investment（*n.*）投资, 投入 make an investment in, large investment

Most successful companies make a significant investment in building brand image.

Text B ● ● ● ● ● ● ● ● ● ● ● ● ● ● ● ●

◆（line 5）... is *expected* to attract 70m visitors ...

expect：→ hope, look for, suppose

［运用］ expect a storm/result/an answer；to be expected, expect of ...

e. g. Parents usually expect too much of their children.

［拓展］ *expectation*（*n.*）预料, 期望 have expectations for, beyond one's expectation

He has little expectation of passing the exam.

［仿写］人们总是期望他们的方法能取得最大的利益。

◆（line 14）... *representing* the common wish ...

represent：→（*vt.*）display, show, reveal

［运用］ represent the country/the group, represent that ...

e. g. The Foreign Minister represented the country at the conference.

［拓展］ *representative*（*n.*）代表, 代表性人物 sales representative 销售代表

Hello. This is a representative of Zhongyou Department Store.

［仿写］我们将和你方代表在广州交易会上讨论这个问题。

◆（line 16）... a central *concern* of the international ...

concern：→（*n.*）interest, anxiety, worry

［运用］ great/main/public concern, concern about/with/over, of/with/without concern, have a concern in, have no concern for ...

e. g. The children's education is the teacher's uppermost concern.

［拓展］ *concern*（*v.*）有关于, 关系到；使担忧, 使烦恼 be concerned in/with

More than two students have been concerned in this affair.

concerning（*prep.*）关于, 涉及 concerning environmental pollution/the future

Please inform me of any information concerning this matter as soon as possible.

［仿写］这是关系到我们公司前途的大事。

◆（line 18）... 2% of the *global* population ...

global：covering, influencing, or relating to the whole world

［运用］ global economy/market/problem/event

e. g. A global environmental meeting is going to be held here.

［拓展］ *globe*（*n.*）地球, 世界 around the globe, all over the globe

There are so many issues all over the globe that are very difficult to solve.

globalization（*n.*）全球化 economic globalization

［仿写］从文化界到经济界, 世博会已经得到了全球的关注。

◆（line 21）... as *estimated* by the ...

estimate：→（*vt.*）figure, evaluate, value

[运用] estimate the cost/number/time/size

e.g. The gardener estimated that it would take him four hours to weed the garden.

[拓展] *estimated*（*a.*）估计的 an estimated weight/cost

An estimated 300 million people carry this disease.

[仿写] 她对自己所作估计的项目成本确信无疑。

◆（line 37）... to *avoid* missing ...

avoid：to prevent from happening

[运用] avoid mistake/accident/doing something

e.g. He avoided answering my questions by commenting my dressing style.

[拓展] *avoidable*（*a.*）能避免的；可回避的 avoidable delay/mistake/error ...

People fall into avoidable errors because of a failure to reason correctly.

[仿写] 他忍住了怒气，避免了一场殴斗。

◆（line 41）... World Expositions *attended* independently ...

attend：to be present at（an event, meeting, etc）

[运用] attend school/a meeting/conference/party/class/lecture

e.g. He insisted that we attend the lecture.

[拓展] *attendance*（*n.*）出席，出勤 regular/full attendance

He missed three attendances this year.

attendant（*n.*）服务人员 flight attendant, ring for the attendant

Being a good flight attendant means making your passengers feel relaxed.

[仿写] 公司代表每年要出席很多重大商务会谈。

◆（line 43）... Chinese *regarded* the World Exposition ...

regard：→consider of, think; relate to; concern

[运用] regard ... as ... ,

e.g. Shaoxing wine is regarded as the national wine.

[拓展] *regarding*（*prep.*）关于 regarding sb./sth.

He set up a new opinion regarding the project.

[仿写] 关于处罚，你有何意见？

◆（line 51）... China's first official *participation* in ...

participation：the act of sharing in the activities of a group

[运用] encourage/promote/allow participation

e.g. The scheme aims to encourage increased participation in sporting activities.

[拓展] *participate*（*v.*）参加，参与 participate in

He has invited the all campus companions to participate in his wedding party.

[仿写] 我们十分重视参与国际会展的机会。

◆（line 65）... World Expo *reflected* the ups and downs ...

reflect：to form an image of something; to show or express

[运用] reflect sunlight/opinion/thoughts

e.g. Does this letter reflect how you really think?

[拓展] *reflection*（*n.*）倒影，反映，深思 on reflection, after long reflection

On reflection, we decided to change our plan.

[仿写] 这句广告词能反映出我们产品的特色。

Translation of Texts

Text A

广交会

广交会，又称中国进出口商品交易会。由于它在中国目前历史最长、层次最高、规模最大、商品种类最全、到会客商最多、国别地区最广、成交效果最好、信誉最佳，而被誉为"中国第一展"。广交会创办于1957年4月春，每年分春秋两季。

广交会由48个交易团组成，有数千家资信良好、实力雄厚的外贸公司、生产企业、科研院所、外商投资/独资企业、私营企业参展。

广交会贸易方式灵活多样，除传统的看样成交外，还举办网上交易会。广交会以出口贸易为主，也做进口生意。另外，还可以开展多种形式的经济技术合作与交流，以及商检、保险、运输、广告、咨询等业务活动。来自世界各地的客商云集广州，互通商情，增进友谊。

第106届中国进出口商品交易会

1. 举办时间：第106届中国进出口商品交易会

第一期:2009 年 10 月 15 日—19 日

第二期:2009 年 10 月 23 日—27 日

第三期:2009 年 10 月 31 日—11 月 4 日

期限:每期持续 5 天

2. 举办地点:中国进出口商品交易会展馆

3. 展出

1)展出分为九个产品区:机械设备、小型车辆及配件、五金工具、建材及厨卫设备、电子信息及家电、日用消费品、装饰品及礼品、食品及农产品、原材料。

2)各展出如下图所示安排在不同的日期

展出时间	第一期: 2009 年 10 月 15 日—19 日	第二期: 2009 年 10 月 23 日—27 日	第三期: 2009 年 10 月 31 日—11 月 4 日
展品	大型机械及设备 小型机械 自行车 摩托车 汽车配件/车辆 五金 工具 工程机械(户外) 电子产品 家用电器 计算机 通讯产品 卫浴设备 建筑及装饰材料	厨具 餐具 家具 家居饰品 园林用品 家居用品 个人护理品 钟表 玩具 节日用品	男装 女装 童装 运动服 休闲服 内衣 革皮羽绒制品 服饰配件 家用纺织品 箱包 办公文具

4. 展位价格

1)光地价格:3 000 元/平方米

2)标准展位价格:30 000 元(9 平方米,含标准展具配备)

3)广交会将为境外参展商提供免费展位或 7.5 折的优惠价,以鼓励境外企业参展。优惠措施如下:

a)经联合国确立为最不发达国家的参展商将获得免费展位。

b)其他国家和地区的参展商可享受 7.5 折的优惠价,例如:进口展区光地价格可以优惠到 2 250 元/平方米,而单独的标准展位(9 平方米,含标准展具配备)则只收 22 500 元。

5. 申请参展

1)申请条件:凡符合《第 106 届中国进出口商品交易会进口展区参展条款》要求的境外企业均可报名参展。

2)申请方法:各企业可以直接向中国对外贸易中心(以下简称 CFTC)提出申请,或者通过中心代理机构申请参展。

6. 参展流程

参展商将《参展申请表》填好于 2009 年 8 月 21 日前交至组委会认定。收到《申请表》后,组委会将与申请人确认。组委会将会分配安排展位,并寄发《第 106 届中国进出口商品交易会进口展展位确认通知》和《第 106 届中国进出口商品交易会进口展服务指南》。在收到《展位确认通知》后 3 个工作日内,请参展商将实际展出场地的各项费用汇入组委会指定账号。所有账目将在大会结束后结清,届时余额将根据具体情况支付给其中一方。

Text B

中国即将到来的盛会

有时候,中国似乎已在"登峰造极"方面令他国望尘莫及:最大、最快、最廉价、最好。如今,这个国家正在筹划有史以来最盛大的全球展会:上海世博会(Shanghai World Expo)。上海世博会于 2010 年开幕,历时 6 个月,预计将吸引 7000 万人次的参观者,其中外国参观者 350 万人次。

上海希望被载入史册,与世界其他几个伟大的展会并驾齐驱:1851 年的伦敦万国博览会(Great Exhibition),举办地在水晶宫(Crystal Palace);1889 年的巴黎世博会(Universal Exposition),艾菲尔铁塔就是那时落成的;1893 年的芝加哥哥伦布世博会(Colombian Exposition),第一座摩天轮由此问世。

本届世博会的主题是"城市,让生活更美好",这代表了全人类对于未来美好城市生活的共同愿望。这个主题显示出国际各界对于政策制订、城市策略和可持续发展的关注。19 世纪,全球人口只有 2%住在城市;到了 1950 年,这个数字就上升到 29%;进入 21 世纪,世界人口几乎有一半搬进了城市;到 2010 年,联合国预计,城市人口将占总人口数的 55%。

这次世博会将设国家、企业及其他各类展馆。有些展馆将以大豆纤维制成墙壁,使用河水驱动的空调系统以及太阳能电池板供电的灯具,旨在向民众展示更洁净、更健康、更可持续的未来城市面貌。

世博会无疑将在近期内拉动上海经济发展、提升国家声望——特别是在国内游客中。显然,成功举办世博会是上海市政府的首要工作,其重要性与去年奥运会对北京的重要性相仿。上海希望世博会名垂青史。上海将会竭尽全力,抓住这一极其宝贵的机会。

　　回顾历史,中国因世博会而向世界开放。最初参观世博会的中国人是单独前往的。王韬参加了1867年巴黎世博会并且游览了伦敦的水晶宫。当时这个中国人把世博会看作是"一堆奇怪的东西大展示",这说明了那时中国人还没有深刻地思考科技会如何改变世界、影响和发展全新的公民价值。1876年,一个名为李贵的中国人作为中国工业贸易界的代表参加了费城世博会。他精明勇敢,并且撰写了一本书记录费城世博会的盛况。这是中国第一次官方层面的参加世博会。中国的展品价值2万两白银,装进了520个箱子。中国的展馆比日本的要小,甚至可以说是不够用来作为常规展览的。这是因为当时中国没有打算展示这么多产品。西方国家的产品和生产力深深地触动了国人。到了1915年,中国参加了巴拿马世博会,茅台酒获奖。之后,由于战争,中国参加世博会受限。直到1982年美国诺克斯威尔世博会,中国才又回到了世博会舞台。中国的魅力和精神再次获得世界的关注。中国参加世博会的历史也反映了中国起伏跌宕、由衰至兴的历史。

Explain these words and expressions through their context or with the help of a dictionary.

run(Para. 1)　进行,运行(*v.*)
e. g. The meeting will run three hours.

concern(Para. 3)　关注(*n.*)
e. g. Global warming has become a big concern all over the world.

miss (Para. 5)　错过(*v.*)
e. g. Don't miss his lecture because his speech is very humorous and meaningful.

demonstrate(Para. 6)　证明,说明(*v.*)
e. g. The experiment demonstrated a failure but a brave try.

Reading Skills Exercises：

1

Write down the main idea after you have read Text B.

 Key

The article tells us China will host Shanghai World Expo . In addition, the article shows us the history of China's participation in World Expo .

2

Complete the blank according to Text B.

 Key

The theme of the Expo 2010 Shanghai is Better City , Better Life.

3

Could you please discuss the importance of Expo？

 Key

Expo can boost China's economy.
Expo can represent the people's common wish.
Expo can raise China's reputation.
Expo can help to raise the awareness of sustainable development.

Language practice

Vocabulary

1

Finish the list of nouns.

 Key

Verb	Noun
apply	application
participate	participation, participant
promote	promotion, promoter
construct	construction, constructor
organize	organization, organizor
purchase	purchase, purchaser
inspect	inspection, inspector
exhibit	exhibition, exhibitor

2

Match the words to make word partnerships.

 Key

1. organize a fair
2. boost economy
3. apply for a booth
4. construct a pavilion
5. purchase tickets

3

Fill in the gaps with words from the box.

 Key

1. "Shanghai Expo <u>Promotion</u> Week" has been launched in Tokyo, which involves exhibitions and forums.
2. The Expo organizer assigned two travel agents to handle <u>ticket sales</u> in US, announcing that the US residents can start booking tickets from next week.
3. A conference for all the national <u>participants</u> of the Shanghai 2010 World Expo took place.
4. The <u>theme</u> of Expo 2010 is "Better City, Better Life," representing the common wish of the whole humankind for a better living in future urban environments.
5. Many <u>events</u> and activities will happen during the Expo.

6. The Expo <u>Site</u> is at the waterfront area on both sides of Huangpu River.
7. Five statues of Expo 2010 <u>mascot</u> Haibao appeared in Beijing Capital International Airport's second and third terminal building on Thursday.
8. The steel structure of Denmark's 3,000-square-meter <u>pavilion</u> was finished yesterday.

Translation

Translate English into Chinese and underline the pattern. Study the pattern. Then translate the Chinese into English by using the pattern. Please do the followings according to the example.

 Key

1. Our company <u>is located in</u> the city's business district.
   主要句型：……位于……
   中文翻译：<u>我们公司位于城市的商业区</u>。
   他的办公室位于城市的中心。
   English translation：<u>His office is located in the center of the city</u>.
2. Shanghai Textile Import and Export Company <u>mainly deals in</u> textile clothes.
   主要句型：公司经营……
   中文翻译：<u>上海纺织品进出口公司主要经营纺织品服装</u>。
   我们公司主要经营五金。
   English translation：<u>Our company mainly deals in hardware</u>.
3. Our <u>company is noted for</u> its strong capacity in processing.
   主要句型：公司以……著称
   中文翻译：<u>我们公司以强大的加工能力著称</u>。
   这家公司以其悠久的历史著称。
   English translation：<u>This company is noted for its long history</u>.
4. Our company will <u>provide</u> best service <u>to</u> the customers.
   主要句型：向……提供……
   中文翻译：<u>我们公司向顾客提供最好的服务</u>。
   广交会的主办方会向参展商提供服务。
   English translation：<u>The organizer of Canton Fair will offer services to exhibitors</u>.

5.　Our company <u>has won</u> the international ISO9002 certificate.

主要句型：……已获得……认证（证明）

中文翻译：我们公司已获得国际 ISO9002 认证。

这个产品已经获得质量证明。

English translation：<u>This product has won the quality certificate.</u>

2.　In our company, great changes have taken place since the new manager came.

3.　This is the coldest winter I <u>had</u> (have had) ever.

4.　They worked on their new design when they <u>were seeing</u> (saw) an opening in the market.

5.　She was planning to attend the Inventors' Fair but she <u>hasn't had</u> (didn't have) time.

6.　We <u>have prepared</u> (had prepared) all the paperwork for our visas before we left for the fair.

7.　He <u>has been writing</u> (has written) the novel which is the best-seller this week.

8.　Our competitors failed to see the gap in the market and missed an opportunity.

Grammar

Grammar Exercises：

Correct the six sentences that use the wrong form of verb.

 Key

1.　Ever since I arrived here, I <u>was living</u> (have lived/have been living) in the dorm because it is cheaper.

Listening

1

Work with your partner to fill in the blanks using the words in the box. Listen and check your answers, and then follow the recording.

 Script

1.　Many excellent *suppliers* are gathering at the fair.

2.　Every session of the Fair has seen a great collection of beautiful *commodities*.

3.　The products made in China are *competitive* with low price and high quality.

4.　We can concentrate on specific *negotiation* with those businesses we are interested in.

5.　We take the opportunity of attending the fair to welcome customers from all over the world to *establish* business relationship.

6.　Different enterprises have shared experiences here, *reached agreements* here, and established relationships here.

7.　The Canton Fair always takes serving China's *foreign trade* as its responsibility.

8.　Chinese Export Commodities Fair was renamed China *Import and Export* Fair in 2006.

2

Listen to the conversation and decide whether the following statements are true or false. Then write key words to support your answer.

Script

A：This is Zhang Ming from Ningbo Garments Import & Export Corporation. May I speak to Mr. Johnson Smith?

B：This is Johnson Smith. What can I do for you, Mr. Zhang?

A：I am calling to book a booth for the fair. Are there any booths available?

B：Yes, we still have some. Could you please tell me what kind of booths you would like to book?

A：I'd like a big one.

B：I suggest a big one facing stairs on the second floor.

A：Great. I am wondering if the booth can be divided into two areas since we would like to have separate space for display and negotiation.

B：I am sure it is big enough. And the booth faces stairs, so you can expect more visitors.

A：That sounds good. Can you tell me the booth number?

B：B 68.
A：Thank you.
B：You're welcome.

 Key

True or false.
1. Mr. Zhang is going to book a booth for the fair. True ✓ False ☐
   I am calling to book a booth for the fair.
2. There's no booth available.
   True ☐ False ✓
   Yes, we still have some.
3. Mr. Zhang doesn't like the booth that Mr. Smith suggests. True ☐ False ✓
   That sounds good.
4. The booth is going to be divided into two areas. True ✓ False ☐
   I am wondering if the booth can be divided into two areas.

3

Listen to the conversation between a sales representative of an exhibitor and a potential buyer. Then fill in the missing information. You may listen to it twice.

 Script

A：Hello, is there anything I can help?
B：Oh, hello, I am just looking at the towel here. The label says it is made of bamboo, is that right?
A：Yes, that's right.
B：Aha, how interesting.
A：Yes, isn't it? How should I address you, sir?
B：My name is Tom Score, and I work for Shine Trading Company in England.
A：Nice to meet you, Mr. Score. I am Ellen Yang from Good Day Textile Company from Shanghai, China.
B：Nice to meet you too, Miss Yang. Are bamboo fiber towels your company's main products?
A：Yes, they are. Besides, we also make bamboo fabrics and bedding products. These products are green and natural.
B：Could I have a look at your introductory brochure?
A：Certainly, here you are. You may keep it.
B：Thank you.
A：As you can see from the brochure, our company specializes in designing, and manufacturing all

kinds of garments and textile. And the bamboo fiber product is a new line developed by our own R&D department and has become one of our best sellers.
B：Sounds very impressive.

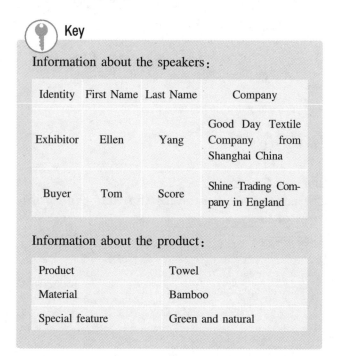 **Key**

Information about the speakers：

Identity	First Name	Last Name	Company
Exhibitor	Ellen	Yang	Good Day Textile Company from Shanghai China
Buyer	Tom	Score	Shine Trading Company in England

Information about the product：

Product	Towel
Material	Bamboo
Special feature	Green and natural

4

Listen to the conversation. A new buyer is going to Canton fair but he is wondering how to get an invitation. After talking with the organizer, he writes down the following information.

Script

Buyer：Excuse me. My company is going to attend the fair as buyer. I am wondering if you can tell me how to apply for the invitation?
Organizer：It is my pleasure to explain to you, sir. You can apply on our official website *www. cantonfair. org. cn* by registering your company's information online. Once your application gets confirmed, you will receive our reply within one week, to inform you of the User Name and Password. With the User Name and Password, you can log in the Buyer E-service Tool (BEST) to print your E-invitation and enjoy the relative services. If you apply for Paper Invitation, it will be sent to you by post.
Buyer：Thanks a lot.
Organizer：You are welcome.

Key

I need to log onto the official website *www. cantonfair. org. cn* and register *the company's information* online. Once my application gets confirmed, I will receive the reply *within one* *week*. I will be informed *the User Name and Password*. With the User Name and Password, I can log in the Buyer E-service Tool (BEST) to print the E-invitation and enjoy the relative services. If I apply for *Paper Invitation*, it will be sent to me by post.

Speaking

1

Role-play a conversation according to the following situations. After the practice, change roles.

Role Cards

Role A: Helen Lee, the sales representative of the exhibitor, should greet the visitors in a polite way and try to ask for any contact method.

Role B: Mr. Smith, who is coming to visit the fair, should show a bit of interest in the product.

Flow Chart

Helen	Mr. Smith
Welcome and greet the visitor.	Greet.
Self introduction and ask for the name of the visitor.	Tell her your name.
Suggest that you have time to show him around the booth. Or you can offer him your brochure.	Show your appreciation.
Briefly introduce your company and main product.	Show your interest. And express that you would like to visit for a while on your own.
Give him your name card and ask for his name card.	Give her your name card.
Show you are ready to give help at any time.	

Suggest Word and Expressions

Helen	Mr. Smith
May I have your name card?	Nice to meet you too.
Our products are well known for their fine quality and fashionable design.	Your booth is very nice.
Our products are famous for . . .	May I have your brochure?
Our products are renowned for . . .	Could you please introduce your company and product for me?
This is our catalogue and company's brochure for your reference.	They're amazing.
This is our samples for your reference.	I am wondering how many sizes your products are available in?
Please take your time.	Then I'd like to look around the exhibition here.
Nice talking to/meeting you.	Nice talking to you.
And if you need help, I am here.	It's very impressive.
Please feel free to ask me any question if you need help.	
I'm always available if you need any help.	

Reference

A: Good morning, Sir. Welcome to our booth. I am Helen Lee. Can I help you?

B: Good morning, Miss Lee. I am Peter Smith.

A: Nice to meet you, Mr. Smith.

B: Nice to meet you too. Your booth is very nice.

A: Thanks. This is our catalogue and company's brochure for your reference. I am sure you'll find something you're interested in. We have a unique collection of clothes.

B: Thanks. Could you please tell me about your company and products?

A: It's my pleasure. Our company offers a wide range of garments such as coats, jackets, pants, shirts and others. Our clothes collection uses silk, cotton as raw materials. And our style tends to be casual and relaxing. Our products are well known for their fine quality and fashionable design. You're welcome to appreciate them since there are samples.

B: They're amazing. China is famous for silk. I am wondering how many sizes your products are available in?

A: They are available in all sizes from S to XL.

B: Very impressive. Then I'd like to look around the exhibition here.

A: Mr. Smith, please take your time. And if you need help, I am here. This is my name card. May I have your name card?

B: Thanks. Here you are.

A: Nice talking to you, Mr. Smith.

B: Me too.

2

Work with your partner to make up a dialogue involving the following situation.

Role Cards

Role A: Sales representative. He is from Shanghai Mobile Phone Import & Export Corporation. He should introduce products in a professional way and demonstrate the function of the new product.

Role B: Miss Green, who comes to the booth and feels interested in the product, should ask questions about the product such as price, function and so on.

Flow Chart

Sales representative	Miss Green
Greetings.	Greet and show your compliment to the booth.
Ask how to address the visitor.	Self-introduction.
Introduce the company and ask the visitor what product she has interest in.	Tell the sales representative her preference.
Introduce the item in detail.	Ask about price.
Explain the pricelist (offer).	The initial price negotiation (counter-offer).
Explain the method to get discounts (counter-counter-offer).	Show interest and tell the sales representative about the possibility of cooperation. Ask for more brochures.
Show your willingness to send more brochures.	Show your appreciation for his introduction.
Say goodbye.	Say goodbye.

Suggested Words & Expressions

The sales representative	Miss Green
Welcome to our booth.	Nice to meet you.
Our products are well known for their fine quality and fashionable design.	It's impressive.
This is our catalogue and company's brochure for your reference.	I would appreciate if you could show me around.
May I ask you if you are interested in any item? Would you please have a seat? I can introduce it to you in detail.	I am wondering if you can send us a sample?
It has a bigger screen. It is multi-functional. It has 8GB internal memory. It's fashionable.	Could you please tell me about it?
And we can manage to offer/provide/present ... special discount for large order, like more than 1,000 pieces.	May I have some ideas of the price?
Thank you for your interest in our product. We do look forward to future cooperation with your company.	Thanks for your introduction. I am impressed by your exhibition as well as your friendly conversation.

Reference

A: Good morning, Miss. Welcome to our booth.

B: Your booth is arranged very nicely. I'd appreciate if you can show me around.

A: Thanks for your compliments. Please this way. May I know how to address you?

B: Thank you. My name is Sena Green.

A: This is my name card. I am Zhang Ming, the sales manager of this company.

B: Please accept mine.

A: Oh, Miss Green, may I ask you where you are from?

B: Actually my company is located in the middle of America, mainly selling mobile phones.

A: Our company has a good reputation for importing and exporting mobile phones. Our products are well known for their fine quality and fashionable design. May I ask you if you are interested in any item?

B: I do like XP12. I think it feels comfortable and fashionable.

A: It has a bigger screen. It is multi-functional. It has 8GB internal memory. It's fashionable.

B: May I have some ideas of the price?

A: Sure. Here is the price list. The one you are interested in is, let me see, is 3000RMB.

B: OK. I see. Are these prices on FOB or CIF basis?

A: FOB from Shanghai China.

B: Mum, I guess it is a bit high. Is this final offer or negotiable?

A: Negotiable. All the quotes here are subject to final confirmation. And we can manage to offer special discount for large order, like more than 500 pieces.

B: Well, you see, I need to report the head office when I go back to see what possible cooperation we may have. I am wondering if you can send us some brochures.

A: Sure, we are glad to.

B: That is very kind of you. And I think we can have further discussion later.

A: Yes. Please feel free to contact me.

B: Thanks for your introduction. I am impressed by your exhibition as well as your friendly conversation.

A: Thank you for your interest in our product. We do look forward to future cooperation with your company.

B: So do I. Goodbye then.

A: Goodbye, Miss Green.

Writing

Business card

1

Look at this business card and answer the questions

 Key

CORUSCANT AUTO SALES

Aaron Wagner
Sales Consultant

office: (928) 3379 2281
cell: (928) 0406 726 831
fax: (928) 3379 2281

Coruscant Auto Sales aaronw@ coruscant. com
6838 Eastlake Rd.
Wayland, Massachusetts, 01778

1. What position does Aaron Wagner hold? <u>Sales Consultant</u>
2. What's the company name? <u>CORUSCANT</u>

Learning for fun

Read the story and then retell it in class.
(Omitted)

3. What does this company do? <u>Sells automobile</u>
4. What's the zip code of this company? <u>01778</u>

2

Make an English version of the following business card.

Hanson Electrics

Wang Kaizhi   general manager
office: (86)0769 – 2226 7878
fax: (86)0769 – 2226 7881
mobile phone: (86) 136 4873 9752
email: kaiserwang@ e-hansheng. com
14F Guangtian Building/Tower.
3321 Guantai Street, Dongguan.
Guangdong, 523009, China

3

Design your business card.
(Omitted)

Unit 6 Travel

Objective

- **Career skills**
  Organizing group trips.

- **Reading**
  1. Reading for main idea(s)
  2. Skimming/Scanning
  3. Reading for general information and details

- **Writing**
  Practical writing: itinerary

- **Listening**
  1. Listening for key words/expressions
  2. Listening for general information and details

- **Speaking**
  1. Buying train tickets
  2. Booking flight tickets

- **Language focus**:

Key words and phrases		
consider	accommodation	ascertain
take into consideration	take up	draw up
book	disappoint	
instead of	budget	

Teaching Arrangement

Warm-up & Unit task (Text A)
1) Time schedule: 2 periods
2) Suggested lesson structure
    Warm-up: 10 minutes
    Text A: 10 - 15 minutes
    Unit task step 1 (pre-task): 10 minutes
    Unit task steps 2 - 5 (while-task): 30 - 35 minutes
    Unit task step 6(post-task): 20 minutes

Reading (Text B)
1) Time schedule: 1 period
2) Suggested lesson structure
    Language points: 20 - 25 minutes
    Language practice: 20 - 25 minutes

Listening
1) Time schedule: 1 period
2) Suggested lesson structure
    Listening exercise 1: 10 minutes
    Listening exercise 2: 10 minutes
    Listening exercise 3: 10 minutes
    Listening exercise 4: 15 minutes

Speaking & Writing
1) Time schedule: 1 period
2) Suggested lesson structure
    Speaking: 20 - 25 minutes
    Writing: 20 minutes

Teaching Procedures

Warm-up

Match the following pictures with the information in Column A and Column B.

Target:
Ss learn some famous scenery spots in the world by identifying some pictures.

Guidance:
- Ss read Warm-up.
- Ask Ss to look at the following pictures and the information in Column A.
- Ask Ss to match pictures with the information in Column A.
- Ask Ss to match the pictures with the information in Column B.

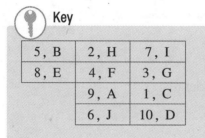 Key

5, B	2, H	7, I
8, E	4, F	3, G
	9, A	1, C
	6, J	10, D

Background Information
- **Package tour**

A package tour is usually a combination of travel services bought as a package, for example flight & hotel or hotel & service, such as a formula ticket, diving course or car hire. Package tours can also be tailored according to the traveler's wishes.

A package tour is usually paid for in advance and organized by a responsible tour operator. A package tour will always include at least the travel and accommodation, or one of these together with some other significant travel service.

- **Independent tour**

An independent tour is a great way to travel to the country if you don't want to travel as part of a group, or your travel dates don't match our group tour dates. With an independent tour you can choose your dates of travel and also the itinerary can be tailored to suit your requests.

Unit task

Read Text A and practice a series of real tasks of organizing a group trip supposing that you are a HR assistant and you are going to organize your colleagues to visit Hong Kong Disneyland.

 Task Map(任务导航)

外出旅游不仅能丰富大家的业余生活,而且能增进出游者之间的感情交流。因此能否组织好外出旅游活动决定了这次活动的成功与否。

特此要求学生根据假定的情景模拟身份来策划组织一次集体出游活动，通过文章的学习，了解如何组织好外出旅游活动。

本单元任务分为6个步骤，第一个步骤让学生阅读文章，了解组织集体旅游的步骤以及各步骤的注意事项；第二个步骤通过给出具体情景及相关信息，让学生比较票价从而选择出游的方式并制定出合理经济的路线；第三个步骤要求学生根据所给出情景及要求，设计出电话预订酒店的对话以了解如何预订酒店；第四个步骤要求学生根据所给出图片，选择其对应的主题公园，然后根据所提供的景点信息，选择计划游玩的娱乐活动；第五个步骤要求学生根据所提供的情景，列出需带物品的清单；第六个步骤要求学生根据上述步骤所得做一个出游活动的行程安排。

Process Break-down

Pre-task：

Step 1   Divide the whole class into groups of 6 – 8 students. Ss read the passage and fill in the blanks with the expressions given in the box. By finishing this step, Ss will have mastered the main steps of organizing a group trip.

While-task：

Step 2   Each team needs to decide their reasonable and economical route by choosing the proper transport.

Step 3   Each team needs to organize a dialogue between Jack and the receptionist. And role play this dialogue with their partner.

Step 4   Ask students to match the pictures with the information in box A and B. And then ask them to choose the attractions they are planning to visit according to the information.

Step 5   Ask Ss to discuss what needs to be carried on the trip. And then ask them to make a list.

Post-task：

Step 6   Work out a two-day itinerary of this trip according to Step 2 – 5 and present it orally.

Step 1

Find out the procedures of organizing a group trip in the text and fill in the blanks according to the box below.

任务过程控制关注点
Minefield

提醒学生根据文中内容并且结合实际，列出主要步骤，并按顺序排列。

Target：

Know how to organize a group trip.

Guidance：

- Ss read the passage by themselves and get to know how to organize a group trip step by step.
- Invite 1 – 2 Ss to present their answers.
- Teacher can do a little explanation afterwards.

🔑 **Key**

1. b　2. c　3. d　4. f　5. g　6. e　7. a

Step 2

任务过程控制关注点
Minefield

　　提醒学生根据所提供的航班、火车和汽车相关信息,比较各方式所需的时间,所需要的路费,制定出合理经济的路线。

Suppose you are the HR assistant in your company. Your company is planning to travel from Shanghai to Hong Kong to visit Disneyland from Nov. 5th to Nov. 6th. Now read the following information, then decide how to go and work out a reasonable route and tell us your reasons.

Target：

Know how to work out a reasonable route.

Guidance：

- Finishing the Step 1, Ss have already known how to organize a group trip.
- Ss need to decide how to go according to the time budget.
- Ss need to compare the prices of flights and then work out the route.
- Invite 1 – 2 Ss to present their answer and give some reasons and do a little explanation afterwards.

Reference：

　　Take flight MU8977 to Shenzhen Bao'an International Airport, and then depart from Shenzhen Bao'an International Airport to Disneyland by bus.

------------------------- **Expressions Pool** -------------------------

1. cheap/inexpensive/economical . . .
2. expensive/costly/high-priced . . .
3. convenient/fast/comfortable . . .
4. I am going to take a plane/train/bus to get there.
5. It will take a long time to . . .
6. We are going to take a morning/noon/afternoon flight MU × × × to . . .
7. We are going to depart from . . .
8. We will arrive in × × very late.

Step 3

任务过程控制关注点
Minefield

- 提醒学生在电话预订酒店前要统计清楚具体人数,男女各多少。
- 在电话预订时要告诉对方打算预订什么类型的房间,预订间数分别是多少。
- 要明确预订哪一天的房间,打算订几天。询问相关价格,是否提供折扣。

Role-play a conversation about booking rooms on the phone.

Target：

Know how to book rooms on the phone.

Guidance：

- Finishing the Step 2, Ss have already known the reasonable and economical route from Shanghai to Hong Kong Disneyland.
- Ss need to organize a dialogue between Jack and the receptionist according to the information.
- Invite 1 – 2 groups to role play this dialogue with their partner and do a little explanation afterwards.

------ **Expressions Pool** ------

Mary：
1. Good morning, × × Hotel. May I help you?
2. What rooms do you prefer? / Single or double-room?...
3. For which dates, Mr. / Ms × ×?
4. A double room with a bath is × × per night, a single room with a bath is × × per night.
5. There is a 20 percent discount.
6. How long do you intend to stay in this hotel? / How long will you be staying?...
7. Could I take your name and contact number, please?

Jack：
1. I'd like to reserve rooms for my group.
2. We have × × people. × × doubles rooms with a bath and × × single rooms with a bath, please.
3. From ... to ... / On Nov. 5th.
4. How much do you charge? / What is the rate, please?
5. Is it possible for me to get a discount? / I was hoping to pay a little less.
6. For × × night(s). / We'll be leaving × ×.

Step 4

Suppose the group will be arriving at Hong Kong Disneyland at about 1 p. m. on Nov. 5.

任务过程控制关注点
Minefield

- 提醒学生搭配时，可以借助图片的文字及相关信息来做判断。
- 提醒学生在选择游玩景点或娱乐项目时，要充分读懂题中给出的时间信息，安排好时间及选择可能游玩的景点。

Target：
Know "attractions they are planning to visit"

Guidance：
- Ss read the situation.
- Discuss in groups and match the pictures with the information.
- Ss read the information and choose the attractions they are planning to visit.
- Teacher may guide Ss to get more information online.
- Ss can choose the attractions according to their interests.
- Invite 1 − 2 Ss to present their answer and do a little explanation afterwards.

A

 Key

1. C, d   2. D, c   3. A, b   4. B, a

B

Now look at the following attractions in each theme park and choose the attractions you are planning to visit.

Reference：
I would like to go to Fantasyland as soon as we arrive at Disneyland. I am going to watch the stage show "the Golden Mickeys", because I love Micky and I know there are performances shown there around 2 p. m. And you know what, Disney on Parade will go through Fantasyland. It will be fantastic.

Attractions：（suggested translation）

美国小镇大街	幻想世界
★「星梦奇缘」烟花表演	★「小小世界」
★ 迪士尼巡游表演	★ 米奇幻想曲
★ 歌舞青春热跳速递	★ 米奇金奖音乐剧
★ 动画艺术廊	梦想花园
★ 动画艺术教室	★ 小熊维尼历险之旅
布公仔流动实验	睡公主城堡
小镇大街古董车	

明日世界	探险世界
★ 飞越太空山	★ 森林河流之旅
★ 巴斯光年星际历险	★ 狮子王庆典
★ 幸会史迪仔	木筏及泰山树屋

Background Information
Disneyland Map

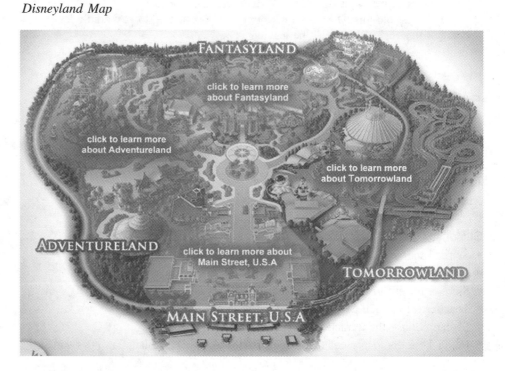

Disneyland Timetable
Disneyland Attraction and Entertainment

Park Hours　　　　　　10:30AM－7:30PM
This is a peak park day.
This is a block-out day for Value Annual Pass.

Parade and Firework Times

Disney on Parade　　　　　　3:30PM
See parade route on Guidemap

"Disney in the Stars" Fireworks　7:30PM
This spectacular fireworks show
transforms the sky above Sleeping
Beauty Castle into a stunning evening
spectacle.

Special Hours

Main Street, U.S.A.
Animation Academy　　　　10:40AM－7:00PM
(Show performs in Cantonese)

High School Musical: LIVE!

High School Musical: LIVE!
Sleeping Beauty Castle Forecourt
The entertainment phenomenon
inspired by the smash hit Disney
Channel Original Movie comes to life in
High School Musical: LIVE, an
immersive show for the whole family
at Hong Kong Disneyland.

Stage Shows
Adventureland
"Festival of the Lion King"　12:15PM　2:00PM　4:30PM
　　　　　　　　　　　　　　　6:00PM

Tomorrowland
"Stitch Encounter"
Please check for show times in your
preferred language (in Cantonese/in
Putonghua or in English) at the
attraction entrance.

Character Greeting Times
Characters appear occasionally at the
following locations, see map for
locations:
Main Street, U.S.A.
Town Square　　　　　　10:30AM－5:00PM

Fantasyland
Fantasy Gardens　　　　　12:00PM－2:30PM
　　　　　　　　　　　　　4:00PM－6:00PM
Sleeping Beauty Castle　10:30AM　11:30AM　12:30PM
　　　　　　　　　　　　3:00PM　　4:30PM　　5:30PM
Tomorrowland　　　　　　11:00AM－5:30PM

任务过程控制关注点
Minefield

- 提醒学生在旅行前,要上网了解需要提前准备什么证件。
- 要了解什么东西可以携带,什么东西不允许携带。
- 然后,把要带的东西一一记下,这样不易落下重要的需带的东西。

Step 5

Make a list.

Target:
Know what needs to be carried on the trip.

Guidance:
- Discuss in groups. Ss should learn what things must be taken according to the relevant laws.
- Ask Ss to write down the other things they should take during the trip.
- Invite 1 - 2 Ss to present their list and teacher will do a little explanation afterwards.

Expressions Pool

1. first-aid box/ bandage/ medicine for fever . . .
2. personal care product/ tooth paste/ tooth brush/ soap/ shampoo . . .
3. wallet/ money/ credit or debit card/ traveler's check . . .
4. wear or take comfortable shoes . . .
5. umbrella/ raincoat . . .
6. comfortable clothes/ sports coats/ jackets/ cap . . .
7. dry fruits/ food/ water bottle . . .
8. cell phone/ digital camera/ TV camera . . .
9. identity card/ Permit for Proceeding to Hong Kong and Macau
---

Step 6

Work out a two-day itinerary of this trip according to Steps 2 - 5 and present it orally.

任务过程控制关注点
Minefield

提醒学生根据文中的相关步骤, 按
时间顺序, 做出行程安排。

Target:

Summarize the whole process and work out the itinerary.

Guidance:

- Ask Ss to work out the itinerary according to steps 2 - 5. The itinerary should include how many days the group is going for, what places of interest to visite, the stopovers, when and where to stop for meals and highlights of the trips.
- Invite 1 - 2 students to make an oral presentation and teacher will do a little explanation afterwards.

Expressions Pool

1. Day 1 Nov. 5th/ meet at . . . / . . . a. m. Depart from . . . station
2. . . . a. m. Arrive in × × by Flt. × × . . .
3. . . . a. m. Arrive at . . . Hotel and check in
4. . . . a. m. / p. m. Eat lunch at . . . Hotel
5. . . . p. m. — . . . p. m. Visit . . .
6. . . . p. m. Dinner at Disneyland
7. 7:30 p. m. Watch "The Star Fireworks" in Main Street, U. S. A.
8. . . . p. m. Return to . . . Hotel
9. Day 2 . . . a. m. Breakfast
10. Return to Shanghai

Action research
（教师自己的教学行动研究）

任务完成中的观察、反思（日志、随笔）   备忘

Language Points

Text A • • • • • • • • • • • •

♦ (line 15) ... **you do not want to *disappoint* them** ...

disappoint：fail to be or do sth as good, interesting etc. as was hoped for or desired or expected by (sb.) 使(某人)失望

[运用]   disappoint sb.

e.g. I'm sorry to disappoint you. 不好意思,让你失望了。

[拓展]   disappointment (*n.*) 失望 disappointed (*a.*) 失望的 disappointing (*a.*) 令人失望的
She couldn't hide her disappointment. 她无法掩饰自己失望的情绪。

♦ (line 17) ... **or the campsite is already *taken up* by some other group.**

take up：occupy (time, space, etc.) 占有(时间,空间等)

[运用]   take up time/space ...

e.g. I don't want to take up much of your time. 我不想占您太多时间。
Too many extracurricular activities take up too much of our precious time for study. 课外活动太多,占去了我们很多宝贵的学习时间。

[拓展]   take up 开始从事   take off 脱掉,起飞 take over 接任;接管   take on 承担

♦ (line 36) ... **how much money to *budget* for fuel** ...

budget：make a budget 做预算

[运用]   budget for the project/budget one's time/ budget for the coming year ...

[拓展]   budget (*n.*) 预算 budgetary (*a.*) 预算的 budgeter (*n.*) 预算编制者

e.g. a family budget 家庭预算 a government budget 政府预算

Text B • • • • • • • • • • • •

♦ (line 1) ... **I *mention*ed taking an American couple** ...

mention：to refer to, especially incidentally 提到

[运用]   mention sth. to sb.

e.g. Did you mention this to my sister? 你对我姐姐说到这件事了吗?
Don't mention it. 不要客气,不用谢。

[拓展]   not to mention (= without mentioning) 更不必说,更谈不上
(not) worth mentioning (不)值得一提

at the mention of 在(听人)提到……时
make mention of 提到……,说到……

e.g. Gaining weight didn't help her health, not to mention the high blood pressure that ran in her family.

[仿写]   昨天他打电话时,我听到他提起这件事。

♦ (line 4) ... **first timers to China, full of *enthusiasm*** ...

enthusiasm：great excitement for or interest in a subject or cause 热情

[运用]   his enthusiasm for table tennis/enthusiasm for English/enthusiasm for labour ...

e.g. What struck me was their enthusiasm for the work.
使我深有感触的是他们的工作热情。

[拓展]   arouse enthusiasm in sb. 引起某人的兴趣
arouse the enthusiasm of 激发……的积极性
be full of enthusiasm about 热衷于
enthusiastic (*a.*) 热心的,热情的 enthusiastically (*ad.*) 热心地,热情地

e.g. Jim had an enthusiastic reception when he returned home.

[仿写]   来访的客人受到了热情的接待。

♦ (line 5) ... **full of enthusiasm, *curiosity*, and** ...

curiosity：a desire to know or learn 好奇心

[运用]   be full of curiosity, curiosity about sth.

e.g. My little brother is full of curiosity. 我的小弟弟充满好奇心。
His curiosity about the world was insatiable. 他对宇宙的好奇心是无止境的。

[拓展]   curious (*a.*) curiously (*ad.*) 好奇地

e.g. It is good to be curious about the world around you.

[仿写]   他无止境的好奇心让爸爸很苦恼。

♦ (line 5) ... **with regard to respecting local customs.**

with regard to：concerning 关于,就……而论

[运用]with regard to sb./sth.

e.g. She is speaking with regard to her family's safety.
她正在讲有关她家庭安全的事情。

[拓展]   in regard to, regarding sth. 关于,regardless of sth. 不管;不理会

e.g. Regardless of what you say, I'm still going to the club tonight.

[仿写]   他不顾众人反对,执意要开除她。

◆ （line 6） **They were also pretty *adventurous* when . . .**

adventurous：eager for or fond of adventure；full of danger and excitement.

［运用］ adventurous life/man/holiday . . .

e. g. John is an adventurous man, unafraid of risks. 约翰是个喜欢冒险的人，不怕危险。

［拓展］ adventurously （*ad.*）爱冒险地 adventure （*n.*）冒险，冒险的经历

adventurer （*n.*）冒险家 adventurism （*n.*）冒险主义 adventurist （*n.*）冒险主义者

e. g. *World of Warcrafts* offers a sense of real adventurism and creates a high level of excitement for the players.

［仿写］ 这里是冒险家们的乐园。

◆ （line 8） **In their *imagination* they were also . . .**

imagination：the ability to think of new ideas

e. g. Poets and artists have imagination. 诗人和艺术家都有想象力。

［拓展］ imaginative （*a.*）富于想象的；有想象力的

e. g. imaginative writers/poet 富于想象的作者/诗人

imagine （*v.*）想象，设想 imaginator （*n.*）想象者，幻想者

e. g. I can't imagine what he looks like.

［仿写］ 这件事的复杂程度超出你的想象。

◆ （line 11） **. . . but it was a common *fantasy* for foreigners . . .**

fantasy：imagination or fancy，esp. when completely unrelated to reality

e. g. George lives in a world of fantasy. 乔治整天生活在幻想的世界中。

The whole story is a fantasy. 这整个故事只是一个虚构。

［拓展］ fantastic （*a.*）幻想的，奇异的 fantast （*n.*）幻想家，梦想家

e. g. The whole thing was so fantastic that I couldn't help being amused.

◆ （line 17） **. . . *washed down* by cold Qingdao beer.**

wash down：eat food accompanied by lots of liquid

［运用］ wash the dry cake down with tea/drink . . .

e. g. The best way to wash down one of these sticky cakes is with a cup of Chinese tea.

吃这种甜腻的食物最好是就着一杯中国茶.

［拓展］ wash against 洗刷；冲洗 wash away 洗掉；洗净；冲走；冲坏 wash off 洗掉，冲走

e. g. Can you wash away the blood stains on my shirt?

［仿写］ 他就着热咖啡吃完了面包。

◆ （line 23） **So excited and *grateful* were they . . .**

grateful：showing or expressing thanks，especially to another person

［运用］ be grateful to sb. for . . .

e. g. I am grateful to you for helping me. 感谢你的帮助。

［拓展］ gratefully （*ad.*）感激地 gratefulness （*n.*）感激

e. g. I wish to express my gratefulness to you for instructing my child.

［仿写］ 我写这封信就是为了表达我的感激之情。

◆ （line 28） **. . . when they *bumped into* a group of older Japanese tourist ladies . . .**

bump into：to encounter especially by chance

［运用］ bump into sb. /sth. . . .

e. g. How nice to bump into you! 碰到你真高兴！

My car ran bump into the wall. 我的汽车猛然撞上墙壁。

［拓展］ bump off ［俚］杀死，干掉；用力推开

bump up 突然增加；提高

e. g. They bump off the landlord. 他们杀死了地主。

You need a good result to bump up your average.

你需要一个好成绩来提高你的平均分数。

◆ （line 44） **. . . This seemed to *confirm* that these were indeed the chefs . . .**

confirm：to support or establish the certainty or validity of；verify.

［运用］ confirm sth/confirm that . . .

e. g. Please confirm your telephone message by writing to me.

请给我来封信，好进一步证实你在电话中传达的消息。

My employer will confirm that I was there on time.

我的雇主将会证实，我是准时到达的。

［拓展］ confirmable （*a.*）可以确定的

confirmation （*n.*）证实，确认，批准

confirmative （*a.*）确定的，证实的

e. g. confirmative sale 售货确认单

We are waiting for confirmation of the news.

［仿写］ 很快，这个坏消息得到了证实。

Translation of Texts

Text A

如何组织一次集体旅游

要成功的组织一次集体出游,你需要考虑组成这个团队的人以及这个团队的人数。这是因为不同的群体有不同的需求,不同的期望,不同的兴趣。对一个家庭群体来说合适的活动不一定适用于喜欢户外活动的青少年群体或者年轻人。如果你将计划一次帐篷旅行,为了安排交通、住宿和吃饭,你也需要考虑出游团队的大小。你要确保出行车辆有足够的空间,特别是要在路上行驶很长时间的旅行。

在确定了团队大小和旅游目的地之后,重要的一步就是提前预定好住宿。到最后一分钟当每个人都十分兴奋并且准备出发的时候,你绝不希望让大家失望地听说酒店都已经预定满了,或者野营地被其他团队占据了。根据团队大小,也许很有必要选出一位团队负责人,在计划安排旅行期间可以和他联系。团队负责人能够代表团队成员发言并且在旅行过程中能够负责组织管理团队。

另一个重要的就是行程安排。制定一份旅游的行程安排。行程安排中表明了团队计划出游几天,将要参观哪些名胜古迹,中途在哪里停留,何时何地吃饭,以及旅行的亮点。行程安排之所以重要的另一个原因就在于它是一种工作计划,否则,你会发现大家时不时的会各自走散,之后,你就必须花费时间去寻找他们。等到结束的时候,你会发现时间不是花在旅游上,而是花在找人上。行程安排对于计算旅行费用也是有帮助的。因为你可以从行程安排中了解到团队将要离开几个夜晚,将去哪里(如果是开车旅行,对于确定燃料预算是有必要的),这将有助于你计算旅行费用,了解所需的预算。

在旅行前,花点时间和团队做个简短的交代是有必要的。这样,你可以就一些疑问做出回答并且消除大家可能出现的误解,如:旅行需要带什么东西,出发时间,集合地点,还可以了解大家是否有什么特定的需求。如果可能的话,做两次简短的交代。一次在计划旅行之前,一次在旅行前几天。

综上所诉,当组织一次旅游时,了解诸如团队成员,团队大小,旅游目的地,如何去,以及预定住宿非常重要。制定出游行程安排也很重要。在出游前和大家碰面,以便回答任何成员可能存在的疑问。

Text B

商务旅行:畅游长江

在本辑博客开头,我提到过,我曾在1978年带领一对美国夫妇乘船游览长江。

他们是第一次来中国,充满了热情与好奇,满怀尊重当地风俗习惯的善意。在品尝中国地方菜的时候,两人也表现得颇具冒险精神。

在他们的想象中,他们还是深入白人甚少涉足的中国内陆地区的英勇先驱。这当然是无稽之谈,但早期来中国的外国人普遍抱有这样的幻想。

美食体验的高潮发生在重庆登船前的第一顿饭上。时值八月,重庆成了中国的三大火炉之一。我们在宾馆畅饮冰凉的青岛啤酒,享用了一顿非常可口的中餐。

我的美国朋友彻底爱上了当晚的饭菜。他们在美国从没有吃到过正宗的川菜。尽管这家宾馆的菜肴并不是令人倾倒的重庆正宗麻辣口味,但也十分好吃。

饭后,他俩满怀兴奋与感激的心情,都想亲自去谢谢厨师。于是,两人起身走向厨房,我留下来结账。

我结完账,去找他们,看到他们还没走出去多远,就遇到了一群刚吃完晚饭准备离开餐厅的日本老年女游客。

我的美国朋友误把这些日本女游客当成了厨师。

"你们就是给我们做了这顿美餐的厨师吧?"红头发的美国人面带灿烂而友善的笑容问道。"味道好极了!"他的太太在一旁插话。

这群日本老太太一句英文也不会说。她们搞不懂,这对美国夫妇为什么如此热情地向她们示好。所以,她们采取了以往在此种场合遇到不明情况时的做法。

她们深深地鞠躬。

美国夫妇把鞠躬理解为中国话里的"别客气"。看来可以确定,这些老太太的确是厨师,而且是非常讲礼貌的厨师。

　　于是这对美国夫妇也深深地鞠躬,作为回礼。

　　那群日本老太太见状,也再次深鞠躬。

　　这对美国夫妇又以鞠躬回礼。

　　当我赶到现场时,这场鞠躬表演正因为体力耗尽而慢慢停下来。最终,那群日本老太太继续"开路"了。

　　我向那对美国夫妇报告了实情,并问服务员,能否让真厨师出来接受道谢。厨师出来了。这次没人再鞠躬了。

---

5. make（Para. 7）　成功做到某事（v.）

e. g. Don't worry. I can assure you that we can make it since the movie is three hours from now.

6. clueless（Para. 10）　没有线索的, 茫然的（adj.）

e. g. The words in the article is so difficult that the students are totally clueless as to what the article mainly talks about.

7. bow-fest（Para. 16）　不停鞠躬（n.）
fest：（slang）much of a certain action

e. g. a music fest, chilifest, fashion fest

Explain these words and expressions through their context or with the help of a dictionary.

1. when it comes to（Para. 2）　提到……, 谈到……

e. g. When it comes to learning a foreign language, reading extensively is necessary.

2. board（Para. 4）　上（船, 飞机等）（v.）

e. g. What time can I board the plane?

3. personally（Para. 6）　亲自（adv.）

e. g. The chief executive saw the important client off personally.

4. settle（Para. 6）　结帐（v.）

e. g. Good morning. I am leaving today. May I settle my hotel bill now?

Language practice

Vocabulary

1

Fill in the blanks with words given below. Change the forms where necessary.

 Key

1. ascertain　2. disappointed　3. misconception
4. consider　5. expectation　6. depart

Reading Skills Exercises：

1

Match the words to their definitions.

 Key

1—B, 2—D, 3—A, 4—C, 5—E

2

Scan the text and mark each of the following statements True（T）or False（F）.

 Key

1. F　2. F　3. F　4. T　5. F　6. T　7. F
8. T

2

Fill in the blanks with words given below. Change the forms where necessary.

 Key

1. takes up　2. instead of　3. On behalf of
4. take ... into consideration　5. in charge
6. draw up

Translation

Translate the following Chinese sentences into English by putting the given words and expressions into right order.

 Key

1. I can't carry it on my own; it's too heavy.
2. Whether the game will be played depends on the weather.
3. I bumped into an old friend in town today.
4. As to where to go, they haven't decided yet.
5. I do not want to deal with him. He makes me nervous.
6. She washed down her bread with a cup of tea.

Grammar

Grammar Exercises

1

Rewrite the following sentences according to the model.

 Key

1. After throwing up, he felt better.
2. After selling his old car, he bought another one.
3. After taking the exam, she went on the holiday.
4. After doing his homework, he went to bed.
5. After making an appointment, I went to the doctor.

2

Fill in the blanks with the words given below.

 Key

1. before   2. When   3. because   4. If   5. so that   6. Even though

Listening 🎧

1

Work with your partner to fill in the blanks using the words in the box. Listen and check your answers, and then follow the recording.

 Script

1. Every year, it seems more and more people are going on holiday abroad.
2. Alas, this means that more and more people are also experiencing the discomfort and frustration of foreign travel.
3. This often starts at the airport, irrespective of which airline you are using.
4. At least at peak holiday times, there are bound to be queues at the check-in and then more queues at passport control as you go into the departure lounge.
5. Then, there is often the misery of delayed flights. These tend to be more common if you are traveling by charter flight, but they are by no means unknown on scheduled flights.
6. Sometimes such delays are due to technical hitches or to the very large numbers of planes which now take off and land. However, some, in Europe at least, are the result of industrial action by staff.
7. The holiday season is a favorite time for baggage handlers, air-traffic control personnel, or other airport staff to take such action. Still, eventually you get to the departure gate, board the plane, find your seat and fasten your seat belt ready for take-off.
8. Members of the cabin crew will very likely serve you with food and drink and unless you are on a long-haul flight, it will seem a relatively short time before you land.

2

Listen to the dialogue three times and fill in the blanks.

 Script

Railway Travel
A ticket to London, please.

Paul: What time does the <u>next train</u> to London leave?
Clerk: At 16:35, from platform 8.
Paul: Is it a <u>direct train</u> to London?
Clerk: No, you have to <u>change</u> trains at Birmingham.
Paul: I see. One ticket to London, please.
Clerk: <u>Single or return</u>, sir?
Paul: Single, please.
Clerk: 64 pounds, please.
Paul: <u>Here you are</u>.
Clerk: Here's your ticket and change, sir.

3

Listen to the dialogue three times and answer the following questions.

 Key

1. Australia
2. Pleasure. He is visiting his relatives.
3. Three weeks.
4. He works as an accountant for an Australian telecommunications company.
5. Yes, he has a return ticket.

 Script

At passport control:
Do you have a return ticket?

Immigration officer: Good evening. Where have you come from?
Paul: Australia.
Immigration officer: May I have your passport and form I-94, please?
Paul: Here you are.
Immigration officer: What's the nature of your visit? Business or pleasure?
Paul: Pleasure. I'm visiting my relatives.
Immigration officer: How long are you going to stay in the United States?
Paul: Three weeks.
Immigration officer: What is your occupation?
Paul: I work as an accountant for an Australian telecommunications company.

Immigration officer: Do you have a return ticket?
Paul: Yes, here it is.
Immigration officer: That's fine. Thanks. Enjoy your trip.
Paul: Thank you.

4

Listen to the passage three times and then mark each of the following statements True (T) or False (F).

 Script

How to Become a Travel Agent

The need for experienced travel agents is increasing as more people travel for business and pleasure. Although this is not a high-paying career, it has the major benefit of deep travel discounts.
Step 1
Realize that larger travel agencies may require an agent to have a liberal arts or business degree.
Step 2
Learn to speak a second language. This skill is invaluable for a travel agent, especially in agencies that focus on international travel.
Step 3
Take a 6-to-12-week travel agent course at a community college to learn the basics of the career.
Step 4
Consider working as a ticketing agent to gain solid experience in the travel industry.
Step 5
Become as computer literate as possible — travel agents conduct much of their business via computer.
Step 6
Check with your state's Department of Commerce for any registration or certification requirements for travel agents.
Step 7
Read a wide variety of travel magazines to keep up with current trends in the industry.
Step 8
Work toward receiving your certification as a Certified Travel Counselor (CTC) after you have gained experience.

 Key

1. T 2. F 3. T 4. T 5. T

Speaking

1

Role-play a conversation according to the following situation. After the practice, change roles.

Role A: Peter is going to visit Beijing next week. Now he is booking flight ticket(s) in Shanghai Eastern Airlines.

Role B: John is a reservations clerk of the booking office of the Shanghai Eastern Airlines.

Suggested Words and Expressions:

cost; the price of the ticket; one-way; round-trip; instructions; at the airport; book; the first flight; morning/noon/afternoon flight; first/economic class

I'd like to book ... ticket(s) to ... on ...

Just a moment, I'll check the schedule.

I prefer a morning/... flight.

What's the first/economic class fare from ... to ...?

Will that be one-way or round-trip?

Is ... available on ...?

What kind of flight do you prefer?

How long will it take to arrive in Beijing?

How much does that cost?

The total fare is ...

Is it possible to get a discount?

Here is your ticket. Enjoy your trip.

Reference:

A – Peter B – John

A: Good morning.

B: Good morning, sir. What can I do for you?

A: I'd like to make a flight reservation.

B: OK, what is your destination?

A: Well, I'd like to book one ticket from Shanghai to Beijing on February 13.

B: Just a moment, I'll check what flights are available.

A: OK.

B: What time would you like to leave?

A: I prefer a morning flight.

B: There are two flights still available that morning. One is due to leave at 7:00. The other is at 10:00. Which do you prefer and would you like a business class or economy class?

A: Economy class, please. That would be much cheaper. How about the fare for the two flights?

B: The fare for the flight at 7:00 is ￥780. And the other one is at 10:00, which costs you ￥920.

A: Let's go with the cheaper one.

B: Would you like a one-way ticket or a round-trip ticket?

A: I need a one-way ticket. I'll be staying in Beijing for some time.

B: OK. Would you like to buy flight insurance?

A: Yes, please.

B: The total fare is ￥880.

A: That's all right.

B: OK. I'll confirm your reservation for a one-way economy ticket to Beijing at 7:00 on Feb. 13.

A: Yes, that's right.

B: May I have your ID card, please?

A: Here you are. Shall I pay now?

B: Yes.

A: (Hands over the money.) By the way, how long will it take to arrive in Beijing?

B: The flight is due to arrive in Beijing at 9:10.

A: Thanks.

B: Here is your ticket. The flight number is MU 5137, at Shanghai Hongqiao Airport. Please arrive at the airport one hour before departure.

A: I will. Thank you very much.

B: Have a good trip. Goodbye.

A: Goodbye.

2

Work with your partner to make up a dialogue involving the following situation.

Tell your partner, if you have enough time and money, where you would like to travel most around the world. Why?

Suggested Words and Expressions:

I'd like to visit ... , because ...

The scenery there is stunning/spectacular/marvelous/breath-taking ...

It is famous/well-renown ... as/for ...

I'm crazy for its culture, history and religion ...

There are springs, great lakes and all kinds of flowers.

It's exotic/passionate/natural/attracting/inspiring ...

That's the kingdom of roses/tulips.

That's the hometown of beer/whiskey/chocolates/cheese ...

Writing

1

Translate the sample itinerary into Chinese.

 Key

星期一,四月十八日

下午4:00 乘航班 ZU952 到达北京,由亚洲贸易公司的总裁 Peter 先生到机场迎接

下午4:15 乘车去长城宾馆

下午7:30 参加总裁 Peter 先生举行的晚宴

星期二,四月十九日

上午9:30 在亚洲贸易公司大楼讨论

下午2:00 小组讨论

晚上8:00 英国驻北京商务领事举行鸡尾酒招待会

星期三,四月二十日

上午9:00 讨论

中午12:00 签订意向书

下午1:30 吃北京烤鸭

下午3:30 参观颐和园

晚上6:00 前往上海

2

Write out an itinerary according to the following Chinese.

Reference:

The itinerary for your visit to our company is as follows:

10:30 a.m.　Arriving at our company

10:30 a.m. – 10:50 a.m. Introducing our company to you

10:50 a.m. – 11:30 a.m. Visiting our company on-the-spot

11:30 a.m. – 13:00 p.m. Having lunch

13:00 p.m. – 13:45 p.m. (PPAP)

13:45 p.m. – 15:00 p.m. Negotiating

Unit 7 Public Relations

Teaching Arrangement

Warm-up & Unit task (Text A)
1) Time schedule: 2 periods
2) Suggested lesson structure
   Warm-up: 10 – 15 minutes
   Text A: 10 – 15 minutes
   Unit task steps 1 – 2 (pre-task): 10 – 15 minutes
   Unit task steps 3 – 5 (while-task): 30 – 45 minutes
   Unit task step 6 (post-task) should be completed after class

Reading (Text B)
1) Time schedule: 1 period
2) Suggested lesson structure
   Language points: 20 – 25 minutes
   Language practice: 20 – 25 minutes

Listening
1) Time schedule: 1 period
2) Suggested lesson structure
   Listening exercise 1: 10 minutes
   Listening exercise 2: 15 minutes
   Listening exercise 3: 15 minutes
   Listening exercise 4: 15 minutes

Speaking & Writing
1) Time schedule: 1 period
2) Suggested lesson structure
   Speaking: 20 – 25 minutes
   Writing: 20 minutes

Objective

- **Career skills**
  Planning a press conference; planning an agenda; reporting a summary of the statements.

- **Reading**
  1. Reading for main idea(s)
  2. Skimming/Scanning
  3. Reading for general information and details
  4. Reading for guessing word meaning from context
  5. Reading for looking for supporting details
  6. Reading for key word spotting

- **Writing**
  1. General writing: sentence types
  2. Practical writing: letter of complaint

- **Listening**
  1. Listening for key words/numbers/locations/figures
  2. Listening for general information and details
  3. Listening for identifying degrees in agreement

- **Speaking**
  1. Negotiate on business deals
  2. Giving a report on a meeting

- **Language focus:**

Key words and phrases			
respond	schedule	prospective	promotion
amazing	anticipate	recommend	marketing
engage	departure	coupon	amplify
boost	community		

Teaching Procedures

Warm-up

Look at the following 6 pictures, discuss with your partner and write down more than five words that describe or relate to each picture.

Target:

Ss brainstorm the features of some types of press conferences in the following pictures.

Guidance:

- Ss read Warm-up 1.
- Ask Ss to write several words related to each picture which can describe the content well.
- Invite 2 – 3 Ss to present their answers.
- Ask Ss to combine the words together as complete sentences.
- Add some more description if necessary.

Reference:

A: hall, light, display screen, host, Super Mario . . .
B: Google, man/manager/spokesperson, microphone, platform, logo . . .
C: Yao Ming, spokesperson, speech . . .
D: Apple, screen, stage, curtain . . .
E: Millitary, officers, foreigners, serious-look . . .
F: Manchester, football, reporters, suits, cameras . . .

Background Information

- What is a press conference?

    A press conference or news conference is a media event in which newsmakers invite journalists to hear them speak and, most often, ask questions.

    News conferences are often held by politicians (such as the President of the United States); by sports teams; by celebrities or film studios; by commercial organizations to promote products; by attorneys to promote lawsuits; and by almost anyone who finds benefit in the free publicity afforded by media coverage. Some people, including many police chiefs, hold news conferences reluctantly in order to avoid dealing with reporters individually.

Match the English translation to the Chinese first, then put them into the table in order of priority according to your understanding and state your reasons briefly.

Target:

Ss can learn some major Public Relations (PR) campaigns in this task.

Guidance：

- Ss read Warm-up 1.
- Ask Ss to match the 2 columns and give an order of these methods according to priority.
- Invite a student to present his/her answer of match and 2 Ss of the order.
- Ask Ss the reasons of ordering.

Reference：

1—D 2—E 3—F 4—C 5—B 6—A

Your Order：(Omitted)

Your Reason：I put *Working With the Media* in the first place because media take a very important role in promoting your company ...

I put *Press Kits* last, for it is not very critical to the company's image ...

Expressions Pool

Facilities：conference hall/room, camera, display screen, lights, sound equipment, microphone, stage, platform, projector ...

Staff：moderator, host, hostess, spokesperson, guest, crew, reporters, media ...

Event：launch a new line of product, announce/make an announcement, state/make a statement, opening, closing, publication, clarify/make a clarification ...

I put ... in the first place because media take a very important role in promoting your company ...

I put ... last, for it is not very critical to the company's image ...

Unit task

Read Text A and practice a series of real tasks of holding a press conference.

 Task Map(任务导航)

公司、组织或者公众人物在"公共关系处理"这一工作领域中,常常需要借助媒体来宣布、深入报道或澄清若干信息,即:召开新闻发布会。能否策划并组织一场有效的新闻发布会则决定了信息能否正确被传递,公司或个人形象能否得到正面渲染,等等。

特此要求学生策划组织一场"新闻发布会",通过模拟主办方、发言人、主持人、现场工作人员以及媒体工作人员,围绕发布会主题进行预演,巩固学生用英语计划、建议、询问、描述、声明、提问与回答、强调等能力。

本单元任务分为6个步骤,第一个步骤让学生了解组织新闻发布会的步骤以及各步骤的注意事项;第二个步骤让学生通过练习明白一些常见新闻发布会的主题与目标;第三个步骤要求学生从第二步中挑选一个主题,再根据第一个步骤的认知进行粗略的策划;第四个步骤要求学生通过阅读某饭店的会务条款,根据已有的粗略计划,询问并预定新闻发布会场地;第五个步骤为主任务,学生通过角色扮演,预演发布会流程;第六个步骤要求学生将所有文字材料以及影音材料汇总,制作"新闻资料箱"。任务的安排主要根据活动过程顺序来设定,每一任务为后续的步骤做基础。

Process Break-down

Pre-task:

Step 1   Divide the whole class into groups of 6 – 8 students. Ss read Text A and put several statements in order. By finishing this step, Ss will have mastered the main steps of planning a press conference.

Step 2   Ss need to match WHO with WHAT to do, which provides them 4 topics/events as their options.

While-task:

Step 3   Each team needs to choose their own topic/event to do, and discuss about the entries in the form.

Step 4   Ss read the introduction of the Conference service. Choose the most suitable conference hall or room and write an Inquiry to order the room.

Step 5   Practice roles with the members of your group. Ask one member of each team to take pictures or shoot.

Post-task:

Step 6   Make a Press Kit including plan, agenda, summary of the statements, Q & A notes and pictures.

Step 1

Read the following statements and put them in order.

Target:

Know how to set a press conference.

Guidance:

- Ss read Text A by themselves and get to know how to set up a conference step by step.
- During this step, Ss can also master different ways to express the same meaning, because the words in this exercise are not quite the same with ones in Text A.
- Invite 1 – 2 Ss to present their answers.
- Teacher can do a little explanation afterwards.

 Key

(9) Preview any possible question that would be raised by the reporters afterwards.

(3) Arrange the time and date for the press conference.

(7) Make an appointment with the conference host to control the situation.

(4) Notify the reporters about event.

(1) Clarify why you need to hold a press conference and what message you want to send.

任务过程控制关注点
Minefield

- 提醒学生不要被生词限制住,阅读时引入常识。
- 提醒学生在练习中有意识地进行题目与原文的比对,从中了解不同的表达方式。

---- **Expressions Pool** ----

clarify, message to send, make statements, make an appointment with . . . , arrange the time and date, reserve/make a reservation

（6）Choose a celebrity, a politician or a corporate senior to make statements.

（10）Adjust the projectors, display screens and computers.

（5）Send invitations and make phone calls to your possible guests.

（8）Print enough copies of related materials.

（2）Reserve a multi-function hall to hold your press conference.

Step 2

Divide the whole class into groups of 6－8 students.

Match the following statements classified in the 2 columns. Choose one of the following events as your group's topic to set up a press conference on it.

Target：
Know "What can be our topic".

Guidance：
- Having finished Step 1, Ss have already known how to set up a press conference.
- Ss need to match WHO with WHAT to do, which provides them 4 topics/events as their options.
- Invite 1－2 Ss to present their answer and check whether they have mastered what each event is about.

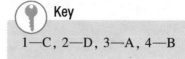 **Key**

1—C, 2—D, 3—A, 4—B

Step 3

Plan a press conference.

Target：
Outline the plan.

Guidance：
- Since each team has chosen their own topic/event to do, discuss in the team about the entries in the form.
- Ss need to understand that the goal of a press conference is not identified with the event itself. For example, SONY presents its new laptop on the press conference with a goal of extending its market in China.
- Elicit the best possible ideas from the team members so that the goal of this press conference can be achieved to the most degree.
- Each group will give an oral presentation of the content.

任务过程控制关注点
Minefield

- 提醒学生开拓思维。看到左栏中的"WHO"后，不要急于到右栏寻找答案。让学生开展头脑风暴，预测可以匹配的事件。
- 提醒学生深入思考。主题事件并不一定是该公司或个人召开新闻发布会的真正或唯一目的。引导学生思考：目标会有哪些？信息公布后会带来哪些相关效应？等等。

---- Expressions Pool ----

Announce the publication of ... ; share ...

Make a clarification about ...

Officially tell the media about ...

Launch the latest product ...

任务过程控制关注点
Minefield

- 提醒学生一切安排都要围绕主题，而非一味地把发布会"做大"，"国际化"，"娱乐化"。
- 提醒学生合理分工，考虑小组成员不同的英语能力水平。

---- Expressions Pool ----

1. On behalf of ... , we are going to hold a press conference to ...
2. ... , ... and ... will be invited as our guests.
3. The agenda is planned as follows：Step 1,... Step 2,... Step 3,...

Reference：

1. *Event*	*Launch the latest cutting-edge product and demonstrate its features.*
2. Goal	Let the public know the newly-launched product.
3. Time（Duration）	2 hours
4. Host/Moderator	PR manager of Sony
5. Guest(s) & Spokesperson(s)	the chief editor of magazine, celebrity
6. Number of Reporters	20
7. Main Steps of the Press Conference（Agenda）	Step 1 welcome speech. Step 2 new product's presentating. Step 3 answer Qs. Step 4 closing speech.
8. Staff（with specific job division）	One clerk in charge of reserving the location, two clerks in charge of inviting guests, one clerk in charge of contacting reporters, two clerks in charge of presenting products, one clerk in charge of agenda.

Step 4

Reserve the location.

Target：

Inquire the location to suit the event.

Guidance：

- Ss read the introduction of the Conference service provided by the Best Western Fortune Hotel.
- Choose the most suitable conference hall or room and other facilities by taking consideration of the specific needs.
- Ss read the inquiry sample, write a new inquiry according to the plan.

--- Expressions Pool ---

1. We are looking for a suitable site for（the event）on（the date）.
2. We will need a conference room or ... that can accommodate（how many people）.
3. We understand that（a conference center）offers a wide range of services from ... to ...
4. Could you please settle（facilities）for us in advance?
5. If not, we would appreciate it if you could send the information before（date）so that we will be able to make adjustment forehand.
6. A list of necessities and detailed requirements is enclosed herewith.
7. Hope to hear from you soon.

任务过程控制关注点
Minefield

- 提醒学生选择场地时要考虑事前所计划的规模和与会人数。
- 提醒学生选择设备不要一味求全，从实际需要和公司预算出发。
- 提醒学生撰写询问函时注意语气礼貌和句式完整。

Step 5

Organize/Rehearse a mini press conference.

In this step, Ss will play roles including the host, the spokesperson(s) and the reporters.

Target:
Test the practicability of the plan and perfect the process of the press conference.

Guidance:
- Teacher guides Ss to think about what will happen all the way through the press conference, and how it will look to reporters.
- Ss outline the POSSIBLE questions or emergencies and Ss' practical answers or solutions.
- Ss practice roles with the members of their group. **If possible, use their camera or cell phone to record the whole process.** It's important that everybody understands his/her role in the event. Ss' rehearsal should include these contents:
  * Host's Opening Speech:
  * Spokesperson/Guests' Statement:
  * Reporters' Question:
  * Host's moderation:
  * Spokesperson/Guests' Answer:

-------- Expressions Pool --------

Good afternoon/evening. Welcome to the press conference of ...
On behalf of ..., I'd like to make a statement on ...
I'm from ... Mr./Ms ..., would you please explain why ...?
Sorry, sir/madam, our main subject for today is ... Next question?
Speaking of/referring to your question,/as you mentioned ..., ...

任务过程控制关注点
Minefield

- 提醒学生开拓思维。回忆自身经历,有没有经历或目睹过会议/活动过程中的小意外。
- 提醒学生进行问题/状况的分类汇总,找出各类问题的负责方,提出解决方案和预警措施。
- 提醒学生换位思考。作为主办方,你想表达的内容有哪些,想避免的话题有哪些;作为媒体工作者,你想窥探的内容有哪些。

Step 6

Press Kit.

Target:
Summarize the whole process and make a visible output of the teamwork.

Guidance:
- A press kit is your background material: fact sheets, news release, text of the statement, and visual materials, such as photographs. It can help reporters to create and produce their stories. Hold press kits in folders or envelopes until the end of the press conference to make sure no one leaves early, getting a jump on their competition.
- Teacher will hand out folders or envelopes to each member.
- Ss are supposed to put their team's press conference plan, agenda, summary of the statements, Q & A notes and pictures (can be sent to teacher by email) into a file and hand on as a Press Kit.

任务过程控制关注点
Minefield

- 提醒学生新闻资料箱包含的材料种类。
- 提醒学生整理分类:文本、照片、音频视频。

-------- Expressions Pool --------

The statement given by the spokesperson is summarized as following: ...
To conclude, ...
In brief, ...

Action research
（教师自己的教学行动研究）

任务完成中的观察、反思（日志、随笔）   备忘

Language Points

Text A • • • • • • • • • •

◆ （line 3）... **make a presentation and** *respond* **to reporters' questions.**

respond：to react；to state in reply

[运用] respond to the question

e. g. The teacher responded affirmatively to the question that student put forward.

[拓展] *respondent*（*n.*）答复者
However, answers varied between categories of respondents.
response（*n.*）回答，答复 in response to
Interestingly, there was no response, no response at all.

◆ （line 21）... **events already** *scheduled* **at the time** ...

schedule：to plan at a certain time

[运用] schedule individuals/timeframes/a project

e. g. It can be useful to work with stakeholders to schedule the most appropriate individuals for each phase.

[拓展] *schedule*（*n.*）时间表，进度安排
He knows everything about the production schedule.

◆ （line 24）... **invitations to** *prospective* **guests** ...

prospective：likely to happen, possible, future

[运用] prospective candidate/employer/bride ...

e. g. She is his prospective mother-in-law.

[拓展] *prospect*（*n.*）前景、前途、希望
She balanced the attractions of a high salary against the prospect of working long hours.

Text B • • • • • • • • • • • •

◆ （line 11）... **is an** *amazing* **accomplishment** ...

amazing→extraordinary, wonderful, remarkable

[运用] what an amazing ... !

e. g. How did David Copperfield perform his amazing feats?

[拓展] *amaze*（*v.*）使大为吃惊, 使惊奇
Your knowledge amazes me.
amazed（*a.*）吃惊的, 惊奇的
He was always amazed by her confidence.

[仿写] 听到你要走，我们都很吃惊。（amazed）

◆ （line 16）... **were** *anticipating* **a rush** ...

anticipate→hope for, await, expect, foresee

[运用] anticipate our needs, anticipate what they will do

e. g. A good general can anticipate what the enemy will do.

[拓展] *anticipation*（*n.*）期盼, 预知 in anticipation of
The animals grew restless as if in anticipation of an earthquake.

[仿写] 不经过研究很难完全预测。（anticipate）

◆ （line 16）... **a rush after the** *promotion* ...

promotion：a message issued in behalf of some product

[运用] product promotion

e. g. He came up with good ideas for the product promotion.

[拓展] *promotion*（*n.*）晋升, 提拔
As a junior assistant manager, he had been selected for promotion.
Congratulations on your promotion !
promote（*v.*）促进, 推动
The organization works to promote the trade between nations

[仿写] 参与国际会展有益于增进各国间的友谊。（promotion）

◆ （line 18）... **in the world of viral** *marketing*, ...

marketing：promoting a product or service

[运用] marketing strategy, marketing campaigns

e. g. A great marketing strategy can leave our competitors in the dust.

[拓展] *market*（*n.*）市场, 销路 a ready market, market share
There's not much market for these goods.
marketer（*n.*）营销人员
In doing so the marketer is likely to find out that different buyers have different needs.

[仿写] 市场研究有助于确定商机。（market）

◆ （line 34）... **also** *requires* **careful management.**

require→need, demand

[运用] require effort/time/skills to do ...

e. g. These systems require significant design to complete the transaction.

[拓展] *requirement*（*n.*）要求, 条件
Your requirement that she wait till next week is reasonable.
required（*a.*）必须的, （学科）必修的 required course

A good degree and real-world experience are required.

［仿写］ 这次聚会要求穿着正装。（require）

◆ （line 55）... **recommends** listening to ...

recommend：to advise as the best choice

［运用］ recommend a good book, recommend wearing safety belt

e. g. My neighbour recommended her own daughter as an excellent secretary.

［拓展］ *recommendation* （*n.*） a letter of recommendation, on one's recommendation

Acting on your recommendation, I have decided to read the article once more.

［仿写］ 经部门主管推荐,她获得了出国进修的机会。（on one's recommendation）

◆ （line 65）... that *engaging* consumers on the Internet ...

engage→involve, get, occupy

［运用］ engage one's attention, engage in doing, engage sb. in sth.

e. g. They often have the power to engage us in a dialogue.

［拓展］ *engagement* （*n.*）约定,订婚

I can't see you on Monday because I have a previous engagement.

John has broken off his engagement to Mary.

［仿写］ 我没时间参加这种没有意义的辩论。（engage in）

Translation of Texts

Text A

如何召开新闻发布会

新闻发布会是自发性地向媒体公布展示某些信息,由你决定什么信息会被公布,如何公布以及谁来公布。召开一场发布会,你要联系媒体、选择时间和地点、公布信息、回答记者提问。

明确目标

在策划之前要明确你的目标。以下介绍了要召开发布会的主要原因:

● 给你的努力成果和面临的问题带来曝光率;

● 得到媒体的广泛报道;

● 吸引更多人参与到你的活动中;

● 培养锻炼员工的技能;

● 体现你的团队优势。

记住:你必须要具备有新闻价值的东西来宣布,值得在发布会上讨论。

主要步骤

● 明确陈述召开发布会的原因:尚未被媒体报道过的、突发的或重要的新闻事件。

● 决定你想借由媒体传达的消息。

● 决定场地。找一个合适的场地,有你所需要的设备,如:电话、话筒、足够的灯源,等等。

● 定好新闻发布会的日期和时间。确保发布会计划召开的那天没有其他新闻争夺版面。

● 邀请媒体。至少在发布会召开前一周给当地适合报道此事的媒体发送告知书。

● 邀请嘉宾,打电话或写书面的邀请函给你所希望出席的嘉宾。

● 准备好发言人向媒体传达消息。通常1—2名发言人较合适,不会出现"你一言我一句"或者信息混淆的状况。

● 与发言人进行预演,发言简单易懂并控制在10分钟之内。

● 选择一位主持人来掌控发布会进程并使记者的提问采访围绕主题。如果有人跑题了,主持人就能提醒"那的确是个有意思的想法,但我们今天讨论的是……",把焦点拉回主题。

● 准备背景资料。记者和嘉宾可能希望得到一份书面的发言稿或新闻稿。准备一个资讯包,装有资料汇总、图表和图片。

● 动用你的员工通过扮演各种角色来练习。设想发布会过程中会发生什么,从记者的角度会怎么看待。要问自己的关键问题就是"如果……该怎么办?"

● 准备好视觉辅助用具。图表、大型地图、照片或其他道具能帮助你更好地渗透想要传达的信息。但记住,幻灯片不适合电视、电台以及平面媒体使用。

Text B

Twitter 与烤鸡促销

英国《金融时报》   蒂姆·布拉德肖

快餐连锁店肯德基（KFC）今年早些时候推出烤鸡时，领教了 Twitter 的一些威力。

肯德基推出烤鸡，有几分告别炸鸡专家称号的味道。奥普拉·温弗瑞（Oprah Winfrey）在她的节目中披露了肯德基的这一举措，并在自己的网站上公布了免费享用烤鸡的优惠券的细节。下载优惠券的网址链接发布到 Twitter 上后，很快就转发给了数百万用户。肯德基表示："在在线讨论我们的免费餐期间，肯德基成为 Twitter 上最热门的话题。对于一个品牌来说，这是一个惊人的成就。如果没有 Twitter，我们可能就无法成功了。"

肯德基及其广告代理商 DraftFCB 预料到促销活动后顾客会激增，但需求如此之高，以至于优惠券下载网页瘫痪，餐厅人满为患。此外，在病毒式营销领域，这次促销活动取得了极大的成功，促使媒体进行了大量免费报道。

如果说消息灵通的营销经理去年必备的工具是 Facebook 网页，那么 Twitter 就是 2009 年众多品牌需要关注和露脸的地方。但随着广告商涌向 Twitter，沿途也留下了受害者。能够放大促销效果和正面信息的力量也意味着，在 Twitter 上的任何过失都是非常公开的。

正如肯德基展示的那样，各品牌公司迅速意识到 Twitter "热门话题"（在用户 Twitter 主页上出现的流行词语名单）的重要性。点击一个热门话题，用户就会看到一长串含有该词或短语的最新 "tweet"。对于商人而言，这会是一个有用的工具，但也需要认真管理。

最近发生了这么一件事。在繁华商业区开店的家具零售商 Habitat 发现，使用了与敏感政治事件相关的短语来推广其邮寄清单后，自己成了 Twitter 上的政治迫害对象，引发了一系列通过 Twitter 组织起来的示威活动。这个信息一经发布就引来了无数质疑的声音。

Habitat 后来删除了令人不快的信息并公开道歉。该公司宣称，这些信息是由一位未具名的实习生发布的。Habitat 在声明中表示："我们一直在倾听 Twitter 上的反馈，越来越了解这个社区希望我们如何与他们打交道。"

Diffusion PR 的董事总经理 D. B. 表示："Habitat 的故事迅速流传开来。他们得到了教训，如果你把发布 Twitter 的责任交给一个没有社交媒体工作经历的人，Twitter 反馈回来的信息就会对你造成伤害。这让许多客户更加紧张。不管他们如何努力，都无法完全不带副作用地解决问题。"D. B. 建议在加入前倾听一下 Twitter 上在说什么，只有这样你才能找到解决问题的办法。"在 tweet 前先想一想"是他的座右铭之一。

最受欢迎的 Twitter 账户，不只是发布品牌公司网站或优惠券链接清单。零售商，如 Habitat，看到了 Twitter 上的机遇，传媒业也同样看到了这个机遇，社会媒体公司 Will McInnes 的联合创始人威尔·麦金尼斯表示，Twitter 上的许多商人已经忘记，在互联网上与消费者打交道需要更加谨慎，而不只是发布自己的信息。"人们需要的是帮助、效用和价值，"他表示。"我们的大多数客户在客户服务上投资了数百万英镑，我们在网上要赢得的就是这些人。"

实际上，许多成功的企业 Twitter 账户与其说是营销部门的一部分，不如说是客户呼叫中心的扩展。

Explain these words and expressions through their context or with the help of a dictionary.

1）departure（Para. 2）   出发，离开（n.）
    a departure lounge   候车室
    departure dates   动身日期
    e. g. His departure created a vacuum in our lives.

2）coupon（Para. 2）   优惠券（n.）
    tear off this coupon   撕下优惠券
    e. g. You get a coupon for every 3 gallons of petrol.

3）amplify（Para. 4）   放大（v.）
    amplify the sound   提高嗓门
    amplify the difficulties   夸大困难
    e. g. The new manager wants to amplify the company.

4）boost（Para. 6）促进，增加（v.）
    boost the economy   促进经济发展
    boost share prices   提高股价
    e. g. We need a holiday to boost our spirits.

5）sensitive（Para. 6）敏感的（a.）

a sensitive issue　敏感问题
e. g. He's very sensitive about his appearance.

6）utility（Para. 9）功用（*n.*）
be of great utility　有效的
primary utility　主要功能
e. g. A fur coat has more utility in winter than in autumn.

restaurants were overwhelmed,
a huge amount of free press coverage
Habitat: the subject of a witch hunt
a series of demonstrations
negative voices followed up

Reading Skills Exercises:

1

List the brands and the effect caused by Twitter respectively according to the article.

 Key

KFC: became the top trending topic,

2

Match the words to their definitions.

 Key

1—B, 2—D, 3—A, 4—C, 5—E

3

Complete each sentence with an appropriate word from the list in Exercise 2.

 Key

1. anticipated　2. community　3. boost
4. unveiled　5. recommend

Language practice

Vocabulary

1

Make the adjectives negative by adding the correct prefix from the box.

 Key

1. impatient　2. inconvenient　3. unreasonable
4. impolite　5. informal
6. inactive　7. irresponsible　8. unemotional
9. uncritical　10. unco-operative

2

Match the words to make word partnerships.

 Key

1—C, 2—E, 3—A, 4—B, 5—D

3

Complete the sentences with the best word from the box.

 Key

1. difference　2. discussions　3. argument
4. conflict　5. disagreements

Translation

Put the following Chinese sentences into English by using the given words. Part of the sentences has been completed.

 Key

1. Before holding a press conference, you are <u>expected to decide</u> what information <u>is presented</u> and how it <u>is presented</u>.
2. Whether the results will be valuable <u>depends</u> partly <u>on our attitudes towards it</u>.
3. It was not until the second year <u>that</u> he has <u>adapted himself to</u> the college life.

4. In <u>handling an embarrassing</u> situation, nothing <u>is more helpful than</u> a sense of humor.
5. That he <u>survived</u> the accident <u>is a miracle</u>.

Grammar

Grammar Exercise:

Connect the words and expressions together and make it a correct inverted sentence.

 Key

1. <u>There comes the bus</u>!

2. <u>Had I known</u>, I might have joined you in the discussion.
3. Not only <u>shouldn't we look down upon</u> those who lay behind, but we should try to help them.
4. Only when <u>I finish my homework can I be allowed to</u> watch TV.
5. No sooner <u>had he got home</u> than the telephone rang.

Listening 🎧

1

Work with your partner to fill in the blanks using the words in the box. Listen and check your answers, and then follow the recording.

 Script

1. To <u>hold</u> a press conference, you contact the media and pick a <u>time and place</u>.
2. Before you <u>plan</u> a press conference you should be very clear about your <u>goals</u>.
3. Clearly state a <u>good reason</u> for holding a press conference.
4. <u>Find</u> an appropriate place that is convenient and has the <u>facilities</u> you need.
5. Usually the best days to get news <u>covered</u> are Tuesday <u>through</u> Thursday.
6. It's <u>good</u> to have just one or two <u>speakers</u> during a press conference
7. If someone goes off <u>subject</u>, the moderator can <u>return</u> the focus.
8. Think about what will <u>happen</u> all the way and how it will <u>look to</u> reporters.

2

Listen to a conversation between Peter, the manager of a bookstore chain, and a website designer. Listen to each part and complete the chart.

Negotiating point	What Peter wants	What the designer wants	What they agree
Schedule for setting up the website	One month, by the end of July	Two months	One month, fewer pages
Payment terms	Fixed amount: $6,000	$50 an hour	$6,000 (half in advance)
Website design	A large number of covers on every page	One big image	Two covers per page

3

Listen again to the 3rd part of the conversation. Note down all the expressions for agreeing and disagreeing. Decide whether they express a) strong, b) polite or c) hesitant agreement or disagreement.

Expressions	Strong	Polite	Hesitant	*Agreement*	*Disagreement*
e. g. Absolutely.	✓			✓	
It's a bit too much, I'd say.		✓			✓
Mmm, I don't know.			✓		✓
Maybe you are right.			✓	✓	
Sounds reasonable.		✓		✓	

 Script:

(P = Peter, D = Designer)

Part 1

P: Let's talk about the time frame for setting up the website. We want it in a month's time. That's the end of July.

D: It's a bit early. I was hoping to have two months to do the job. If I finish in one month, will you agree to reduce the number of pages?

P: Yes, that's no problem. Just do the best you can. Our priority is to have the website up and running as soon as possible.

D: OK then, agreed.

Part 2

P: Now about the payment. You want to charge us 50 dollars an hour. That works out at 400 dollars a day, I believe.

D: Yes, that's the normal fee for the job.

P: Well, we'd prefer to pay you a fixed amount for the work. We can offer you $6,000.

D: I see. Do you mind if I ask you why you want to pay that way?

P: Well, you see, that way we can control the cost of the project. If we pay you per hour, the cost could become high. It could get out of control. This way, we know where we stand.

D: I see. $6,000. Mmm, that could be all right, I suppose, as long as I get some money in advance. How about paying me half when I start the work and half at the end?

P: Yes, I think we could arrange that. OK. I agree to that.

Part 3

D: Now, the design of the website. Will we have book covers on it?

P: Absolutely. I'd like to display a large number of book covers on every page. They'd really attract people's attention. What do you think?

D: It's a bit too many, I'd say. A lot of pictures take too long to download. I'd prefer one big image. How about that?

P: Mmm, I don't know. People like to see the book covers. It draws them into the website, believe me.

D: Maybe you're right. How about two covers per page, then?

P: OK, that sounds reasonable. Now, what else do we need to discuss before you get started?

Speaking

1

Role-play a conversation according to the following situation. After the practice, change roles.
Role Cards

—**Company manager**:

You want:

1. A one-year contract

   You want to see how well the company does the job and if they are reliable before giving them a long contract.

2. To have the website tested every quarter

You want the maintenance cost to be as low as possible. However, you would like to have weekly checks on security of the website.

3. Response time—five hours

You want to contact them at any hour by phone if there is an emergency. You want the maintenance company to solve any problems within 5 hours.

—Website representative:

You want:

1. A four-year contract

This allows you to offer the best service to customers and it will be profitable for you.

2. To test the website twice in a month

This will give the best level of service to the client and increase your earnings.

3. Response time—24 hours

You want the company to contact you by e-mail if there is an emergency. You want up to 24 hours to solve any problems.

Flow Chart

Company manager	Website representative
Greetings.	Reply. Start with the length of contract.
Give the answer.	Show disagreement and state the demand.
Offer another suggestion.	Reluctantly accept.
Move to the frequency of testing.	Give the answer.
Show disagreement and state the demand.	Stick to the first offer and give reasons on a professional stand.
Try to bargain again.	Make a little concession.
Show satisfaction and move on.	Reject the suggestion.
Stick to the offer and inform the other of other website companies' offer.	Accept the offer and try to raise more demands.
Focus the discussion and close.	Close the conversation and show expectation.

Suggested key words and Expressions

1 Stating aims:
  - We'd like to have it in a month's time.
  - We must have delivery by the end of next week.

2 Making concessions:
  - If I have to finish in one month, I'll need to have an extra designer.
  - That could be all right — as long as I get some money in advance.

3 Rejecting suggestions:
  - We'd prefer to pay you a fixed amount.

4 Bargaining:
  - How about paying me half when I start the work?

5 Focusing the discussion:
  - Let's talk about the time for setting up the website.

2

Make an oral report according to the following situation.

Tips: The content in your speech should be based on the results of Speaking activity 1.

The following words and expressions can be of help.

You and your partner can check and assess the performance for each other.

> **1. Opening**
> Good morning/afternoon, everyone.
> If we are all here, let's get started/start the meeting/start.

> **2. Stating the Principal Objectives**
> We're here today to ...　I'd like to make sure that we ...
> Our main aim today is to ...　I've called this meeting in order to ...

> **3. Introducing the First Item on the Agenda**
> So, let's start with ...　I'd suggest we start with ...
> Why don't we start with ...　So, the first item on the agenda is ...

> **4. Closing an Item**
> I think that takes care of the first item.　Shall we leave that item?
> Why don't we move on to ...　If nobody has anything else to add, lets ...

> **5. Next Item**
> Let's move onto the next item.　Now that we've discussed X, let's now ...
> The next item on today's agenda is ...　Now we come to the question of ...

> **6. Summarizing**
> Before we close today's meeting, let me just summarize the main points.
> Let me quickly go over today's main points.　To sum up, ...
> OK, why don't we quickly summarize what we've done today ...

Writing

1

Put the sentences in this letter in the correct order.

 Guidance:

Letter of Complaint

A letter of complaint requesting compensation for delayed, defective or damaged goods or for poor service usually consists of following parts.

◆ Background: describing the situation;
◆ Problem: explaining cause and effect;
◆ Solution: stating exactly what you want to be done about the problem;
◆ Warning: stating measures to take if the problem is not solved;
◆ Closing: ending with a wish to solve the problem.

 Key

1—D　2—F　3—B　4—E　5—A　6—C

2

Write a reply to the letter in Exercise 1.

Guidance:

Letter of Adjustment
Replies to letters of complaint, often called "Letters of Adjustment", must be handled carefully. Here are some suggestions that may help you write letters of adjustment:

- ◆ Refer to the letter of complaint by date.

- ◆ Identify the item or problem that the customer has encountered.
- ◆ If your company is at fault, apologize.
- ◆ Explain how the error occurred.
- ◆ State exactly how you intend to solve the problem.
- ◆ If you cannot solve the problem as they wish, try to make a slight adjustment.

Reference:

INTERNATIONAL
1 Connaught Place

Grissom & Beth Advertising
23 Alexandra Road
Bournemouth

17 May

Dear Mr Slander

Further to your phone call and your letter of May 14th, we would like to apologise for the problems you had.

There was obviously a mix-up over your order and the goods you received were meant for another customer. The correct order was sent by special delivery and should already be with you.

Once again, our apologies for the inconvenience.

We look forward to receiving further orders from you.

Yours sincerely

Jake Grissom

Jake Grissom

Unit 8 Entertainment

Objective

- **Career skills**
Identifying a story's high concept or attractive spot, driving force and conflict; writing script for a short play; knowing expressions used in talks about films and other forms of entertainment; writing reviews of films and other forms of entertainment.

- **Reading**
  1. Reading for main idea(s)
  2. Skimming/Scanning
  3. Reading for general information and details
  4. Reading for guessing word meaning from context

- **Writing**
  1. General writing: sentence patterns
  2. Practical writing: review

- **Listening**
  1. Listening for key words
  2. Listening for identifying procedure
  3. Listening for note-taking
  4. Listening for general information and details

- **Speaking**
  1. Making comments on varied forms of entertainment
  2. Expressing agreement and disagreement

- **Language focus**

Key words and phrases			
entertainment	music	film	play
script	feature	character	conflict
at stake	make one's day		hip-hop
villain	hero	protagonist	
have its share of	hang out	take off	
popularity	go hand in hand with		review

Teaching Arrangement

Warm-up & Unit task (Text A)
1) Time schedule: 2 periods
2) Suggested lesson structure
   Warm-up: 10 – 15 minutes
   Text A: 10 – 15 minutes
   Unit task step 1 (pre-task): 10 – 15 minutes
   Unit task steps 2 – 5 (while-task): 45 – 60 minutes
   Unit task step 6 (post-task) should be completed after class

Reading (Text B)
1) Time schedule: 1 period
2) Suggested lesson structure
   Language points: 20 – 25 minutes
   Language practice: 20 – 25 minutes

Listening
1) Time schedule: 1 period
2) Suggested lesson structure
   Listening exercise 1: 10 minutes
   Listening exercise 2: 15 minutes
   Listening exercise 3: 10 minutes
   Listening exercise 4: 15 minutes

Speaking & Writing
1) Time schedule: 1 period
2) Suggested lesson structure
   Speaking: 20 – 25 minutes
   Writing: 20 minutes

Teaching Procedures

Warm-up

Look at the following pictures and discuss with your partner. Match each picture with the corresponding form of entertainment.

Target:

Ss identify the subject of each picture.

Guidance:

- Ss read Warm-up 1.
- Ask Ss to match the names of different performances with their pictures.
- Invite 1 – 2 Ss to present their answers.
- Ask 2 – 3 Ss to add some more forms of entertainment.

 Key

1. Concert—F   2. Musical theater—A   3. Cinema—B
4. TV series—E   5. Animation—C   6. Straight play—D

Background Information

What is entertainment?

Entertainment consists of any activity which provides a diversion or permits people to amuse themselves in their leisure time. Entertainment is generally passive, such as watching opera or a movie. Active forms of amusement, such as games or sports, are more often considered to be recreation. Activities such as personal reading or practicing musical instruments are considered as hobbies.

Work in pairs. Look at the following descriptions of the forms of entertainment mentioned above. Mark number 1 – 6 in front of the sentences to match them with the forms of entertainment they describe.

---- **Expressions Pool** ----

Entertainment types: Concert, Musical theater, Cinema, TV series, animation, Straight play . . .
Sentence pattern: It is performed by . . . / to go hand-in-hand with . . .

Target:

Ss can understand the difference between various forms of entertainment. Ss can learn some expressions to describe different forms of entertainment.

Guidance:

- Ss read Warm-up 2.
- Ask Ss to work together to discuss the answer with their partners.
- Invite no more than 3 students to present his/her result.
- The teacher may help to explain some difficult language points.

Reference:

1	It's performed by a single musician or a musical band.
2/3/4/5/6	It tells a complete story.
3/4	The performance is pre-recorded by video camera and projected onto a screen.
1/2/6	The actions and dialogues in the show always go hand-in-hand with singing.
2	The actions and dialogues in the show always go hand-in-hand with dancing.
1/2/6	It's a live performance.
5	It's not performed by real actors or actresses.

Listen to five fragments of music, and guess which genre each of them belongs to.

Target:

Ss can understand the differences between various styles of music. Ss can learn some words of music genre.

Step:
- Ss read Warm-up 3.
- Play music fragments one by one, with enough intervals for Ss to take a guess and write down their answer.
- Ask Ss to work together to discuss the answer with their partners.
- Play the fragments again and describe their characteristics.

 Key

1. classic   2. jazz   3. rock   4. rap   5. New age

Background Information

- The term classic music generally refers to the traditional music genre in Europe that took shape and standardized around the 17th century, with Bache, Mozart and Beethoven as representatives in its golden age.
- Jazz is a music style that began in the early 20th century. It has spawned a variety of subgenres, but its most core qualities are still distinctive, which include "swinging", improvising, and group interaction. Its performance is rich in spontaneity and vitality.
- The sound of rock music often revolves around the electric guitar, a strong back beat laid down by a rhythm section of electric bass guitar, drums, and keyboard instruments such as Hammond organ and piano.
- Hip-hop music is distinguished by the rapping technique. Rapping refers to rhyming lyrics spoken or singed to the beat of a strong rhythmic backing music.
- New Age is music of various styles intended to create artistic inspiration, relaxation, and optimism. It is used by listeners as a method of stress management or to create a peaceful atmosphere. The harmonies in New Age music are generally modal, consonant, or include a drone bass. The melodies are often repetitive, to create a hypnotic feeling.

Unit task

Read Text A and practice some real tasks on the topic of entertainment.

 Task Map(任务导航)

优秀的故事脍炙人口,源远流长,电影、戏剧、文学作品,乃至广告策划案等等都离不开创意写作。就最简单的短篇故事而言,要给读者留下深刻的印象,仍然需要非常重要的技巧。短篇故事的写作可以拓展为一系列的任务,如理解构成一篇优秀故事的几个要素,尝试将这些要素应用到自己的创意写作中,以及衍生出的表演短剧、拍摄短剧、乃至影片剪辑等实际操作性极强的活动。创意写作及其衍生任务的各项环节里有大量的英语阅读、听力、写作、口语等的实际应用。

特此要求学生对创意写作及其衍生任务进行具体实践,通过模仿影视作品的故事架构、角色对话进行语言实践活动,巩固学生用英语询问、介绍、建议、提问与回答等能力。

本单元任务分为 6 个步骤,第一个步骤让学生通过阅读了解构成一篇优秀故事的四要素:富有感染力的角色、角色驱动力、人物冲突、前提假设;第二个步骤是学生阅读电影剧情简介,在实例中寻找"四要素",使所学知识迅速得到应用;第三个步骤是学生模仿电影角色进行对话,并注意模仿电影中的语音语调,体会其角色设定和对话设计;第四个步骤是学生分成 4－5 人一组,按照之前学习的"四要素",设计一个简单的故事梗概,学生可以参考书中列举的情景设定;第五个步骤是细化情节设计,角色性格设计和对话设计,参照前文的电影剧本创作短剧;第六个步骤是学生在课上进行表演,或在课后将表演拍摄成录像在课堂播放。该任务主要是针对创意写作进行初步的训练,并试图以较为活泼的方式进行口语实践。现实中,"四要素"未必足以成就一部优秀作品,但为降低难度,该任务中经过简化的四个要素,使创意写作任务的可操作性得以增加。情景剧剧本构思和表演环节可以安排在课下进行,先进行后续课程,等到该单元最后一课时再完成对第六个步骤的考察。

本单元任务的安排主要根据活动过程顺序来设定,每一任务为后续的步骤做基础。

Process Break-down

Pre-task：

Step 1   A Ss need to read Article 1 to get a preliminary idea of the elements crucial to a good story.

B Ss explain each element with their own words or words from the article.

While-task：

Step 2   Ss read the plot summary to bring their understanding of the four elements to practice.

Step 3   Ss perform a play according to the film script and try to imitate the tones and performance of the actor and actress.

Step 4   Ss work together to design a short story, practicing the theory of 4 elements.

Step 5   Ss add details to their story, making the characters alive with personalities and dialogues.

Post-task:

Step 6   Ss make a play according to the script they have written. Ss are encouraged to shoot it with a video camera or mobile phone and show the video at class for appreciation from their peers.

Step 1

A

Group Discussion: Read Article 1 and find keywords describing the 4 magical elements that make a good story.

Target:

Identify 4 elements for good story writing.

Guidance:

- Divide the whole class into groups of 4 - 5 students.
- Ss scan some related information from the text quickly.
- By finishing this step, Ss will have a general idea of the 4 elements' functions, and of how to identify them.
- During this step, Ss can also learn how the theory is supported by various examples.
- Invite one group of Ss to present the answers.
- Teacher can do a little explanation afterwards.

Key

Elements	Function
1. Great characters	Make audience passionate
1. <u>Something at stake</u>	Keep the characters going, whatever difficulties they would go through.
2. <u>Conflict/Obstacles</u>	Prevent the characters from achieving their goals.
3. <u>Hook/High concept/What if?</u>	Attract the audience's attention.

任务过程控制关注点
Minefield

- 提醒学生不要被生词限制住,阅读时需要利用上下文猜测关键词,非关键词可以忽略。
- 提醒学生快速阅读时应采用查读法。
- 提醒学生这个步骤的任务是为接下来需要完成的实际任务提供理论依据。
- 提醒学生可以有多个表达意思相似的关键词。
- 不强调标准答案,只要学生理解了"四要素"即可。

------ **Expressions Pool** ------

(Omitted)

Expressions Pool

1. ... is at stake ...
2. The conflict is that ...
3. must/have to ... but ...
4. What ... if ... ?

Step 2

Group Discussion: Read Article 2 the plot summary of *Roman Holiday*. It's hard to see great characters in a plot summary rather than dialogues and actions, but you can find the other 3 elements that make *Roman Holiday* a good story.

Target:

Test and improve Ss' understanding of the elements to make a good story.

Guidance:

- Ss read the summary quickly to get a general idea of what happened in this film.
- Invite 3 – 4 Ss to present their answer.

 Key

1. What is "at stake" in this film?
   Joe's job is at stake. He must have a special report about Princess Ann's adventure in Rome, or he will be fired by his boss.
2. What is the "conflict"?
   Joe has to expose Ann's personal life to save his career. But Ann must keep her identity as a secret.
3. What is the hook or "What if?" in this film? Is there more than one "What if"? Find as many as you can.
   What will happen if you meet a princess in disguise?
   What will you do if you are torn between your career and your friend, or love?

Step 3

Perform a play according to the following script and try to imitate the tones and performance of the actor and actress.

Target:

Imitate the intonation and stress of the actor and actress.

Guidance:

- In each group, invite a boy student and a girl student to read the characters' lines, with a third student reading the action descriptions as voice-over.
- Teacher may explain new words in the script briefly if necessary.
- Play the video/audio clip. Ask the students to pay attention to how the native speaker speaks.
- Ask each group to read after each line to imitate the actor/actress' intonation and stress.
- Invite each pair to perform a play according to the script.

Expressions Pool

1. Out of my head.
2. I'm terribly sorry to mention it, but ...
3. Can I ... ?

（续表）

4. I'm afraid you'll have to . . .
5. I haven't . . . in years.
6. Will you help me . . . , please?
7. There you are.

Step 4

Work together with your group to design a short play, using the 3 magical elements you find in Step 2! Keep the length of the play between 5 – 10 mins.

任务过程控制关注点
Minefield

● 提醒学生可以分步进行,避免同时考虑因素太多。
● 鼓励学生自由创作,也可以参考、改写书上列举的题材。
● 提示和提醒学生设计时注意要可以表演。

Target：

Practice the elements learnt in previous steps. Know how to use them to design a short story.

Guidance：

● Ss think of 3 elements and link them into a story summary.
● Ss share and discuss their ideas in each group.
● Each group decides a best story to further improve.
● Ss are free to use the listed examples.

Reference：

● A group of friends go to the cinema but find themselves with conflicting choices.
● A young man helped an old lady knocked down by bike, but was mistaken as the perpetrator. How would he prove himself innocent?
● One day you wake up and find everyone including your closest friend is left-handed. What happened? What are you going to do? Can you still trust your friend?
● You're a time traveler. You're mistakenly caught in a crime scene in 1996 (or any year you like). You have no ID. How can you talk the police into believing you as innocent? Or will someone be able to help you?

Step 5

Add details to your play. Now is the time to bring in the first magical element：great characters. Give your characters personalities and catchy lines to make them alive. Write your own play.

任务过程控制关注点
Minefield

● 提醒学生开拓思维。可回顾 Step 3 的对话表达,并在此任务中运用。
● 该步骤占时较多,可安排于课后进行。

Target：

Write a detailed short play.

Guidance：

● Ss read the tips and try to add details into their story summary.
● Ss use dialogue tips to design dialogues.
● Work in groups.

──────── Expressions Pool ────────

be a fly on the wall：be somewhere discreetly to listen and observe.
It's not a bad idea . . .
. . . to have a difficult time . . .

任务过程控制关注点
Minefield

- 提醒学生此任务属于后任务环节,应在课后自己操练。
- 提醒学生要把前面任务的语言进行积累。
- 提醒学生要勇于创新,并记录自己学习或表演的事实。
- 提醒学生重点是进行语言演练及表演,而不要把重点放在道具准备等上。

Step 6

Play it out! And record it with a video camera or a mobile phone.

A: Ss can use software to edit video and audio recording and add in background music to intensify emotional impact. The software is available for free download on Internet.

B: The final cut will be shown in the class. Ss will vote for Best Film, Best Director, Best Actor and Actress and other awards.

Target:

Summarize what have been learned and apply them in practice.

Guidance:

- Ss are supposed to review what they have learned about story writing.
- Ss are supposed to discuss freely.
- Teacher should encourage Ss to make the play or short film after class.
- Teacher should explain the direction clearly.

Action research
（教师自己的教学行动研究）

任务完成中的观察、反思（日志、随笔）	备忘

Language Points

Text A •

Article 1

◆ （line 9）**There is always something at *stake*
in a good movie.**

stake：a sum of money gambled on a risky game

［运用］　have a stake in　与……有利害关系

e. g. Each of us has a stake in the future of our
country.

The mercenary have no stake in this war.

［拓展］　at stake：at risk　面临危险

e. g. His career is at stake.

With enough at stake, he decided to silence the
witness.

◆ （line 22）**... provide what actors love so
much — *CONFLICT*.**

conflict：a struggle or clash between opposing forces

［运用］　be in conflict with, conflict between,
conflict over, thrown into conflict, conflict escalates/
comes to an end

e. g. Government business is in conflict with personal
interests.

The conflict between the two countries began
in 1988.

Conflict over natural resources has been
widespread.

Suddenly her personal and professional lives are
thrown into conflict.

The conflict has escalated over the last month.

［拓展］　conflicting *a.* 矛盾的,冲突的

Her heart is torn by conflicting emotions.

Article 2

◆ （line 2）**She begins to *rebel* against her
restricted schedule.**

rebel：to resist an authority

［运用］　rebel against

［拓展］　*rebel*（*a.*）反抗的,叛乱的

rebellion（*n.*）叛乱,叛乱者

The Imperial forces began their task of tracking
down the rebel alliance.

◆ （line 7）**... Hennessy threatens to fire Joe
for his *failure* ...**

failure：an action that is not successful

［运用］　failure to do, failure in doing, failure of
sth.

The failure of all attempts drove him desperate.

［拓展］　fail *v.* 失败,消亡

When hope fails, duty prevails.

◆ （line 30）**She then *departs*, leaving Joe to
linger for a while ...**

depart：to leave

［运用］　depart from, depart for

e. g. The train will depart from Shanghai at 2：30
p. m.

Sam will depart for Japan tomorrow.

［拓展］　departure *n.* 离开

The freighter was fuming thick black smoke and
ready for departure.

Article 3

◆ （line 18）**Is this the *elevator*?**

elevator：电梯 a moving platform or cage for
carrying passengers or freight from one level to
another, as in a building

［运用］　get in/out of an elevator

e. g. I was trapped inside an elevator during the
blackout.

［拓展］　elevate（*v.*）提升

More successful peasants began to elevate
themselves above their fellows, to accumulate
land and employ their own labourers.

◆ （line 25）**I'm terribly sorry to mention it,
but the *dizziness* is getting worse.**

dizziness：头晕感

［运用］　A moment of dizziness, stumble with
dizziness

e. g. As she rose from the bench, a wave of dizziness
swept over her.

［拓展］　dizzy（*a.*）头晕眼花的

He felt a little dizzy and dropped himself into a
chair.

◆ （line 44）**There you are; you can *handle* the
rest.**

handle 处理

［运用］　handle sth. /some situation

e. g. We can handle it.

There's nothing we can't handle.

［仿写］　这件事你能自己处理吗?

Text B •

◆ （line 1）**Rock *had its day*.**

have one's day：to experience success or prosperity
经历成功和繁荣

e. g. Every dog has its day. ［谚］凡人皆有得意日。

［拓展］　day 此处指兴旺发达的鼎盛时期

　　　　make one's day 使某人的一天生色,使某人高兴

e. g. It'll surely make his day when he knows his son's success.

［仿写］　你的称赞让他高兴坏了。

◆（line 3）... **have** their **roots in** the black community.

have roots in：起源于,源自于

e. g. Many English words and phrases have roots in a Latin origin.

　　His unhappiness has its root in early childhood.

［拓展］　root *n.* 根源

　　　　take root in: to be accepted or established 扎根

e. g. Money is the root of all evil

　　Democracy is now struggling to take root in most of these countries.

［仿写］　成功源自于自信。

◆（line 4）... **rap has faced** *its share of* **criticism.**

one's share of：what is due or enough for someone 属于某人的一份,足够的份额

［运用］　to pay/take/bear one's share of ...

e. g. Every one in this team has done his share of work.

［拓展］　to have one's share of 拥有足够的……

e. g. My husband and I have had our share of job changes and periods of unemployment in recent years.

　　We have taken more than our share of risk.

［仿写］　我们受够了这些年的苦日子。

◆（line 5）... **it's** *more* **popular** *than ever.*

more than ever：比以前更……

e. g. He loves you more than ever.

［拓展］　better/stronger/shorter/... than ever

［仿写］　她的歌唱得比以前更好了。

◆（line 6）Hip-hop refers to the *backing* music for rap.

backing：（音乐）伴奏的

［拓展］　back *v.* 1. 伴奏

　　　　　　　2. 支持

　　　　　　　3. 构成背景

e. g. Federal government backs Australian tourism. （财政支持）

　　There is no fact to back up his argument.

　　Snowcapped mountains back the village.

［仿写］　我们需要用事实来支持我们的论点。

◆（line 9）Baggy jeans, sports jerseys, and baseball hats worn *sideways* ...

sideways：toward or from one side 侧着地,斜着地,歪向一边地

e. g. He jumped sideways to dodge the ball.

［运用］　glance sideways, move sideways

［拓展］　sideways *adj.* 斜着的

　　　　sideways◇direct

e. g. He shot her a sideways glance.

　　He addresses the problem through a sideways approach.

［仿写］　螃蟹侧着身子走路。

◆（line 16）... **a way for inner-city youths to** *publicize* **the problems they faced.**

publicize：bring to public notice；advertise 发布,宣传

e. g. The campaign is intended to publicize the tourist festival.

［拓展］　public *n.* 公众　*a.* 公众的

　　　　publicize→promote, sell, acclaim, announce

［仿写］　公司花了很大力气宣传新产品。

◆（line 21）... **break-dancing, a dance style that** *took off* **around the same time.**

take off：to become successful or popular, esp. suddenly

［拓展］　take off（飞机）起飞,（项目）启动

　　　　take off→launch

［仿写］　这种风格在近两年突然流行起来。

◆（line 24）Originally used by gangs as a way to mark their *territory* ...

territory：area of land；a region 领地

e. g. Our country has a large population, vast territory and abundant resources.

［拓展］　territorial（*a.*）领土的,区域的

［仿写］　我们会拼死捍卫我们的领土。

◆（line 24）..., graffiti *eventually* developed into an independent form of street art.

eventually：finally 最终地

e. g. They eventually come to terms with each other.

［拓展］　eventual（一系列事件后）最终的

　　　　His mistakes led to his eventual dismissal.

　　　　eventually→finally, at last, ultimately

［仿写］　敌人最终还是被击败了。

◆（line 25）..., graffiti eventually *developed* into an independent form of street art.

develop：发展

［拓展］　developing *a.* 发展中的

developed *a.* 发达的

develop *v.* 照片显影；开发；生长发育

e.g. The document is setting unequal limits on carbon emissions for developed and developing countries in 2050.

［仿写］　我国大力发展工业和农业。

Translation of Texts

Text A

是什么成就了好故事?

我们不妨随便猜猜。在你最喜欢的电影中,那些人物角色让你置身剧中,他们能俘获你的感情,牵动你的思绪。看电影的观众们要求的,并不只是感兴趣和在乎银幕上的角色,他们想被他们牵动真情实感,无论是爱是恨。杰出的男主角和女主角能激励我们,杰出的反派则让我们忍不住要扑到屏幕上去!

好电影中总是设计了一些遭遇危机的事物。它不仅仅是某些人物欲求的某种东西,它也可以是不惜代价一定要必须获取的某种东西,比如《法柜奇兵》中的宝物。或者是诸多主要角色都极度渴望的东西。有时它可以是无形的,比如《阿拉伯的劳伦斯》或《甘地传》中一个民族的自由。所有这些因素都在驱使着角色在征途上不断前进,甚至赋予主人公超人的力量。它可以是私密的(爱情),也可以是大公无私的(从外星人手中拯救世界),但它必须是强有力的,并且随着故事的展开,变得越来越迫切、激烈。

阻力是不可或缺的。阻力催生了角色们最喜爱的元素——冲突。这是戏剧的核心元素。有人想得到某个东西,但是不断有其他人和事物插进来阻扰他们达成目标。有时,阻力可以是男主角和反派共有的,最终目标是双方都渴望达成的。冲突和阻碍可以是物质上的,也可以是感情上的。但是你的故事中必须有冲突,否则就会索然无味。在大多数优秀的故事中,主人翁也有一种内在的阻力,一种精神上的或者是心灵上的困扰,这种困扰将在他/她达成外在的、物质上的目标之后得到解决。有人称这种内心的魔鬼为"心魔",也有人称之为"心病"。

你需要一个吸引人的元素。它能攫取公众的注意力。好莱坞有个流行术语叫"高概念"。意思是说某个故事建立在一种简单的假设之上,寥寥数语就可以解释清楚。尽管许多电影评论家对这种设定批评很多,但是对于新手来说,仍不失为一剂良方。更

好的主意可能是单纯地问"如果……会怎样?"。例如《银河追缉令》的概念是"如果一部被腰斩的流行科幻电视剧中失败的演员们被一群把该剧误认作纪录片的外星人拖进一场太空战争会怎样?"。一个出色的"如果",能让你的剧本脱颖而出。这才是为什么人们会放弃舒服的小窝,把辛苦挣来的血汗钱砸进当地的电影院里。

《罗马假日》剧情简介

安妮公主正在游访欧洲诸国的首都,各方媒体高调报道。当她和皇室随从抵达罗马时,她开始反抗限制她自由的访问日程。

一天晚上,安妮溜出房间逃到外面。但是她之前被注射的镇静剂开始发挥作用,使她在街边的长椅上睡着了。一名叫乔·布拉德利的驻罗马美国记者发现了她,并把她带到了自己的公寓。

第二天早上乔迟到没赶上安妮公主的新闻发布会。主编亨尼西威胁要因此辞退他。但是乔意识到睡在他躺椅上的少女就是公主本人,于是许诺会交出一份对公主的独家专访,让亨尼西大吃一惊。

乔自告奋勇带安妮游玩罗马,以便暗中偷拍她的照片。他们骑着 Vespa 摩托车穿越罗马城,观赏各处名胜。安妮向乔吐露了自己渴望平常生活,远离责任与束缚的梦想。当天晚上,政府特工追踪到她的下落,试图将她护送回府。随后双方大打出手,乔和安妮趁乱逃脱。经历这些事情以后,他们渐渐坠入爱河。但是安妮知道这是不可以发生的。她最终没有表明自己的真实身份,而是向乔道别,回到了大使馆。

在这一天中,亨尼西打听到公主并不像大使宣称的那样是生病了,而是失踪了。他怀疑乔知道公主的下落,便旁敲侧击想让他说出实情。但是乔藏起他拍下的照片,矢口否认。

次日,公主出现在推迟了一天的新闻发布会上,发现乔也在新闻记者之列。乔通过暗示让她知道,他会保守她的秘密。她也在不动声色的发布会陈词上暗藏了一条信息,向乔表达了爱意和谢意。她随

后离开,留下乔徘徊半晌,沉思着他们之间未能发生的故事。

Text B

嘻哈音乐的世界

每个时代都有它的音乐。爵士乐曾经称王,摇滚乐也有过风光的时候。现在是饶舌歌当家,盛会方兴未艾。

就像其他源自黑人社区的音乐形式——例如爵士乐与摇滚乐——饶舌歌也同样遭到批评。饶舌歌一度被称为一时的流行,但它却风行了二十年以上,而现在比以前更受欢迎。所谓"饶舌"是指配合节奏说话或唱歌,还要押韵。嘻哈音乐指的是饶舌歌的伴奏音乐,它也代表饶舌文化。

嘻哈不仅仅是音乐,它是一种生活方式、一种文化。环顾四周,只要是有年轻人闲晃的地方,你一定会看到这些形象:宽松的牛仔裤、运动套衫与斜戴一边的棒球帽,这只是其中几样已经在有些街道上开始出现的嘻哈标记。

严格来说,嘻哈是由四项要素组成:涂鸦喷画、街舞、饶舌歌与音乐混音。大部分的人都同意嘻哈文化开始于 1970 年代晚期纽约市的布隆克斯区。早期的嘻哈音乐把注意力放在贫穷的都市贫民区的困苦生活上。居住于都市内部的年轻人以此告诉人们他们所遭遇的问题。嘻哈音乐就非洲裔美国人的问题与这类人群形成了直接的对话。

嘻哈的音乐是饶舌歌。它的乐风建立在节奏和口白上。这种音乐和街舞的关系密切,街舞是大约在同一时期开始流行的舞蹈。唱片混音开始时是被当成一种创造新音乐的省钱方式。另一项要素——涂鸦喷画,长久以来一直是都市文化的一部分。最早它是帮派用来标示势力范围的方式,后来发展成为一种独立的街头艺术。

这就是嘻哈的起源,那么它走向何方呢? 四面八方,老兄,它到处都是。从英国到巴西到日本,嘻哈四处散播,并且快速流传。现在连爱斯基摩人都有嘻哈!

Notes:

Explain these words and expressions through their context or with the help of a dictionary.

1) criticism (Para. 2)   批评(*n.*)
e.g. Criticism should be aimed at helping those criticized.

2) hang out (Para. 3)   常去某处,混在某处
e.g. We should hang out together.

3) trademark (Para. 3)   商标,标志性特征(*n.*)
e.g. The actress's trademark smile spared her a speeding ticket.

4) record (Para. 5)   唱片(*n.*)
e.g. Vinyl records are widely used for distribution of independent artists.

Reading Skills Exercises:

1

Complete the article structure after you have read Text B.

 Key

- Para. 1 hip-hop is the music of this age.
- Para. 2 <u>history</u> of hip-hop
- Para. 3 the broader sense of hip-hop: <u>it's a way of life, a culture.</u>
- Para. 4 the nature of hip-hop: a way for inner-city youths to <u>publicize the problems they faced</u>
- Para. 5 the elements of hip-hop:
  - <u>rap</u>
  - <u>break-dance</u>
  - <u>sound mixing</u>
  - <u>graffiti</u>
- Para. 6 the future of hip-hop

2

Match the phrases to their definitions.

 Key

1—B, 2—C, 3—A, 4—D

Language practice

Vocabulary

1

Finish the list of nouns and adjectives.

 Key

Noun	Adjective
music	musical
rhythm	rhythmical
culture	cultural
element	elemental
territory	territorial
style	stylish
popularity	popular
independence	independent

2

Complete the sentences with the following verbal phrases in their proper forms.

 Key

1. Anybody can <u>make history</u>; only a great man can write it.
2. Women officers <u>make up</u> 13 per cent of the police force.
3. This sentence just doesn't <u>make sense</u>, no matter how you read it.
4. I don't have a nightgown, so you'll have to <u>make do</u> with pyjamas.
5. The fire was too big. They tried to escape but didn't <u>make it</u>.
6. To this day I still can't <u>make out</u> why they did so.
7. The kids <u>made fun of</u> her because she spoke with a southern accent.
8. "Thanks for your news, buddy. You just <u>made my day</u>!"
9. "Turn left. No, no, no, turn right!" "<u>Make up your mind</u>!"

3

Fill in the blanks with words from the box.

 Key

1. The controversial play received much <u>criticism</u> from Christian community.
2. For more than three <u>decades</u>, he had been an advocate for independent film making.
3. Two pilots went missing in enemy <u>territory</u> after their aircraft was shot down.
4. The young man <u>eventually</u> rose to the position of vice president.
5. "Beef" and "leaf" are <u>rhymes</u>.
6. The police know where the thieves <u>hang out</u>.
7. He glanced <u>sideways</u> at her.
8. The author appeared on TV to <u>publicize</u> her latest book.

Translation

Translate English into Chinese and then underline the pattern. Study the pattern. Then translate the Chinese into English by using the pattern.

 Key

1. This election produced <u>its share of</u> surprise.
   主要句型：也同样……
   中文翻译：<u>此次选举也同样有其令人惊讶之处</u>。
   气候变化会谈自身也在产生着碳排放。
   English translation：<u>Climate change conference itself emits its share of carbon.</u>
2. This musical <u>focuses on</u> protagonist's pursuit of dream.
   主要句型：关注……
   中文翻译：<u>这部音乐剧的主题是主人公对梦想的追逐</u>。
   他的电影作品总是关注人性的主题。
   English translation：<u>His films always focus on the subject of human nature.</u>
3. Love and regret <u>go hand in hand</u> in this world of changes.
   主要句型：伴随着……同时出现

中文翻译：<u>在这个变幻莫测的世界，爱情与遗憾总是形影不离</u>。

犯罪活动往往伴随着糟糕的经济状况而来。

English translation：<u>Crime usually goes hand in hand with poor economic conditions.</u>

4. The style really <u>took off</u> among teens.

主要句型：……<u>突然取得成功；突然流行</u>

中文翻译：<u>这个风格在青少年中突然流行开来</u>。

斯皮尔伯格（Spielberg）的《太平洋》是一部突然间大获成功的新电视剧。

English translation：<u>Spielberg's *Pacific* is a new TV series that really took off.</u>

Grammar

Review Test

Choose the more appropriate words to complete the following sentences.

1. They weren't meeting heavy resistance, because the air force <u>had already crippled</u> (had already crippled, already crippled) enemy communications.

2. And if we <u>haven't found</u> (didn't find, haven't found) her by the time Boss gets here, you keep him busy.

3. "Sorry, comrade," he said, regretting <u>his</u> (his, himself) rudeness. "No offense."

   "I know, comrade. <u>None</u> (nothing, none) taken."

4. He <u>can't</u> (can't, mustn't) have been in the library.

5. You <u>don't have</u> (don't have, haven't) to pay me back before Christmas.

6. Either my brothers or my father <u>is</u> (have, is) coming.

7. Neither Mara nor I <u>am</u> (is, am) going.

8. The detective <u>has been</u> (is, has been) tracking her for months. She isn't going anywhere.

9. It <u>had been</u> (has been, had been) bothering him in recent days, ever since he began to think of the delay as having an indefinite timescale.

10. I don't insult people just <u>because</u> (when, because) I don't agree with them.

11. This ship won't leave <u>until</u> (when, until) the last one of you is safely on board.

12. Only when the tension had passed <u>did he go away</u> (away he went, did he go away).

13. Not only <u>had it</u> (it had, had it) built the nest for its mate, but <u>it had</u> (it had, had it) also stocked food for the winter.

Listening

1

Work with your partner to fill in the blanks using the words in the box. Listen and check your answers, and then follow the recording.

 Script

1. The Black Eyed Peas' newest album has brought them six <u>nominations</u> for the 2010 Grammy Awards.

2. Fergie is the band's only female member and the <u>lead</u> singer.

3. Lady Gaga is firing back at a music producer who claims he <u>launched</u> her career and is suing her for $30.5 million.

4. During current period of time, it seems no one could match the <u>popularity</u> of "Brother Sharp" and "Sister Phoenix" on China's Internet.

5. Shahrukh Khan, whose last release *My Name Is Khan* created <u>box office</u> record overseas, was conferred with the Global Entertainment and Media Personality award at the FICCI Frames 2010 Excellence Awards in Mumbai.

6. There's nothing like a good-old celebrity <u>scandal</u> to get tongues wagging.

7. The Count demands that they <u>reserve</u> Box Five exclusively for him.

2

Listen to an introduction of a Yoga pose — the Salutation Pose. Match the instructions you hear with the following pictures.

 Script

The Salutation Pose combines several postures and gestures in a fluid, evolving flow that combines motion, stretching and holds. It delivers great benefits for the back, arms, chest, legs and hips. Regular practice will strengthen concentration and improve balance.

Perform this posture with a sense of reverence and praise. Take a moment to reside in silence and peace as your hands are held at the heart in the gesture of salutation. Keep the intention of praise in mind as you extend your arms skyward. Feel your entire body-mind-heart extending outward in recognition of the sacredness of life.

Follow the following steps:

1. Sit comfortably in the thunderbolt pose.
2. Kneel up on your knees until your back, buttocks and thighs are aligned.
3. Extend your left foot forward bending your left knee at about a 90 degree angle.

4. Place the palms of your hands together at the heart in the salutation.
5. Raise your arms straight up, keeping the palms together while bending the head backward and looking up.
6. Slowly bend backward, stretch the arms backward and straighten out the right leg. Hold this position for as long as comfortable while breathing gently through the nostrils.

 Key

A—1, B—6, C—4, D—3, E—5, F—2

3

Listen to the conversation among four friends: Darman, Roy, Gary and Zoe. Answer the following questions.

 Script

D—Darman   R—Roy   G—Gary   Z—Zoe

D—So guys, what would you like to see?

R—I don't know ... how's that one, *Night at the Museum*? Seems cool to me.

G—It seemed pretty silly to me. The story was too far-fetched. I just couldn't see the point of it.

Z—Well, I don't think you were supposed to take it too seriously. It was just meant for entertainment.

R—Yeah, I totally agree with Zoe. I like to relax my brain after so many days of overwork.

D—Is there any other choice? What about *Laurence of the Arabia*?

G—The acting was first rate! Peter O'Toole is the leading actor. A very well-known British actor.

R—Never heard of ... no, wait a minute, I know that film. I couldn't help falling asleep last time I saw it ...

Z—And for good reason. It lasts more than three hours. It'll be too late to catch the subway when it finishes.

G—Roy, you don't know what you've missed. It's based on a true story about a man who sacrificed his future to win liberty for a foreign nation.

D—Maybe it is too profound for us to understand. What about *Avatar*?

R—You mean the $30 dollar one?

D—Uh-oh ...

G—We can always choose digital 3D version, though. It's only $10.

D—Good point. By the way, what does its name mean?

G—It's Sanskrit, means the incarnation of god in human or animal form.

Z—Gary, you are ever so enlightening ...

R—Is that a science fiction?

G—Yeah, It's James Cameron's newest film. It's a sci-fi about a soldier who tries to save an alien race from humans and falls in love with an alien princess.

R—Hah, I have always had a taste for sci-fi!

D—Same here. So, any objections?

Z—Not really ... As long as it's a romance film.

D—Good. Four tickets for *Avatar*. Digital 3D.

Key

1. What are they discussing?
   They are discussing about what film they should see.
2. How many films are mentioned in the conversation?
   3 (*Night at the Museum*, *Laurence of the Arabia*, *Avatar*).
3. Who seems to know the most about films?
   Gary.
4. Who expressed a liking for science fiction?
   Roy and Darman.
5. What kind of film does Zoe like?
   Romance film.
6. How much are they going to pay for the tickets in total?
   $ 40.

4

Listen again and fill in the blanks.

Key

1. "*Night at the Museum* seems cool to me. "
2. "The story was too far-fetched. I just couldn't see the point of it. "
3. "I don't think you were supposed to take it too seriously. It was just meant for entertainment. "
4. "I couldn't help falling asleep last time I saw it . . . "
5. "And for good reason. It lasts more than three hours. "
6. "It's based on a true story about a man . . . "
7. "Maybe it is too profound for us to understand. "
8. "We can always choose digital 3D version, though. "
9. "It's James Cameron's newest film. It's a sci-fi about a soldier who tries to save an alien race from humans . . . . "
10. "I have always had a taste for sci-fi!"

Speaking

1

Role-play a conversation according to the following situations. After the practice, change roles.

Role Cards

Role A: Sharon is a super fan of Nicolas Cage's new movies.
Role B: Derek is intrigued by Nicolas Cage's old movies especially *Wild at Heart*.

Situation:

Sharon and Derek are talking about the latest movies and famous actors while on the way home.

Flow Chart

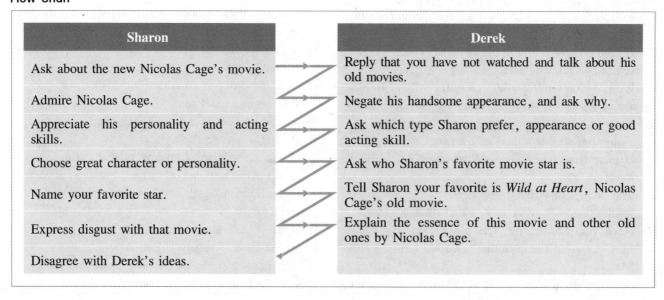

Sharon	Derek
Ask about the new Nicolas Cage's movie.	Reply that you have not watched and talk about his old movies.
Admire Nicolas Cage.	Negate his handsome appearance, and ask why.
Appreciate his personality and acting skills.	Ask which type Sharon prefer, appearance or good acting skill.
Choose great character or personality.	Ask who Sharon's favorite movie star is.
Name your favorite star.	Tell Sharon your favorite is *Wild at Heart*, Nicolas Cage's old movie.
Express disgust with that movie.	Explain the essence of this movie and other old ones by Nicolas Cage.
Disagree with Derek's ideas.	

Suggested Words and Expressions

Sharon	Derek
Did you see the new . . . movie? I just saw it last night with my friend . . . I think . . . is great. His performance is fouching. That's not always true. Let me put it this way: I don't like an actor just because he is handsome. It was disgusting. I almost couldn't watch it. I don't like black humor. I like his new movies.	Which one? No, I haven't seen it yet. But I saw . . . I thought that was good. Really? Why? He isn't very handsome. It's interesting you like him so much. Usually I think women don't like him. So what do you value more? Appearance or acting skill? So who is your favorite then? My favorite Nicolas Cage's movie was . . . . He was perfect for that role. It was a kind of movie that they call black humor. What about *Raising Arizona*? Did you see that? You must see it. That is the classic Nicolas Cage's movie.

Reference

Sharon: Did you see the new Nicolas Cage's movie?

Derek: Which one?

Sharon: *Snake Eyes*. I just saw it last night with my friend Sarah.

Derek: No, I haven't seen it yet. But I saw *Con Air*. I thought that was good.

Sharon: I think Nicolas Cage is great.

Derek: Really? Why? He isn't very handsome.

Sharon: No, but he's got character. His performance is touching.

Derek: It's interesting you like him so much. Usually I think women don't like him. They like more handsome actors.

Sharon: That's not always true.

Derek: So what do you value more? Appearance or acting skill?

Sharon: Let me put it this way. I like some very handsome actors. Like Alec Baldwin. But I don't like an actor just because he is handsome.

Derek: Hmm. So who is your favorite then?

Sharon: Nicolas Cage.

Derek: I used to like Nicolas Cage more than I do now. He used to play more interesting roles.

Sharon: What do you mean? What movies?

Derek: Oh, my favorite Nicolas Cage's movie was *Wild at Heart*. He was perfect for that role.

Sharon: I saw *Wild at Heart*. It was disgusting. I almost couldn't watch it.

Derek: It was a kind of movie that they call black humor.

Sharon: Yes, I know. Black humor is humor with a lot of violence or horrible things in it. I don't like black humor.

Derek: What about *Raising Arizona*? Did you see that?

Sharon: No.

Derek: You must see it. To me, that is the classic Nicolas Cage's movie. He is perfect for it.

Sharon: I like his new movies.

Derek: Well, you should check it out. Maybe you'll love it.

2

Work with your partner to make up a dialogue involving the following situation.

Role Cards

Student A: She found the movie not very entertaining.
Student B: He couldn't agree with student A and regarded the actor to be a genius.

Flow Chart

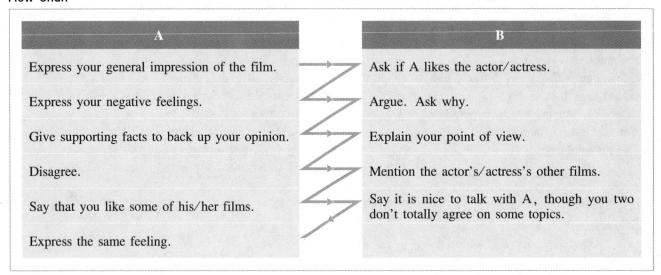

A	B
Express your general impression of the film.	Ask if A likes the actor/actress.
Express your negative feelings.	Argue. Ask why.
Give supporting facts to back up your opinion.	Explain your point of view.
Disagree.	Mention the actor's/actress's other films.
Say that you like some of his/her films.	Say it is nice to talk with A, though you two don't totally agree on some topics.
Express the same feeling.	

Suggested Words and Expressions

A	B
In general, I didn't like it.	Why not?
He seems very arrogant. I think an actor often plays characters that match his real personality.	Maybe it's the characters he plays. I doubt it's always the case.
I almost couldn't watch it.	What about the other film?
What bothered me was . . .	That's what he does best.
I only like his romances.	It's still great to talk with you.

Reference

A: It was entertaining in some ways. But in general, I didn't like it.
B: Do you like Keanu Reeves?
A: No, not at all.
B: Why not?
A: I just think he is a bad person. He seems very arrogant.
B: Maybe it's the characters he plays. Maybe in real life he's a good guy.
A: No, I think an actor often plays characters that match his real personality. They are naturally better at such characters.
B: I doubt it's always the case.
A: And I can sense something about Keanu Reeves. I don't like it. He seems like a jerk.
B: Hmmm. What about the other film? *The BARC*?
A: It was also disgusting. I almost couldn't watch it. The humor was too gross.
B: It was a kind of movie that they call black humor. It wasn't a dirty movie. There wasn't even any nudity.
A: What bothered me was all the jokes about sex, stuff like that. It was too sick.
B: Some new movies are just vulgar. If they become popular, it proves that people are becoming more vulgar.

A: I think American's values are screwed up if movies like that are popular.

B: He is more popular since he started doing action movies. But I always think he should be a comic actor. That is what he does best.

A: I only like his romances.

B: Maybe I can persuade you next time. Anyway, it's still great to talk about films with you. I gotta go now. See you next time.

A: Me too. Good bye!

Writing

Movie Review

Target:

Ss practice how to write a review. Improve Ss' skill of critical writing.

 Guidance

- Ss read examples in exercise 1 and learn how to amplify their sentences.
- Ask Ss to think freely of a film they like or dislike.
- Ss write a film review.

1

See how the following sentences are improved to be more specific. Then write down your specific opinion about a movie.

Reference:

The Sci-fi is wonderful.

—The Sci-fi is full of imagination. And the visual impact is strong. It's vivid.

2

Develop your opinion and write a full review.

Reference

I watched a comedy called *Proposal*. It told a love story between a Canadian lady working in America and a younger American man working as her personal assistant. Once the lady was informed that her visa was about to expire and would be forced back to Canada and lose her job, a stupid idea occurred to her. She decided to get married with her assistant to cheat the authorities. During their preparation of the fake wedding, they got inmate with each other and fell in love finally.

Personally, I appreciate and admire the leading actress a lot. She is an experienced actress who is equipped with amazing talents in acting and a great sense of humor. She can naturally play a professional senior director with a tough appearance and a clumsy, immature woman in love at the same time. She is the key to the success in office box of this movie. To be honest, the story itself is a little vulgar. There have been thousands of movies telling similar stories happening in different counties, with actors and actresses speaking different languages. But this kind of simple story is still touching and relieving.

In a word, I like *Proposal* for its ever-moving theme of love and the actress' acting skills.

Learning for fun

Have your say:

How do you define reality? How can you tell what is real, and what is not?

(Omitted.)

图书在版编目(CIP)数据

创新大学英语综合教程(高职高专版)1 教师用书/何刚总
主编.—上海:华东师范大学出版社,2010
普通高等教育高职英语系列教材
ISBN 978 - 7 - 5617 - 7687 - 2

Ⅰ.创…　Ⅱ.何…　Ⅲ.①英语—高等学校:技术学校—教
材　Ⅳ.①H31

中国版本图书馆 CIP 数据核字(2010)第 069984 号

普通高等教育高职英语系列教材

创新大学英语综合教程(高职高专版)1 教师用书

总 顾 问　何自然
总 主 编　高等职业英语教材编写研究会
　　　　　何　刚
项目编辑　李恒平
审读编辑　姚　望　邓　伟
装帧设计　戚亮轩　丁天天

出版发行　华东师范大学出版社
社　　址　上海市中山北路 3663 号　邮编 200062
电话总机　021 - 62450163 转各部门　行政传真 021 - 62572105
客服电话　021 - 62865537(兼传真)
门市(邮购)电话　021 - 62869887
门市地址　上海市中山北路 3663 号华东师范大学校内先锋路口
网　　址　www.ecnupress.com.cn

印 刷 者　上海商务联西印刷有限公司
开　　本　787×1092　16 开
印　　张　10.25
字　　数　272 千字
版　　次　2010 年 7 月第 1 版
印　　次　2010 年 7 月第 1 次
书　　号　ISBN 978 - 7 - 5617 - 7687 - 2/H·518
定　　价　30.00 元(含盘)

出 版 人　朱杰人

(如发现本版图书有印订质量问题,请寄回本社客服中心调换或电话 021 - 62865537 联系)